Praise for the novels of
GAYLE WILSON

"A writer who combines impeccable craft with unsurpassed storytelling skills. Her books are dark, sexy and totally involving."
—*New York Times* bestselling author Anne Stuart

"Gayle Wilson is a rising star in romantic suspense."
—*New York Times* bestselling author Carla Neggers

"Gayle Wilson will go far in romantic suspense. Her books have that special 'edge' that lifts them out of the ordinary. They're always tautly written, a treasure trove of action, suspense and richly drawn characters."
—*New York Times* bestselling author Linda Howard

"An exhilarating continual-action thriller that never slows down."
—*TheBestReviews.com* on *Double Blind*

"Wilson is destined to become one of the suspense genre's brightest stars."
—*Romantic Times BOOKreviews*, 4 1/2 stars, on *Wednesday's Child*

"Gayle Wilson pulls out all the stops… a thrilling chilling read."
—*ReadertoReader.com* on *In Plain Sight*

"Writing like this is a rare treat."
—*Gothic Journal*

"Rich historical detail, intriguing mystery, romance that touches the heart and lingers in the mind. These are elements that keep me waiting impatiently for Gayle Wilson's next book."
—*USA TODAY* bestselling author BJ James

Also by GAYLE WILSON

THE SUICIDE CLUB
BOGEYMAN
THE INQUISITOR
DOUBLE BLIND
WEDNESDAY'S CHILD
IN PLAIN SIGHT

GAYLE WILSON

VICTIM

ISBN-13: 978-0-7783-2394-5
ISBN-10: 0-7783-2394-3

VICTIM

www.MIRABooks.com

Printed in U.S.A.

For Bill Derryberry, a fine policeman, an excellent teacher and a kind, patient and much beloved friend.

Acknowledgments

Special thanks to Lynda Cooper, Bill Derryberry, Cindy Kelley and Dr. Mollie Thomas for kindly lending your expertise to this project. Any factual mistakes are mine and mine alone—I obviously didn't know the right questions to ask. You guys are the best!

Dear Reader,

I can't imagine what it must be like to lose a child. To lose one in the horrific way the heroine of *Victim* does would surely make any mother understand her actions toward her son's killer, especially when the justice system fails to provide any justice at all for his many victims.

What begins as a simple act of revenge becomes a dangerous cat-and-mouse game between a deadly predator and the woman from whom he has already taken so much. Then the stakes increase as Sarah Patterson's frozen heart finally thaws enough to embrace the possibility of loving someone again.

Mac Donovan, the New Orleans cop who prevents and yet admires Sarah's attempt to bring her son's murderer to task for his crimes, is more than capable of protecting both Sarah and himself. There is another child, however, a boy far more vulnerable than Sarah's lost Danny, who complicates the psychological chess match she and Mac must win in order to prevent a sociopath from claiming any more defenseless victims.

Although the subject matter of *Victim* is admittedly grim, the story line of a child in danger is all too familiar in our modern world. Sarah is a strong, resourceful woman, one who chooses a path few of you might take, but I hope that, given her circumstances, most of you will be able to empathize with the desperate choices she makes on that journey.

And as always, I wish you good reading.

Gayle

Prologue

He liked the darkness. He liked the anonymity of it. And he especially liked the way the lights in that darkness reflected off their faces. Young, eager, and so very beautiful.

His choice was usually a matter of fate, which meant there was no choice at all. This, however… This was so perfect he wondered why he hadn't thought of it long ago.

To be able to move unnoticed through the darkness. Watching them. Their eyes intent. Slim buttocks rotating. Bony adolescent shoulders shifting as they tried, through that unconscious body language, to influence the outcome of whatever game they were playing.

His lips slanted into a slow smile. Playing a game. That's all he was doing. Trying to influence not the outcome, which was predetermined, but the selection of the game piece.

His eyes contemplated the ones he'd singled out for further consideration. He had made his initial choices as he moved through the crowded room, almost rubbing shoulders with them.

Even their smell excited him. Hormonal sweat. The sharp, sweet scent of sex. Cigarette smoke, caught in the faded cotton of their tees and in the denim of their jeans. The occasional whiff of marijuana, which reminded him of his own adolescence, when that forbidden gratification had been almost all he had found pleasure in.

His gratifications were more comforting now. Their forbiddenness so much more exciting.

He made another slow circuit of the room, doing nothing that would draw attention to himself. Taking one last look at each of them, weighing this all-important decision.

When he was absolutely certain, he headed toward the service door at the back, the one that led to the delivery alley behind the mall. He had parked his van there. It would be waiting for them in the shadows, as nondescript as he himself.

He opened the door, looking up and then down the alley. There were bare bulbs above the loading platforms, but they cast only enough light to chase the shadows from the top of the ramps. Not enough to threaten his plans.

Before he closed it again, he checked the strip of tape that had been laid over the protrusion of the latch to keep the door from locking. The young men who worked the arcade had taken care of that detail.

During the course of the evening, they would come out into the alley in groups of twos or threes to smoke.

Meticulous in his planning, he had watched them, too, so that he knew they were all inside now. Their needs had been satisfied, providing him with this narrow window of opportunity to satisfy his.

He turned, his stride purposeful. His groin ached with its sudden engorgement. This moment was almost as fulfilling as the other. Its surge of anticipation almost as powerful as the release.

As he went back down the hall, he grabbed one of the blue aprons off the line of hooks and slipped it over his head. He wrapped the strings around his back and tied them in front. Then, taking a deep breath, he put his trembling hand into his pocket, stilling the jangle of tokens it contained.

As he reentered the game room, he kept his face turned slightly down. Other than that precaution, there was nothing furtive about his movements. He had watched the employees long enough that he had perfected their slouching, self-important posture as they moved among the machines. And as long as none of them stopped him…

He paused behind the boy he'd chosen, watching him play. The child's face changed constantly, following the fortunes of the game. A grimace. A wince. And then…

The lights on the machine flashed, bells ringing loudly. No one looked around. This happened often enough to be a non-event. His were the only eyes that watched as elation washed tension from the soft, unformed face.

"All *right,*" the boy said, his lips widening into a grin. There was a glint of metal over teeth too big for the mouth they occupied.

Seeing the braces, he felt a momentary disappointment. Momentary, because otherwise the boy was perfect, possessing every feature that pleased him. Perfect, he assured himself again.

Deliberately he delayed, letting anticipation build in slow, roiling waves of pleasure. It roared through his body like a drug, fueling his need. Seconds merely, and then…

The child put his initials beside the score, and they, too, were perfect. Everything perfect.

"We got the new version of this one in this afternoon."

His accent wasn't exact—he hadn't been here long enough—but it would do. Certainly not different enough to draw attention to him or to make the kid suspicious.

The boy's eyes flicked upward from the score, meeting his. They were almost unfocused, still full of the thrill of victory.

It made a connection between them. A union. Toward a more perfect union.

"So much better than this," he added, feeling the adrenaline rush as he drew out the first word. "You wouldn't believe the difference."

"Cool." The kid seemed interested for the first time.

"You oughta try it."

The boy's narrow shoulders moved upward, almost a shrug, and then the blue eyes darted back to the screen, eager to play again. "So when's it gonna be on the floor?"

"We got it set up in the back. Been playing all afternoon. What the boss don't know…" He smiled, and in response the boy's grin again exposed the metal bands on his teeth.

They were slightly green in the reflected light from the game. The sight was jarring. Throwing him out of sync, like hearing a wrong note in a familiar piece of music. Maybe this wasn't the one. Maybe—

"I still got tokens," the kid said.

"We got it rigged to play for free. You want to try it?"

"Sure."

"You can't let anybody know," he warned. "They'd all want to come."

"Okay."

"You here with somebody?"

"My dad. He went next door."

"If he's gonna miss you and raise a stink—"

"He's in the music store. I'm good for half an hour at least."

He hesitated a few seconds, as if he were calculating the risks. "You see that door in the back? Under the exit sign?"

The kid turned, looking toward the other side of the room. The back of his head was exposed, a small endearing cowlick at the crown. Again the sense of rightness descended, blocking the momentary doubt.

This was the one. This one.

"Yeah?" the boy said, turning back to face him.

"I'll go first. When I get into the back hall, you follow, but not so's anybody's going to notice you."

"Okay," the kid said.

"If the others see what I'm doing, they'll stop us."

"Nobody'll see me."

"Okay."

He looked around the room, his eyes finding and checking off the employees. A couple were standing at the front, watching the girls parade along the mall outside. Another was intent on watching the numbers build as one of the regulars played the most popular game in the room, well on the other side. All of them accounted for.

He looked back at the boy, whose eyes were focused on his face, their eagerness seeming to match his own. He nodded, the movement small and controlled, and then he began to walk, making his way toward the exit sign. Toward the door and the alley and the van.

He knew that the boy would follow, never questioning his destination. Even if he had, it was one he could not possibly imagine. Not in a million years.

And that was perhaps the greatest of all the multiple anticipations and releases he found in his game. The pleasure of seeing the final realization of what was about to happen invade their stupid, trusting little eyes.

One

"Unfortunately for the state, Mr. Evans, the product of an illegal search cannot later be used as justification for having made it. Nor do I find compelling Officer Gateau's observation that the defendant seemed overly concerned about the damage to the back of his van. That would be a common enough reaction to a traffic mishap, however minor. I cannot see how, in that situation, it can possibly be construed to constitute probable cause to search Mr. Tate's vehicle."

Each word of the ruling was pronounced in the precise, almost pedantic accent Judge Marlene Wexler had adopted long ago to hide her rural Mississippi upbringing. The only black female on the Orleans Parish criminal bench, Wexler's assignment to this case had been, from the beginning, the district attorney's worst nightmare.

Her rulings were carefully grounded in the law, but

courthouse scuttlebutt had long ago put her down on the side of defendants' rights versus the police. She had never been overturned. It was obvious she didn't intend to be on this.

"Ms. Siddons has testified that she clearly heard Mr. Tate deny permission for the officer to open the rear doors of the van. And deny permission for him to search the suitcase discovered inside. In both instances, Officer Gateau chose to do so, despite the defendant's objections."

"Your Honor—"

"Leaving me no option," Wexler went on, speaking above the prosecutor's attempt to protest what they all knew was coming. "*No* option," she repeated for emphasis, "but to grant the motion to suppress all evidence found during the course of those searches. As well as," she continued inexorably, her tone daring the district attorney to interrupt again, "all evidence recovered during the subsequent search of Mr. Tate's home."

Because of the political ramifications of this case, if not for other, more humanitarian concerns, District Attorney Carl Evans was forced to take up that challenge, no matter how much he might dislike the position it was going to put him with the judge. "The warrant for that search, Your Honor—"

"Was obtained from Judge Fischer based on evidence found during the illegal search of the van. Fruit of the poisonous tree, Mr. Evans, as you are very well aware. It is not going to come in. None of it is."

The last phrase was very soft, each word distinctly

enunciated. And only after the sibilance of the last syllable had died away, the pause lengthening unbearably, seeming to echo throughout the courtroom, did Judge Wexler speak again.

"Do you have any other evidence that would justify holding this defendant, Mr. Evans?"

The prosecutor's mouth had flattened. Now it pursed, as if he were reluctant to open it. There was, however, only so long he could delay the inevitable.

"No, Your Honor," he said finally.

Wexler's dark eyes settled briefly on the rookie cop who had performed the search that was about to put a serial killer back on the streets. The media had already had a field day with this case. Given the events of this morning's hearing, that would only get worse.

"Then, Mr. Tate," Judge Marlene Wexler said, "you are free to go."

"He's gonna walk," the voice in his headset warned.

"Son of a bitch," Mac Donovan said.

The utterance wasn't forceful. Mac had learned long ago that he could do nothing about the vagaries of the system he served. He was sworn to uphold it, even when it was wrong. As it had been today.

"Taking him out the back?" he asked.

"That's what they say."

"Everybody in place?"

"He may not cooperate. He's like that, you know," Sonny Cochran said, the last phrase sarcastic.

"Good," Donovan responded, the single syllable sharp, abruptly cut off. "Maybe somebody'll shoot the bastard."

There was soft laughter in his ear. "We should be so lucky."

They had all known how this would play out. The uniform who'd responded to a fender bender had screwed up. As a result, the evidence he'd discovered in the back of Samuel Tate's van, the so-called murder kit that would link him to the deaths of more than a dozen adolescent boys, wasn't going to come in.

This morning's hearing had been little more than a formality. There might have been some wiggle room if it had been the cop's word against Tate's, but Phillip Gateau had managed to conduct his search in front of the woman who'd bumped into the back of the killer's van. Once she'd been subpoenaed by Tate's very expensive lawyer, everybody within reach of a newspaper headline had known he was going to walk.

"Okay," Mac said. "Let's assume he won't cooperate. We have to cover all our bases on this one."

Given the nature of Tate's crimes, the department would keep him under surveillance. In light of the ruling that had just come down, they couldn't legally justify that tail, so it wouldn't be acknowledged publicly. Nor could it be obtrusive enough to allow Tate to scream harassment to the judge.

But the bastard wouldn't be able to take a piss without somebody analyzing its color and the smell. Every move, every breath he took, somebody would be watching Samuel Tate.

Damn little satisfaction, Mac Donovan acknowledged, but right now, it was all he had.

* * *

Long shot, Sarah Patterson thought, crossing her arms over her breasts. She put her gloved fingers in her armpits to keep them warm.

She had known that waiting out here might be wasted effort, but then, she had nothing to lose. Her lips tightened at the unintended melodrama of the phrase. She had tried very hard during the last three years to avoid that kind of self-pity.

She turned her head, her gaze sweeping the portico at the front of the courthouse. There were people moving up and down the steps, as there had been all morning. Heads down, briefcases dangling as they climbed, going about their normal business.

All the excitement was inside and out back. The media was waiting in force at the rear of the courthouse, along with a few of the other parents. And the cops.

Which meant that's where they intended to take him out, just as the television news this morning had speculated. The media had better sources within the justice system than she did. They always seemed to know what was going on.

All she knew was Tate. She had made it her mission to know.

Once he'd been arrested, she had pored over every scrap of information available. Every article. Every psychological assessment. Every speculation. And there had been a lot of those.

She knew as much as there was to know about Samuel A. Tate. Which was why she was waiting here instead of at the back with the others.

Tate wasn't going to do what the cops wanted him to. He had beat the system, and he was going to glory in it. He was going to publicly thumb his nose at the fools who couldn't even get arresting him right.

Even if the evidence they'd uncovered had been allowed in, he would still have found some way, Sarah thought, her bitterness building. Some sleazebag lawyer. Another idiot judge.

The internal tirade dissipated in an explosion of adrenaline as her eyes focused on the slight figure emerging through the double doors. She blinked to clear her vision, needing to be absolutely sure.

When she was, her chest tightened, squeezing the air from her lungs. She didn't notice, since she had already forgotten to breathe. She watched Tate instead, tracking his movement across the porch toward the top of the granite steps.

A couple of flashbulbs went off. Apparently she wasn't the only one who had suspected Tate might come out here rather than at the back. A microphone was thrust into his face, but he pushed it away with one hand. He said something to the reporter who held it, but she was too far away to hear the words.

Or maybe she hadn't heard them because after her identification of her son's murderer, a cone of silence seemed to have settled over her, blocking any distractions. Her entire consciousness was focused on the man at the top of the steps.

She didn't move until he reached the first of them. Then, unconcerned that someone might be watching, she slipped her right hand into the opening of her purse, its long strap still over her left shoulder.

As her fingers closed around the butt of the pistol it contained, she began to climb the steps, going up them on the diagonal as Tate began to descend. He came straight down, head high, pushing arrogantly through the few members of the media who'd been waiting for him.

They followed, mouths moving, throwing questions at him. Tate continued to ignore them, heading purposefully down the steps.

Sensing that purpose, for the first time Sarah's concentration shifted, tracing the trajectory of his descent. At the foot of the stairs a taxi waited. If she didn't hurry, she realized with a jolt of panic, he would be inside it before she could get close enough—

She began to run, no longer climbing the steps, but going straight across them. She was aware subliminally of other people, all of whom seemed to be converging on the spot where she was headed. Their presence had no impact on her determination.

There was still no sound. The action played out in front of her like a silent film. And now the only other actor—the only one who mattered—was less than a dozen feet away, slightly above her and to her side.

Sarah stopped, holding the pistol in her outstretched right hand. Her left settled under it, steadying the weapon. Just as she had been taught, she pointed the muzzle like an accusing finger at the man coming down the steps. Infinitely calm, now that the moment was finally here, she locked on her target, leading it slightly.

Don't talk. Just shoot.

The words careened through her brain, as her hands and her eyes continued to track her prey. Dan must have said them in a hundred darkened movie theaters through the years. Transfixed by what was occurring on the screen, he would whisper those words, offering his warning to countless heroines tremblingly holding a gun on the bad guy.

Shoot him. Don't talk to him. Just shoot him, you stupid bitch.

That was exactly what Sarah had planned to do. She had even uttered Dan's words over and over, preparing for this moment.

Now, despite what her intellect was telling her—had told her from the moment she had thought of this—she knew that she needed him to know. She needed Tate to understand for which of them he was dying. In some sense, perhaps, what she was doing would be for all of them, but the only way it would ever make any difference to *her* was if Tate knew her son's name.

"Daniel," she shouted.

The dark, well-groomed head turned, everything happening in slow motion. She had time to watch his eyes meet hers before they fell to the gun. When they lifted again, they were slightly widened, but there was no panic in them. Fastened on hers, they were exactly the same pale, clear blue her son's had been.

"His name was Daniel Patterson," she said, no longer shouting because he was near enough she knew he could hear her. And because she had his full and undivided attention.

His head moved up and down. In agreement? Did that mean he had known Danny's name? Or did it simply mean he understood for which of them he was about to die?

Tate's descent had begun to slow, his gaze still locked on her face. *Shoot, don't talk.* Now she could. Now she could kill him because she had told Tate Danny's name.

Her finger closed over the trigger, beginning the slow deliberate squeeze. Concentrating fiercely on the man in front of her, she was totally unaware of the one rushing at her from the side.

He reached her before her finger could complete the move it had begun. He wrapped his arms around her, the momentum of his dive carrying them both down the steps.

The gun was jarred out of her hand as they landed. She fell on her left shoulder and hip, hitting the granite with incredible force. They slid down the last few steps, their bodies locked together.

Stunned by the impact of her fall, Sarah wasn't sure at first what had happened. One second she'd been standing on the courthouse steps, pointing Dan's pistol at the man who had murdered their son. The next she was lying on the sidewalk, unable to breathe. Unable to escape the crushing weight of the man who had brought her down.

She turned her head to the side in time to watch Samuel Tate duck into his waiting cab. She was near enough that she could smell the fumes of the exhaust as it pulled away from the curb and disappeared into traffic.

Only when it was gone did she become aware that pandemonium had broken out around her. Someone was screaming. Someone else—and the sound of this was very close—cursed, the words low and intense.

The noises rushed through her head like water over the stones of a brook. Meaningless babble.

She looked up at the sky, the thick winter clouds over her head mottled and gray until they blurred with her tears. Despite the growing cacophony of noise around her, it was Dan's voice that echoed again and again in her head.

Shoot, don't talk. Just shoot him, you stupid bitch.

Two

The woman he'd tackled was so still Mac thought at first she'd been knocked unconscious. Then he pushed up far enough to see her face.

Her lashes rested like fans against her colorless cheeks. Under them, glinting over shadows the color of old bruises, moisture gathered as he watched.

"You hurt?" He continued to push onto his elbows, trying to take some of his weight off her.

She opened her eyes then, looking straight into his. The irises were a dark gray-green, lightly flecked with brown. Even viewed through the veil of her tears, the fury in them was obvious. "You bastard."

Patterson. The name that went with this face floated unexpectedly to the surface of Mac's memory. Danny Patterson. Tate's second local victim.

"You can't take the law into your own hands, Mrs. Patterson." The hypocrisy sickened him, even as he mouthed the words.

Cops, especially in this town, took the law into their own hands every day. Besides, who the hell was he to try to tell this woman what she should or shouldn't do? It wasn't his kid that butcher had slaughtered.

"He killed my son, and you just let him go. You released him, so he can go out there and kill another child."

It was hard to argue against that logic. They *had* let him go. That was the way things worked. Mac didn't have to like it, and neither did she, but it was the law.

"He'll be followed. The first time he does anything we can pick him up for—"

She laughed, the sound without amusement. Then she turned her head, looking in the direction in which Tate's cab had disappeared. She was still breathing in small, ragged inhalations.

"Get off me," she demanded without looking at him again. "Just…get the hell off me."

"If you'd killed him, Mrs. Patterson, you'd have been charged with murder."

She looked back at him again. The tears were gone, but the fury was still there. The dark pupils expanded, widening into the rim of color. "Do you think I care? He tortured my son to death. You really think I care what they do to me?"

In the silence that fell after that unanswerable question, Mac became aware of the growing commotion on the courthouse steps. The reporters who had been waiting here on the off-chance that Tate might use the front entrance were clustered around them.

The two of them had now become the show. Not Tate. Tate was gone. He was old news.

Mac glanced up, right into the black eye of a camera. Obviously whoever held it had been shooting the exchange between him and Danny Patterson's mother.

Which meant they'd probably shot the events that had preceded it as well. And if they showed that tape…

Scrambling awkwardly to his feet while trying to avoid a more intimate contact with the Patterson woman, Mac reached out, putting his palm over the lens and pushing the camera away from him. The cameraman never stopped filming.

Ignoring him, Mac held his hand out to the woman he'd tackled, but she was already in the process of getting to her feet, pointedly ignoring him. He realized for the first time that she was far smaller and a lot more fragile than she had appeared standing there with that big pistol in her hand.

The wail of sirens converging on the courthouse reminded Mac that what she had done would be considered a criminal act. Attempted murder? If anybody had the gall to push it.

"I want that tape," he said, turning to hold the hand she'd rejected out to the cameraman, palm up.

The demand was unexpected enough that the guy took his eye off the viewfinder. "You're kidding, right?"

"You can give me the tape or you can give me the camera. I'm not picky."

"Come on, man. You don't expect me to just hand over—"

Mac's hand closed around the lens. He jerked once,

hard enough that he almost succeeded in wrenching the camera from the man's hold. The anchor, the one who'd thrust his microphone into Tate's face, began to argue something about the first amendment. In the background the sirens grew louder, drawing the eyes of the news crew to the street.

Seizing the opportunity, Mac gave another jerk. This time the camera slipped out of the man's hand. As soon as it did, Mac let go. It bounced down a couple of the granite steps before it came to a rolling stop on the sidewalk.

As if dazed, the cameraman watched its journey. When it landed, he turned back to Mac, mouth gaping in shock.

"I want that tape," Mac said again, his voice menacing. To punctuate the message, he flipped open the leather case that contained his badge, holding it under the cameraman's nose. "If I don't get it, you two are gonna have a hell of a time explaining to a judge why you refused to turn over evidence to an officer of the law."

Apparently the tone, normally reserved for uncooperative suspects, worked on reporters as well. There was a few seconds' hesitation, and then the news team looked at one another, eyes meeting briefly before they skated away. During that exchange, they had either decided he was crazy, and therefore dangerous, or that they weren't perfectly sure of their legal standing. Mac didn't care which it was, as long as it got him the tape.

Reluctantly, the cameraman walked down the remaining few steps and, stooping, retrieved his camera from the sidewalk. He removed the tape cartridge and held it out. "You'll be hearing from the station's management."

Mac controlled the urge to laugh, taking the tape instead. As threats went, that one lacked a certain something. "I'll let you all know when you can have it back."

He turned, looking for Danny Patterson's mother, but she had disappeared. His eyes searched the crowd, whose numbers seemed to have increased exponentially in the few minutes since Tate had ridden off.

Pushing past the reporter, who was still standing belligerently in front of him, Mac took a couple of steps to his left, looking for the weapon he'd knocked out of the woman's hand. It had vanished as well.

Chalk one up for the victims, he thought in satisfaction.

He couldn't be expected to arrest her if she wasn't there. That was going to be his story, at least until somebody challenged it.

He glanced to the top of the stairs where his partner was standing. Sonny gestured down the street with a tilt of his head. Mac turned to look, but if that's where she had headed, there was no sign of her now.

He started climbing the steps, aware of a couple of aches and pains he hadn't noticed before. The result of that off-the-bench tackle. He'd pay a bigger price for that tomorrow, he knew. She would, too, because she'd taken the brunt of their landing.

Maybe that's what had precipitated her tears. That and not the fact he'd stopped her from shooting Tate. He knew that it wasn't true, but the thought was comforting.

"Jesus, man. What the hell were you thinking?" Sonny asked as he approached the top. He had lowered his voice so that the question was audible only to Mac, despite the reporters who trailed him. "You shoulda let her pop him. Save us all a lot of trouble and the taxpayers some money. Besides, if anybody has the right…"

Samuel Tate deserved to be shot down like the rabid dog he was, and, as Sonny said, if anyone had the right, it was the mother of one of his victims. According to the law, however, no one but the state could execute Tate. If she'd killed him, Mrs. Patterson would have been a murderer.

"Seemed like a good idea at the time." Mac brushed past his partner, pushing open the door of the courthouse.

"What're you gonna do with the tape?" Sonny followed him inside.

"What would you do?"

"Lose it. Some place nobody'd ever find it."

"Got a lighter in your desk?" Mac pushed the button that opened up the cartridge.

Sonny was in perpetual "I'm quitting smoking" mode. This week it had been "I've finally done it."

"I could probably find one," Sonny evaded, watching him pull tape out of the case in a long black ribbon. "Or we could stop by a convenience store on our way back to the station. Lighter, little lighter fluid, empty garbage can. Problem solved."

Problem solved. The words reverberated in Mac's head, seeming too glib.

He'd get rid of the tape. They'd keep an eye on Tate.

Now that they knew who he was, that shouldn't be any harder than any other routine surveillance.

Problem solved. Except if it were, Mac couldn't figure out why there was this nagging uneasiness in the back of his mind that none of this was going to be that simple.

"The station's pretty upset about the damage to their camera." Mac's supervisor looked even more sour than he normally did.

It apparently hadn't taken long for the news crew to follow up on their threat. "They should take that up with their cameraman," Mac said. "He's the one who dropped it."

"He says you threw it down the steps."

"I didn't have any reason to do that. I told them I wanted the tape, and they refused to cooperate."

"So you broke their camera."

"I showed them my badge and told them their tape might be evidence."

"Evidence you can't produce."

"I told you. I pitched it after I looked at it. There was nothing on the thing. I don't know. Maybe the guy damaged it taking it out of the camera." Mac added a shrug for effect.

"And maybe," Captain Morel said, "you should think very carefully about what you're saying, Mac. If you tampered with evidence—"

"There was nothing on the tape, Captain, I swear."

"Everybody outside the courthouse yesterday morning saw what happened."

"Sir?" A little sucking up couldn't hurt, Mac decided.

He'd not done enough of that through the years, but playing departmental politics had never been his thing. That's why Morel, who'd joined the force the same year he had, was where he was, and Mac was still a detective.

Not that he wanted to be anything else, he told himself. His normal conviction rang slightly hollow this morning.

"Sarah Patterson tried to kill Tate, and you stopped her."

Sarah. Mac hadn't remembered her first name yesterday, and he hadn't had time since to look it up. Not after the surveillance team lost Tate, throwing the task force into a near panic. The cab had dropped him off at the French Market where he'd disappeared into the crowd of shoppers.

Tate had never returned to his apartment and, although they had it staked out in case he did, it was looking more and more as if he'd had a contingency plan in place in case he was ever arrested.

All of which had put pressure on everyone in the department. They had blown it with Tate, not once but twice, and the public and the media were very unhappy.

Rightly so, Mac acknowledged.

"I thought she had a gun, too," he said aloud. "At least at first."

"You *thought*?"

"Apparently she just wanted to say something to Tate about her kid. We'd all been afraid someone might try to get to Tate. When I saw Mrs. Patterson approach him, I guess I kind of overreacted."

"So you're saying she *didn't* have a gun."

"That's what I'm saying."

Morel's eyes rested on his face a long time. If he was trying to induce some kind of guilt trip for that lie, it wasn't going to work. Sarah Patterson had suffered enough.

"Then why were you so interested in obtaining the tape of the incident?" the captain asked finally.

"I knew her face would be all over the evening news."

"It was," Morel said.

For that matter, Mac's had been, too. Despite the blow of losing Tate, despite whatever Morel was going to do to him, Mac could take satisfaction in the fact that nobody had film showing what had really happened to run alongside those stills. As a result, Danny Patterson's mother wasn't up on a charge of attempted murder this morning.

"The media wants your head," Morel said. "Actually, I think they'd like a collection of heads, but right now, you're at the top of their list."

"They'll get over it."

He had more important things to do than worry about some irate TV station. If that frigging camera really had been damaged, they could damn well afford to have it fixed, given the increased coverage the department's screwup would give them.

"Two weeks," Morel said.

Mac tried to fit the words into the context of the conversation. *Two weeks to catch Tate?*

"Without pay," the captain added. "That should cover the cost of replacing their camera."

"You're *suspending* me?"

"Call it administrative leave. Pending an investigation of your actions, of course. With all the department's got going on right now, I figure that will take at least a couple of weeks."

"Captain," Mac protested, only to be cut off.

"I don't like being yelled at. Not by the media. Not by the commissioner. Nobody does. Most of all, I don't like being lied to by my own people. Two weeks should give you enough time to think about using the resources of this department for your personal agenda. Sarah Patterson tried to kill a man yesterday. And because you destroyed evidence, she walks."

"Just like Tate." Mac didn't bother to hide the sarcasm. "We must be playing hell with the D.A.'s conviction rate."

Morel's lips tightened in anger, but he maintained control. "We can't afford to appear to condone vigilante justice here, or we'll have the family of every homicide victim in this city carrying weapons into courtrooms and plotting their own revenge."

"Do you remember what Tate did to her son?"

Morel did, of course. Not that it would make any difference.

"Tate's an innocent man until the courts prove he isn't. That's the way it works. You know that, Mac."

"All I *know* is that I've forgotten more about Tate than anyone else in this department knows," Mac argued.

He was the N.O.P.D.'s representative on the multi-jurisdictional task force that had been organized when they had finally figured out they had a serial killer on their hands. Something it had taken them way too long to do, in Mac's opinion.

"I need to be out there working this case," he went on. "You *need* me out there. Suspending me right now is insane, and *you* know *that*," he mimicked the captain's last words.

"Three weeks." The red that had started in Morel's neck spread upward to his cheeks. "That should give Internal Affairs time enough to determine whether we should add tampering with evidence to blatant destruction of property."

"Look—"

"Enjoy your time off, Mac. I imagine we'll be able to get a handle on Tate without your expertise." The last was as coldly biting as Morel allowed himself to get.

"I'll pay for the frigging camera." As he said it Mac wondered how much that was going to set him back.

"Yes, you will. And you'll pay for lying to me, too. Starting now."

"You really want to send a woman to prison for trying to shoot the maniac who tortured her kid to death?"

"I want her and anybody else who's got a beef with Tate out of the way, so this department can deal with him. I really wish you were going to be around to help with that."

"Don't worry. From what I've seen of the department's ability to deal with this guy, I'll be back in plenty of time."

"Four weeks," Morel said. "And no, you won't."

Three

"Want me to walk him for you?"

Sarah turned at the question and then wished she hadn't. Of course, it wouldn't have done any good to ignore him. The child was nothing if not persistent.

"I saw you were limping," he added. "Did you hurt your foot?" Blue eyes, filled with what appeared to be genuine concern, lifted from her sneaker to her face.

Sarah resisted the urge to smile at him. She'd been resisting it since she'd moved into the building three months ago.

"Old age. Thanks for the offer, but I need the exercise."

"You aren't old."

The boy fell in beside her, taking a couple of steps to each of hers in order to accommodate her longer stride. She was trying not to favor the leg that had taken the brunt of yesterday's fall, but every step she took jarred her hip. It had hurt like hell all last night, despite the ibuprofen she'd ended up popping every few hours.

The bruises on that side of her body, viewed in the mirror this morning as she'd dressed for work, had been nothing less than spectacular. She knew from experience that they'd become more colorful before they faded, but she also knew they'd be less painful tomorrow. Right now she just needed to grit her teeth and bear it—at least until after she had taken Toby for his evening walk.

"Older than you," she said, glancing down at him.

Why the hell couldn't she leave it alone? Ignore him, and eventually he'd get tired of trailing along beside her. After all, other than the attraction the dog held for him, it didn't make a lot of sense that he'd persisted this long. It wasn't as if she'd been friendly.

One afternoon shortly after she'd moved in, the boy had been in the foyer when she'd come down the stairs with Toby. The dog, inveterate admirer of all things small and male, had wagged and slobbered as if the child were his long-lost brother.

Or his master, her heart reminded, cutting a clean, sharp path through her pretended cynicism.

"So how old *are* you?"

The boy was skipping a little to keep up as Toby pulled her along, faster than was really comfortable. After being cooped up in the apartment all day, the dog was eager to reach the small neighborhood park and its bushes.

"Thirty-four." She'd had to think about it. Maybe because she felt a hundred. At least today.

Most days she found it hard to believe she was almost thirty-five. She had been nineteen when she and Dan married. Twenty-one when Danny was born.

Every step along the way, her life had sailed along just as it should. The major events nicely timed. Orderly. Well-planned. And then one day—

"You're supposed to ask me now," the child prompted.

Her eyes considered the top of his head, bobbing beside her. Just as she had had to deny the urge to smile at him, Sarah fought the mother-impulse to run smoothing fingers over that badly cropped hair.

Ridiculous. She didn't even know his name.

And I don't want to.

Maybe he hung around her so much because he didn't have any friends. She had never seen him with anyone else, although there were plenty of children in the neighborhood. He had never been among those she watched from behind her curtained windows as they played ball or ran shrieking through some variation of hide-and-seek along the alley behind the building.

"Okay," she said. "I'll bite. How old are you?"

"Nine nearly ten."

The words were pronounced so quickly they came out of his mouth as one. Obviously he had said them innumerable times in exactly that way. Or, she amended, remembering his solitary existence, maybe they always were right there, ready to be offered to anyone who could be goaded into asking for them.

Nine nearly ten.

Third grade? Multiplication tables and long division. Cursive writing. Too old, probably, for puzzles and coloring books. And not yet old enough for—

She jerked her mind away from the image, refusing

to let it form in her brain. This was why she had avoided this child. This particular child.

"I go to Davidson," he added helpfully.

For a moment Sarah drew a blank, and then she remembered that Davidson was the elementary school that served the neighborhood. A run-down brick building surrounded by dirt playing fields and rusting jungle gyms. In the winter grayness, which was the only way she'd ever seen it, it looked as uninviting as the aging, boarded-up properties around it.

"Mrs. Sharpton is my teacher."

At least she wasn't having to talk, Sarah decided, giving in to the ache in her hip and allowing herself to limp. It couldn't hurt to listen. He seemed willing to fill any dead air by telling her things she couldn't possibly want to know. And as for the ones she did want to know…

"What's your name?"

"Dwight David Ingersoll."

Again the words had no spaces between them. And this time there was a singsong inflection to them that surprised an upward tilt at the corners of her mouth.

When she was a little girl, her grandfather had sung some silly song about a man named John Jacob Jingleheimer Smith. The child's recitation of his name sounded enough like that to evoke an almost pleasant nostalgia.

"That's a pretty big name for…" She almost said for such a little boy, but before she finished the sentence, she realized he wouldn't appreciate that.

Rustier than I thought.

"For a kid," she finished.

"I was named for a president. What's your dog's name?"

Obviously a more important question than what her name was.

"His name's Toby. He *wasn't* named for a president."

Actually, she didn't know who the mutt had been named for. She'd let Danny choose both the dog and the name, and she hadn't questioned the process that had resulted in either.

She had a sudden mental picture of her son walking, big-eyed and almost solemn, along the metal cages at the Humane Society. He had weighed his selection so carefully that she'd hoped at the time he didn't realize the implication for those animals he didn't choose.

Naming the white-and-tan mutt he'd selected had occurred that same day. In the car on the way home, actually. There had been no announcement. No "I'm going to call him…" No "What do you think I should name him?"

He had simply begun calling the dog by his name. And Toby had responded as if he had known it all along.

"That's a nice name." The boy put his hand on the top of Toby's big head as if in benediction.

"Thank you."

Not so hard. She had managed to get through the entire sequence of the dog selection memory without wanting to cry or scream.

It had taken her a full year after Danny's death to be

able to do that. Every passing day of the next two years had been easier, until she had finally gotten to the point of actually being able to remember the good times. To relish her memories of him. And then Samuel Tate had been arrested, and with the media circus she'd been right back at ground zero.

"I can't go any further." The boy stopped at the curb, balancing dramatically on the balls of his feet and windmilling his arms to maintain that position. "To the end of the block, but not into the park. That's what my mama said. She worries about me."

Sarah nodded, feeling the burn of tears she'd just congratulated herself for not entertaining. The boy didn't notice, stooping to wrap his arms around Toby's neck. The dog leaned into his thin body, looking up at Sarah over the child's shoulder.

"Dwight or David or Dwight David?"

"Dwight," the boy said, looking up at her, too.

It would be, she thought, feeling a surge of bitterness toward the mother who supposedly worried about him. The ridiculously old-fashioned name fit with the jacket that was too short in the sleeves and the scuffed tennis shoes with their knotted laces and the poorly cut hair.

"You better run on back home then."

"You gonna stay out here long?"

"Probably not. It's pretty cold."

The current cold snap was as low as the temperatures ever got in New Orleans. The wind off the river carried a wet chill that seeped through clothing and settled under it, against the skin.

"If he had a ball, you could throw it, and he could chase it."

Another flash of memory. This one she banished as quickly as it formed. "I think I'm too old for playing ball."

"If you asked my mother sometime, I bet I could come with you and throw one for him." The tone was as hopeful as the eyes looking up at her.

Unable to deny either, Sarah said, "We'll see."

Like "nine nearly ten," those words had been too accessible. Familiar. They had come out of her mouth as if she had last said them yesterday rather than three years ago.

"You better go on home now," she said again, her voice low.

After another fierce hug, the boy released Toby and stood, moving from that awkward, semi-kneeling position with the unconscious grace of childhood. "I think my uncle may have a ball. I'll ask him if we can borrow it."

Unable to speak for the thickness in her throat, Sarah nodded again. He nodded in return, and then he began to run back along the way they had come. Halfway down the block, he turned around to face her, running backwards.

When he saw that she was watching him, he waved. A thin, white wrist poked out of the dark sleeve of his jacket like a bone, his hand moving from side to side.

Unable to stop herself, she lifted her own hand, waving back at him in the same way. When he turned around, he increased his pace, hopping over the lines in the sidewalk. Making a game of it.

Just as she had done as a child. Just as Danny had always done. *Step on a crack, break your mother's back.*

And in spite of Toby's efforts to draw her on to the park, she watched until the boy had disappeared into the lengthening shadows at the end of the street.

"So what are you gonna do for four weeks?" Sonny asked.

Mac muted the television, considering the people on the screen, now mouthing words they had been speaking only seconds before. Good question, he thought, switching the phone to his right ear. What the hell was he going to do while everybody else was out hunting Tate?

"Catch up on my laundry."

Sonny would know what he was feeling. It didn't have to be put into words. Not between the two of them.

Mac had had plenty of time to think about what had happened. And he'd decided he didn't regret anything he'd done, except maybe a couple of remarks he'd made to Morel on which he could have toned down the sarcasm a decibel or two.

"So what's the word on our boy?" he asked, his eyes following the action on the screen.

There wasn't a lot of furniture in his living room, but the television was top of the line and the couch wasn't a bad place to catch a couple of hours of sleep when the bed felt like the last place he wanted to be. As it had last night.

"We got nothing," Sonny admitted. "He ain't been

back home. Bank account's not been touched. Credit cards silent. He must have had a stash somewhere."

"Locker at the bus station," Mac suggested. "Or the airport."

"Yeah, well, if either of those were where it was at, he hit 'em before we got there."

"Maybe he'll just lay low."

"You believe that?"

"No," Mac said. "I think that's why he was out roaming around that night with his neat little kit in the back of his van. Considering the time between the last one and now…"

"He's due." Sonny's voice was full of resignation.

"Bingo," Mac agreed softly.

That was the bad part. Knowing you had a guy who was going to kill again, as sure as the sun was going to come up tomorrow, and not being able to anticipate who or where. Some kid. Some poor, unsuspecting kid…

"I gotta go," Sonny said. "Want me to bring you something by on the way home?"

"I got pizza from last night. Let me know what you hear."

"No news is good news," Sonny said.

The sudden dial tone in Mac's ear signaled the conversation was at an end. He laid the phone on the cluttered coffee table, pushing the button on the remote. The silence of the apartment obediently filled with the sound of canned laughter.

No news is good news.

Not with Tate, he thought. No news was just that. No

news. Because there was no doubt in anyone's mind, certainly not in Mac Donovan's, that the bastard was going to kill again.

"That's all you're getting," Sarah said. "Eat it or don't eat it. I don't care."

Soulful black eyes lifted from their contemplation of the contents of the can she had just dumped into Toby's dish. They held on hers as hopefully as the boy's had earlier. Ignoring them, too, she used the foot pedal to open the garbage can and tossed the empty can inside.

When she turned back, the dog was still watching her. Still ignoring him, she walked across to open the freezer compartment on the refrigerator, looking at the three frozen dinners that remained from her last foray to the grocery store. They looked about as appetizing as what was in the dog's bowl.

She pulled the middle one out of the stack and walked over to the microwave, aware that Toby's eyes followed every move. She opened the box, split the plastic with her thumbnail, and without consulting the printed instructions, shoved the black tray in and punched up a number. Maybe it wasn't the right one, but when the buzzer went off, she'd eat whatever came out.

Most nights went exactly as tonight had. They got home from the obligatory twice-a-day drag through the park, and then she would dump a can in Toby's bowl and put a carton in the microwave, usually without looking at either of them.

"It's beef and liver. You like beef and liver."

She couldn't remember when she'd started talking to the dog. Maybe when the silence around her had gotten so deep she could hear echoes of the voices that had once filled its current emptiness. Danny's laughter. The sound of him yelling about whatever was happening on his Playstation. Hers and Dan's fights. The creak of the old bed as they made love. At some point talking to the dog had become preferable to remembering any of those.

Almost delicately, considering his size, Toby picked one small chunk out of the rest. He had finished almost half of the can, one unnatural cube of pseudo-meat at a time, before the buzzer on the microwave went off behind her.

She jumped at the sound, although the dog seemed oblivious to it. She opened the door and picked the black plastic container up by the edges with her hands. She set it down on the counter and peeled back the sheet of cellophane. Taking a spoon out of the drawer beside her, she stirred the contents.

As she did, she realized she was hungry. Which seemed almost sacrilegious. Tate was out there somewhere, looking for his next victim, and she was thinking about food.

If that bastard had left me alone…

Tamping down her anger, she picked up the microwavable tray and walked back over to the refrigerator. She could hear the dog's tongue slurping around the rim of the bowl, cleaning out the last bit of juices from his dinner.

She set hers down and opened the door to take out

a can of Diet Coke. Holding that in one hand and her supper in the other, she crossed the kitchen. Without thinking, she pushed against the swinging door that led to the rest of the apartment with her left shoulder.

"Son of a bitch," she said aloud as the bruises protested.

The door opened enough to allow her through. She walked over to the couch and set the tray and Coke on the coffee table. She sat down and picked up the remote to turn on the TV.

All she wanted was background noise. The local news should be over by now, and if it wasn't, she'd switch stations. She had seen enough pictures of herself last night and today to last a lifetime.

Sitcom, she realized, relieved. She popped the tab on the Coke and then felt around beside the plastic tray for her fork. She couldn't find it, and after a few seconds she realized that she hadn't gotten one out of the drawer.

She stood up and had started back to the kitchen when she noticed that the light on the message machine was blinking. That was unusual enough that it stopped her. She stared down at the small red eye, trying to think who might have called.

She didn't believe anyone had left a message in the entire three months she'd lived here. She couldn't remember, other than the manager of the restaurant where she worked and her ex-mother-in-law, to whom she had given this number.

Probably someone looking for a quote or an interview. They'd shown an old black-and-white newspaper photo of her on all the broadcasts last night. No one had accused her outright of trying to shoot Tate, probably out of fear of a lawsuit, but anyone with half a brain could have figured out what they were getting at.

And from somewhere they'd found out about the animosity that had existed between her and Dan. The fact that she'd blamed her ex-husband for not keeping an eye on Danny that night.

She had already started by the machine when, moving almost of its own volition, her hand reached out and pushed the Play button. After all, there was always the possibility that the message was from Dan's mother. If Louise had seen the news reports yesterday, she might well have wanted to talk, either about Danny or about what they'd said.

Instead, when the tape began to play, the recording was of an unfamiliar male voice. And the message one that filled her with horror.

"I just thought you might want to know. You were the one Danny cried for as he was dying."

Four

With her initial phone call, she had wound her way up the chain of command until she'd finally been given the name and number of the detective who represented the N.O.P.D. on the national task force tracking Tate. Instead of calling, she'd decided to come downtown to speak to him in person.

Now, less than five minutes into this conversation, she knew that had been wasted effort. Detective Cochran had been attentive, his features arranged in the proper attitude of concern, but the horror of what she'd felt as she heard the message on her machine had not been reflected in them.

"I appreciate how much something like that would shake you up, Ms. Patterson. And you did the right thing to come in to talk to us, but…"

"But…?" she prompted when the pause stretched too long.

"That wasn't Tate."

"Then who the hell do you think it was?"

"Could have been anybody. Somebody who saw you on TV and thought leaving you that message would be…" Cochran lifted beefy hands from where they'd rested on his desk, moving them up and then out. The gesture seemed to indicate she should know what it would be.

She didn't. She had no idea why he thought someone other than Samuel Tate would call her to describe her son's dying. "Would be what?"

"Some kind of a joke. They saw you on television and… I don't know. They decided to get in on the action. Maybe they wanted to rattle your cage. Or rattle ours."

"A *joke*," she repeated. "You think someone would joke about how my son died?"

"You'd be surprised what people will do, Ms. Patterson."

When she had digested that disclaimer, the initial anger she'd felt at Cochran's suggestion surged again. "No. No, I wouldn't. Not anymore, Detective Cochran. Three years ago, maybe I could still be surprised by the depths of depravity the human race can sink to. Tate cured me of that in one night."

She stood, knowing she wasn't going to get any further with the police than the district attorney had gotten with that idiot judge yesterday. For some reason she had believed the cops would want to know about Tate's message. Naively, she'd even believed they would do something about the fact that he'd called her.

"Ms. Patterson, I understand that you're upset, and you have every right to be—"

"It was Tate," she interrupted, her voice low and intense. Controlled. "It wasn't a joke."

Cochran moved his shoulders, almost a shrug. "You might want to think about getting an unlisted number. What with the publicity and all." His hands rose again, the gesture more restrained this time.

"My number *is* unlisted. It's never *been* listed. And it's fairly new, so I guess whoever this is has some pretty good sources of information. I wonder how he did that with the cops watching him so closely. Having him under such tight surveillance."

The dark eyes reacted. She hadn't been quick enough to read the emotion in them before it was shuttered.

Surprise? Or…something else?

"Serial killers have certain patterns they follow, Ms. Patterson." Cochran's voice was reasoned and patient. "They have ways in which they…work. They stick to those methods because those things make them feel comfortable. Secure. Calling and leaving a message on your machine doesn't fit Tate's pattern."

"Maybe that's because I'm not an eleven-year-old boy. He's not raping and murdering me, Detective. He's only harassing me. Maybe his 'pattern,' as you call it, is different for that."

She could tell he wanted to argue with what she'd said. Mouth tight, he refrained from correcting her again, nodding instead as if he got her point.

"You want to go ahead and file a complaint?"

"Would that give you grounds to pick him up?"

In that case, she'd be willing to fill out the paperwork, despite Cochran's attitude. She'd be willing to do just about anything that would get the son of a bitch off the streets.

They couldn't hold him long on a harassment charge, but it would buy some time. Buy some other kid a reprieve, maybe. The hours they held Tate, at least he wouldn't be out prowling for his next victim.

"You'd be welcome to file one," the detective said.

She turned the phrase over in her mind, trying to figure out what bothered her about it. "I'd be welcome to file it, but...you still won't pick him up?"

"I didn't say that."

Cochran seemed evasive, yet she couldn't think of any reason why he would be. The cops should want Tate off the streets as much as she did. So why wasn't he jumping at a chance to pick him up for something? For anything?

"You don't know where he is," she said, speaking her realization aloud. "He told me they'd follow him. The cop who jumped me yesterday. He said you'd keep a close eye on Tate's every move. But instead..." She shook her head in disbelief. How many ways could they screw this up? "You let him go, and now you clowns don't have any idea where that murdering son of a bitch is."

The silence lasted long enough that she knew she was right.

Donovan. The name of the big cop who'd told her that had been in the *Picayune* this morning. She had skimmed the article before she'd folded the paper in disgust and stuck it back into the stack of others at the restaurant.

Maybe *he'd* listen to what she was trying to tell them. At least he'd seemed to give a damn yesterday. Not like this idiot.

"Is Detective Donovan here?"

"Donovan's on leave. Be back next month."

"A little vacation." She made sure he didn't miss the sarcasm this time.

Cochran's mouth tightened again, but she didn't care. The cops had a guy who killed children on their hands, and one of their detectives was taking the month off.

"Detective Donovan was suspended."

"Suspended?" The word surprised her. They wouldn't have suspended him for preventing her from killing Tate. They would probably have thought he deserved a medal, so…

"For what?"

"The station didn't like him taking their tape."

The TV station? The one whose cameraman Donovan had confronted after he'd jumped her?

"He told them it was evidence."

"That tape could have been used to bring a charge of attempted murder against you, Ms. Patterson. After Mac took it, it kind of conveniently disappeared. That didn't set too well with some people in the department."

"I don't understand."

"Detective Donovan refused to verify that you were trying to shoot Tate, Ms. Patterson. And he confiscated that tape so it couldn't be used to *prove* that's what you were doing."

"And then it...disappeared? Are you saying he *made* it disappear?"

"Mac Donovan did you a favor. One that cost him big time."

She didn't want to feel gratitude. Not to any of them. But certainly not to Mac Donovan.

No matter what his motives had been, Donovan had kept Tate alive. When she remembered the message that had been left on her machine, she couldn't find it in her heart to forgive him for that.

"And I'm supposed to be *grateful?* Sorry. Maybe the next mother whose child Tate tortures to death will be willing to thank him for both of us."

Cochran's eyes held hers, but she didn't back down. After a moment, he broke the contact between them by glancing down at the phone on his desk. His lips pursed, and then he looked up again, obviously conceding defeat in his attempt to induce guilt over Donovan's suspension.

"We can ask the phone company to let us know where the call came from, but ten to one, it'll turn out to be a pay booth somewhere. Or, if you want to go that route, we can put a trace on your home phone." Cochran's voice was carefully neutral.

"Don't bother. I'm sure you've got more important things to do than to chase people who are just 'making jokes.' After all, I wouldn't want anybody here to go out of their way to try to catch *this* guy either."

Sarah's anger built as she descended the stairs from the second floor office where she'd told her story. Eyes lowered as she hurried down them, she didn't realize there was someone coming up them until he spoke.

"Mrs. Patterson?"

She looked up, straight into the eyes of the man who'd tackled her yesterday. The man who, according to the guy she'd talked to upstairs, had been suspended for confiscating the video tape of that incident.

Apparently, she couldn't believe anything they told her. Not if it concerned Tate.

"Mackenzie Donovan." He added the identification when she didn't respond to his greeting. "We met yesterday after the hearing."

"Is that what *you* call it, Detective? A meeting?"

She hadn't realized until now how tall he was. No wonder she ached all over. Big and dark, with a shock of coal-black hair that seemed out of place with his blue eyes.

"Sorry. I hope you didn't suffer any ill effects. I thought… I thought you had a weapon."

"You know damn well what I had." She started down the stairs again, intending to edge by him.

"They call you in?"

The question stopped her. Or maybe it was his tone, evoking the same response as it had yesterday. He sounded as if he really cared.

Or maybe, if the cop upstairs had been telling the truth, he was regretting that his sacrifice had been in vain. And if he *had* been suspended—

"I thought you weren't supposed to be here."

"I left a few personal things I decided to come by and pick up."

Apparently the detective upstairs hadn't lied. At least not about that.

"They told me you got into trouble because of what you did with the tape."

His mouth moved slightly. One corner had definitely ticked upward before he quickly controlled the motion.

The concern in his voice was replaced by a hint of amusement. "Let's just say that today I'm even less the fair-haired boy around here than I normally am. No big deal."

"It is to me."

The words were too conciliatory. Almost the gratitude she had been determined not to express. After all, if it hadn't been for Mac Donovan—

"You didn't admit to anything, did you?" he asked. "Without that tape they got nothing. I was the closest to you. If we stick to the same story, they aren't going to pursue charges because they'll know there's no point."

He was still under the impression that she'd been brought in for questioning. She supposed she owed it to him to clear up that misunderstanding.

"Whatever you told them about what happened, I guess they bought it. Actually, I came about...something else."

She had almost told him about the message. She wanted to, and that, too, surprised her.

With the other detective's reaction, she decided she'd made a big enough fool of herself for one day. Besides, she didn't want to be under any greater obligation to Mac Donovan than she already was.

She started down once more, but he didn't move, evidently waiting for her to go by him. Just before she stepped onto the stair where he stood, under a compulsion she didn't completely understand, she raised her head to glance at him again. Up close the blue eyes were more remarkable, surrounded as they were by a fringe of thick, black lashes, which made them stand out against the darkly tanned skin.

"You know they lost him."

"Tate?" he clarified.

She nodded, controlling the surge of bile that hearing his name always created.

"He'll make a mistake," Donovan said. "Use a credit card. Visit one of the places here he was known to frequent. He'll do something. His patterns are too rigid. And when he does, believe me, Mrs. Patterson, they won't lose him again."

Something in the depths of his eyes had changed as he talked. You would think a man accustomed to dealing with the scum of the earth would be better at lying. *She* was probably better at it. Or maybe she was simply better at spotting the telltale signs.

"Before or after?"

"Ma'am?"

"Will they find him before or after he kills the next one?"

A muscle tightened in Detective Donovan's jaw, but he didn't respond. He didn't look away either, holding her eyes until she chose to break the contact. Finally she moved past him and continued down the remaining stairs.

She didn't stop when she reached the outside door, pushing through it and out into the cold, moisture-laden air. She took a deep breath, filling her lungs with it, trying, futilely, to erase the smell of the police station.

She hadn't said thank you to Donovan, although he was being punished because he'd tried to keep her from being charged with the attempted murder of her son's killer. Maybe she should be grateful to him for destroying that tape, but whatever she should feel about that was negated by how bitter she was that he'd kept her from doing what she'd intended.

Maybe Donovan hadn't gotten what he deserved, but then neither had she. Neither had Danny. Neither would the next child Tate selected.

That was something she couldn't find it in her heart to forgive any of them for. Not even herself.

"Says he left a message on her machine last night."

"What kind of message?" Mac asked, trying to fit that information into what he knew about Tate.

He had wanted to know what the hell was going on. And, although he was less willing to admit to this, he had wanted some human company besides the talking heads on TV. Until this afternoon, he'd had no reason to discover how bad daytime television really was.

"Telling her how the kid cried for her while he died."

"Jesus." Mac's voice was subdued by the horror of the image.

"Somebody looking to rattle her cage. Seen her on TV. Figured to be cute."

Mac nodded. It made more sense than Tate taking time to hunt up Sarah Patterson's number while he was evading the police. The guy was probably in Mexico by now. Some place far from New Orleans, anyway.

"What'd she say when you told her it wasn't him?"

"That I was wrong. That it had been Tate. Yada, yada. The call really spooked her. Took the time to file a complaint for harassment. So, you see our guy out there someplace, arrest him for harassment, okay?"

That was the kind of humor cops used when nothing was funny about the job they did.

"You talk to Morel?" Mac asked.

"About you?"

"Yeah, about me," Mac said. "What'd you think about?"

"I thought maybe about Tate. I told him about the call to Ms. Patterson. He agreed with me that it was some prankster. Bastards."

"I need to be on this, Sonny. I was the department's representative to the task force, for Christ's sake. I know this guy better than anybody here."

He was preaching to the choir, but frustration at being forced to stand on the sidelines while every cop in a hundred square miles was looking for Tate was getting to him. And he was only a few hours into this month-long suspension.

"I'll talk to him again," Sonny said, his voice free of any emotion Mac could read.

His partner understood everything he was feeling. Whining about the injustice of this wasn't doing either of them any good. He'd known there were risks when he'd destroyed that tape. He had just never imagined Morel would go so far.

"So what'd you think about her?"

It took a second for Sonny to shift mental gears. "The Patterson woman?"

Mac nodded. Then he turned one of the files on Sonny's desk around so he could pretend to read while he waited for his answer.

"Okay. If you like 'em thin. Got a mouth on her. I know why she's divorced."

"According to the news yesterday, she always blamed her husband." Mac wasn't sure why he felt the need to defend Sarah Patterson, but he didn't deny that he did.

"For the kid?"

"He was supposed to be watching him. He let him loose in the arcade at the mall while he went to the store next door. Left him there alone for more than an hour. He comes back. The kid's gone. Nobody saw a thing."

Sonny shook his head. "Bet she made his life hell."

"They say a kid dying is the hardest thing for a marriage to survive. And that's not just if it's something like what Tate did. That's illness, accident, whatever."

Mac couldn't remember where he'd read that. Maybe because of the murders, it had stuck with him. And it had come back to him yesterday.

In the case of the Pattersons, it made a lot of sense. How could you not want someone to blame if your kid was abducted and then brutalized in ways most people couldn't imagine one human doing to another?

People usually blamed the police. Or society. Sarah

Patterson had blamed her husband, who was supposed to have been watching his son.

"Yeah? So where was she when it happened? Working nights or something?" Sonny's question sounded judgmental.

Maybe it was meant to be. His wife stayed home with their three kids.

"I don't know. The paper didn't go into that. Just that the kid was supposed to be with his father."

Sonny nodded. "I'd like to get my hands on the guy who thought it would be cute to leave that message. Takes a sick mind, you know, to come up with something like that."

If there was one thing Mac had learned in the fifteen years he'd been a cop, it was that there were a lot of sick minds out there. Not just the Tates of this world, but guys like the one who'd left that message on Sarah Patterson's machine.

Sickos. Nutcases. Psychos. Cops called them all kinds of things. And they came in all degrees of craziness, from Tate to the homeless guy down on Esplanade who thought he was Jesus.

That had been one thing the profiler kept saying that really bothered him. That Tate wasn't insane.

Mac knew the legal definition of insanity was different from what most people thought of when they said the word, but it seemed to him that someone who could do the things Tate did to a kid would fall way on the other side of anybody's insanity scale. And he didn't. At least not according to the Bureau.

The psychologist one of the local stations had interviewed after they'd finally figured out they had a serial killer on their hands had called Tate a sociopath. No conscience. No empathy for those he hurt. No more than the normal person would have for killing a roach or a worm.

Mac understood that to do what Tate did, he would have to have that kind of mentality. What he hadn't been able to grasp, on anything other than an intellectual level, was that it didn't make him insane. Just…a sick mind.

There was that phrase again, bumping around in his head too strongly. He didn't like having it there. And he could imagine that Danny Patterson's mother had liked it even less.

Through the years, he had sometimes wondered how people endured what they endured. Remembering what had been in her eyes as she'd looked up at him from the sidewalk where he'd thrown her down, he knew exactly what had kept Sarah Patterson going.

And he wondered if Tate had any idea how lucky he had been that Mac was there yesterday morning.

Five

Sarah couldn't stop thinking about the words left on her machine yesterday, not even in the middle of the lunch hour rush. Normally, the best thing about her job was that with the hundred things she had to think about, there wasn't a lot of time for her brain to engage in that useless cycle of blame and regret.

Today, however, she couldn't get any of what had happened the last two days out of her mind. Her fury with the cops hadn't lessened during the nearly sleepless night she'd spent after her visit to the police station.

She kept thinking that if Tate could get her unlisted number within hours after his release, he probably wouldn't have any trouble finding out where she lived. And despite the nature of the decaying neighborhood that surrounded it, security at her building was a joke.

Like Detective Cochran thought that message had been.

"Your ex is out on the patio," Paul Reagan told her

as she came back through the swinging door into the restaurant's kitchen. "Wants to know if you've got a minute to talk."

All I need, Sarah thought.

Considering what she felt if she ever allowed herself to think about Danny's last few hours of life, as she had been since she'd listened to the message on her machine, Dan was the last person she wanted to see right now.

Glancing at her watch, she saw that it was after two. The lunch crowd had begun to thin, and most of her orders were up. Apparently Dan had figured out enough about her shift on his infrequent visits here to choose a time when it would be pretty hard to plead she was too busy to see him.

Besides, she would have to deal with him sooner or later. Like going to talk to the cops last night, this, too, was something she should just get over and be done with.

"Can you get 12 for me when it comes up?" she asked Paul. "I need to take care of this."

"Got it covered," Reagan agreed. "Go on. He giving you a hard time?"

No one at work had hassled her. They hadn't mentioned the media coverage, although the knowledge that she'd tried to kill the man who'd murdered her son had been in the eyes of some of her coworkers. They had met hers and then shifted uneasily away.

"Probably wants to float a loan," Sarah said as she headed toward the door leading to the patio.

Actually, that was the one thing she was sure Dan wouldn't try to do. He was making a hell of a lot more money than she was right now.

Located on the fringes of the Garden District, the restaurant where she worked had fewer drunks and lower tips than the ones in the Quarter. That had seemed a more than reasonable trade-off when she'd taken the job.

She hadn't even objected when she'd been assigned the day shift. She would have made more working after dark, but unlike a lot of the wait staff, she had no family to support. No one other than Toby, she amended.

Dan's company, on the other hand, was flourishing. He'd taken over his dad's contracting business when his father died fifteen years ago.

The company had specialized in repairs rather than home construction, and Dan had done well enough at it. After the hurricane, however, like most contractors in the region, Dan had more work than he could handle and at any price he wanted to name.

When they'd first married, Sarah had worked right along beside him. She'd handled whatever needed to be done, from bookkeeping and fielding calls to setting up appointments and wielding a hammer or nail gun during those times when Dan couldn't get enough help to complete a project by deadline.

As soon as Danny was old enough, he'd pitched in during the summers and when he had breaks from school. It had been, of necessity, a family business. Back when they had been a family.

Dan's way of coping with Danny's death had been to throw himself into his work. It must have helped, she admitted, because he had gotten over it a lot better than she had. And she still resented the hell out of that.

She fought a familiar sense of failure as she stepped through the outer door. After the interior warmth of the restaurant and the demands of the lunch hour rush, the bite of the cold air felt good.

The patio, which was nothing more than row of small wrought-iron tables and chairs set on bricks laid in sand between the restaurant and the sidewalk, was popular in the spring and fall. The area wasn't open to customers this time of year, which was why Dan had chosen it.

He was sitting at one of the tables, watching the traffic move up and down St. Charles. He was smoking, the cigarette held between his thumb and index finger.

His hands were large, perpetually callused, and deeply tanned from the hours he worked outdoors. To her, they had always been one of his most attractive features. Even now, despite everything that lay between them, the accusations and the bitter arguments, at the sight of them there was a brush of desire, hot and aching, in the bottom of her stomach.

Need, she amended. Not desire. Pure, unadulterated physical need. And considering how long it had been since those needs had been satisfied, this was nothing she wouldn't have felt for any attractive man. Especially one with whom she had a long and satisfying sexual history. Out of all the things that had gone wrong in their marriage—and at the last almost everything had—sex hadn't been one of them.

As he stubbed out the cigarette with a characteristic impatience, Dan turned his head and caught her watching him. She moved forward, pulling out the chair across the table.

Before she completed the motion of sitting down in it, he asked, "What the hell did you think you were doing?"

I did what you should have done.

Exactly the kind of thinking that had led to their divorce. The kind the counselor had repeatedly warned her against. She had finally succeeded in preventing herself from voicing those thoughts, but she had never been able to deny them a place in her consciousness.

"I would think that would be obvious, Dan. Even to you."

"If you'd killed him, they'd have fried you."

He must have gotten that from the news. Dan wasn't exactly into cause and effect.

"*They* can't manage to fry *him*. At the time, however, I wasn't real worried about what the cops were going to do to me."

"If you're going to try something like that, you don't do it in public. On the steps of the fucking courthouse, for God's sake."

"Is that what you came here for? To tell me what I did wrong?"

Shoot, bitch. And don't talk.

"Ma's worried about you. I came because she asked me to."

That was probably the truth, Sarah decided. After all her years of experience, Dan's motives were pretty much an open book.

"Tell her I'm fine. Tell her..." She couldn't think of a single comforting thing to tell Dan's mother.

Danny's death had devastated her mother-in-law

almost as much as it had the two of them. Of course, Louise had looked after Danny a lot when he was little and they'd been trying to get the business back on its feet after her father-in-law's long illness.

Their divorce had been another blow, especially since Dan's mother had understood the reasons for it. She had known Sarah blamed Dan for Danny's death and that she couldn't find it in her heart to forgive him.

As a result, her mother-in-law seemed to have aged ten years during the last three. Maybe they all had, but it showed more on Louise. For the first time since Sarah had known her, she seemed old.

"Tell her I'm okay," she said finally. "And that I said not to worry."

"She sees you all over the TV, with them saying you're trying to shoot somebody, dredging up the dirty details of our divorce, she's going to worry. You know that, Sarah. I don't know what the hell you were trying to prove."

"I wasn't trying to prove anything. I heard they were going to let him go. I didn't think that was right."

"You can't take the law into your own hands. That's why they got courts. You've got to let them handle it."

That was the same thing the cops had said. It made even less sense to her coming from her ex-husband.

"He called me last night." She hadn't intended to tell Dan about the message, but somehow the words were in her brain and then out of her mouth.

Dan's forehead furrowed, his brows coming together over the bridge of his nose. "Who?"

"Tate. The cops said it was somebody playing a joke, but it wasn't. It was him. I know it was him."

"You *talked* to him?"

She shook her head, wondering for the first time if he would have talked to her if she'd been at home. And then wondering if he had somehow known she wasn't.

"He left a message on my answering machine."

There was a small silence, but Dan had to ask the inevitable question. "What kind of message?"

She hadn't had any trouble saying the words to the detective she'd talked to last night. She had repeated them with the same sense of disassociation she'd struggled to maintain when she read through the speculation about Tate's background and his personality after his arrest.

They were just words, she'd told herself. With only the power she gave them. But for some reason, she couldn't say them now.

It was harder for men to protect themselves against the impact of something like that message. They weren't allowed to cry. Instead, they put guns in their mouths or they drank too much and drove head-on into a bridge abutment.

"Just taunting me," she lied, protecting Dan out of habit and instinct.

"Because of what you tried to do?"

She nodded.

"He threaten you?"

"It wasn't like that. It was…gloating."

He didn't ask again what Tate had said. She could tell from his eyes he didn't want to know. And because she had once loved him, a long time ago, she didn't repeat those terrible words to him.

"He scare you?"

She shrugged. Then, just as she had while she'd waited outside on the courthouse steps that morning, she crossed her arms over her chest, running her hands up and down them. She was beginning to feel the damp cold through the thin white cotton dress shirt that, with a black vest and red bow tie, comprised her work uniform.

"It was… I don't know. Hearing his voice, it was like he'd been there. Inside my apartment. You know?"

He nodded, his eyes concerned. "You want to come stay with me and Ma for a few days?"

She shook her head. "You know I can't do that. It isn't good for any of us, but…especially not good for her."

"What are the cops going to do about it?"

"I told you. They said it wasn't him. I went ahead and filed a complaint. That way, if they catch him killing somebody else, they'll let me press charges for harassment."

"They can't pick him up for leaving the message?"

"Maybe. If they knew where the hell he is."

"They didn't follow him when he was released? Stake out his house or something? Shit, what were they thinking?"

"The impression I got is that they don't have a clue where he is. Comforting, isn't it?"

"Assholes. This has been nothing but a fuck-up from the start. They don't even know what he's doing until the bodies start piling up. They mess up the arrest and have to release him. Then they can't even keep up with the guy."

As much as she agreed with Dan's assessment of the police work, she couldn't afford to get into assigning blame for Tate's success. That kind of thinking triggered the endless round of anger and bitterness she needed to avoid in order to stay sane.

Besides, the two of them had said these same words, or ones like them, a thousand times in the first year after their son's murder. Nothing had ever changed. When she woke up in the morning, Danny was still dead.

"I've got to go," Sarah said, interrupting the pattern they'd fallen into in the only way she'd ever figured out to interrupt it. By running away. "Tell Louise I really am okay. And that what she saw on TV… Tell her… Tell her I won't do that again."

She wasn't sure that was the truth, but she thought her mother-in-law would like to hear it. Maybe Dan would, too. Maybe it would reassure him.

She was sorry now she'd told him about Tate's call, but she had needed to tell someone. Someone who would be as outraged as she was. Someone who would buy into her conviction that it had been Tate.

"I could put you in a security system."

She had already risen and started toward the door that led inside when Dan's offer registered in her tired brain. She turned back, her expression questioning.

"Motion sensors. An alarm," he added.

"You know how to do that?"

"I can figure it out. Get the stuff at cost with my license. You'd have to pay if you want monitoring, but I could rig it to where the alarm goes off if somebody tries to come into the apartment. They wouldn't know if it was connected to a protection service or directly to the cops."

"I don't think that's necessary," she said, but the more she thought about it, the more tempting it was.

"I can do it for almost nothing. It'll make me feel better about you being there by yourself. It'd make Ma feel better, too."

"The cops said Tate wouldn't do something like that. Call me, I mean." After his generosity, she felt she should be honest with Dan about what she'd been told. "They said it didn't fit his pattern. But…I don't like the idea of somebody having my phone number."

"Let me come over and take a look. See what I can rig up. You got nothing to lose."

The phrase she'd avoided yesterday. Nothing to lose.

So many mornings since Danny had been killed, she'd opened her eyes and wished she was dead. Then last night, because of the message on her machine, she had taken Dan's gun out of the drawer and put it on top of her bedside table. And that hadn't been so she could use it on herself.

"You sure?" She was a little surprised by her willingness to think about what Dan was proposing, considering the possible emotional pitfalls involved.

"You got a spare key, I'll go by there now. We're pretty much caught up."

"I don't have it with me," she said.

"What time you get off?"

"Four-thirty."

"I could meet you. Take a look at your place. See what I need to pick up. You give me the key then, and

certainty that it was Tate had lessened through the course of the day. Still, no matter who had left that message, she didn't want to leave a key lying around.

When the lock clicked, she pushed the door inward, letting Toby's waiting nose edge through. He barked once in greeting, and then, as the opening widened and he saw the boy behind her, the entire back end of his body began to wag.

"I have to get his leash," she explained, unwilling to invite the kid inside. This apartment was a refuge from the very feelings Dwight Ingersoll evoked.

"Okay."

Dwight bent, putting his arms around the dog's neck as he had yesterday at the curb. Toby was too eager for his run to respond as calmly as he had then. Despite his impatience, he managed to bestow a few perfunctory licks across the kid's mouth and chin.

Dwight looked up at her, eyes wide, mouth rounded with surprise and pleasure. Apparently, she'd been forgiven. Or, in one of those quicksilver mood shifts common to his age, he'd forgotten her initial reluctance to take him. After all, Toby was genuinely glad to see him.

While he and the dog renewed their acquaintance in the doorway, she set her purse on top of the bookcase. Her eyes automatically found the indicator light on the answering machine. It wasn't blinking.

Only with the resulting wave of relief did she realize how much she'd been dreading a repetition of last night. In a fit of anger, she had erased that message as soon as she'd gotten home from the police station. That she had done so had been another thing she had worried about during her nearly sleepless night.

She slipped her keys into the pocket of her slacks as she pulled the elastic-backed bow tie off over her head. She tossed it on the bookcase and unfastened the top button of her shirt as she crossed the room to grab Toby's leash from among the books and magazines stacked on the coffee table.

Seeing it in her hand when she turned, the dog broke from Dwight's embrace, beginning his nightly "I need to go" dance, nails clicking like castanets on the scarred hardwood floor.

Spare key, she remembered as she started toward him. Damn Dan. Why couldn't he ever get anywhere on time?

She debated putting the leash on Toby and letting Dwight hold him while she went into the kitchen to retrieve her extra key. In his hurry to get to the entryway, the mutt would probably pull the kid down the stairs. Toby had thrown her off balance a couple of times, and she was a lot stronger than Dwight.

"Sarah? You up there?"

She stuck her head out of the door the child was propping open as he watched Toby cavort. Her ex-husband was coming up the stairs, one hand on the banister, the other holding a metal carpenter's tape.

His eyes found hers briefly before they dropped to the boy squatting at dog's-eye level in the doorway. Dwight had pivoted to face the stairs as soon as he heard Dan's voice.

When her ex-husband glanced up again, his expression was quizzical. Sarah found there was nothing about this she wanted to explain. Especially not the part about why she had a kid camped out on her doorstep.

"I was just about to take Toby out," she said instead.

"Hey, Tobe," Dan said. "What ya doing, you old fleabag?"

The dog lunged past Dwight, making for Dan, who reached down to ruffle his fur, smiling at the boy as he did.

"I'm Dan. Who are you?"

"Dwight David Ingersoll."

The words weren't quite as singsong, but they caused Dan's lips to twitch before he reasserted control.

"So…you a friend of Toby's?"

The boy looked back at Sarah, as if asking permission to answer. Or maybe for confirmation that he was.

When she realized she was smiling at him in reassurance, she forced her eyes to focus on Dan's hand instead of the child's face. Those long, tanned fingers were massaging the spot behind Toby's ear that turned the dog into a slobbering, mindless love slave.

"I'm *her* friend," Dwight said. "Toby's a *dog*." The last held a hint of scorn for anyone who didn't understand the subtleties of friendship.

Dan's eyes, filled with amusement, again met Sarah's, but he continued to address the boy. "You've never heard the expression 'man's best friend'? That's Toby. You are, aren't you, old boy?"

"We have to go."

Her words, clipped and unfriendly, brought Dwight's gaze back to her face, his brow wrinkled in concern. She wondered if he could possibly be sensitive enough to recognize the strained dynamics of her relationship with Dan.

"Toby needs to go out," she explained, trying to soften the harshness of her tone.

Somehow, she and Dan had fallen back into their old patterns of behavior. Dan, being charming and laid back, making points with both the dog and the boy. And she, put into the position of having to remind all of them of priorities and duties. During her marriage, it had sometimes felt as if she were rearing two children rather than one.

"We may not be back before you're through," she went on, determined to be clear with Dan about exactly why he was here. She didn't intend to repeat the mistake she'd made yesterday with the kid. "You don't have to wait. Just make sure the lock's on before you close the door."

"Key?" Dan reminded, straightening from his bending stance over the dog. She must have looked blank, because he added, "So I can come by tomorrow and put this stuff in, remember."

"I'll get it. It's in the kitchen."

She handed him the leash and then headed back inside. Behind her, she could hear Dan talking to Dwight. Admiring the ball. Throwing the occasional conversational tidbit to Toby, who was probably wondering what the hell was going on.

This was the most excitement the dog had had since they'd moved in. She could only hope that and the delay in taking him out didn't lead to an accident.

She fished the extra key out of the small china vase she kept it in. As she set the container back on the kitchen shelf, she noticed that her coffee mug and cereal bowl from this morning were still sitting in the sink. She thought about washing them and putting them away before her ex-husband saw them.

Which would be the height of hypocrisy, she admitted.

She had constantly stayed on Dan and Danny about picking up their things. Working the hours she did, she'd complained that she didn't have time to run around behind them and put their stuff away. That didn't mean she couldn't damn well leave a dish in her own sink if she wanted to.

As she walked back into the living room, leaving the swinging door to the kitchen open, she could see Toby darting up and down the hall, legs comically spread to avoid the leash that trailed between them. He was barking at the ball, which Dan and the boy were throwing back and forth, bouncing it once at a midpoint between them.

She stepped out into the chaos, intending to remind them that her neighbors probably wouldn't be thrilled with the noise. Before she could, Toby reared on his hind legs, knocking down Dwight's last awkward, overhand throw.

The dog pounced on the ball as it ricocheted off the wall. It was almost too large for him to grip with his teeth, but somehow, maybe because some of the air had seeped out as it aged, he got his mouth around part of it. Tail wagging, he carried the ball over to the child and dropped it at his feet.

Dwight's laughter was clearly delighted. And he

wanted someone to share his joy in the dog's antics. His eyes found Dan's face first and then hers.

"Tell him he's a good boy," Dan suggested.

"Good boy," the child repeated obediently, stooping to hug the dog. "Good Toby."

"If you two aren't careful, you're going to be cleaning up after that 'good boy.'"

Had she always been like this? she wondered, hearing the note of censure. Why couldn't she just let them have fun instead of anticipating problems?

Because someone has to anticipate them. Someone has to be the grown-up. Someone has to think of all the things that could happen. And Dan, of course, had never done that. Maybe if he had—

She jerked her mind away before it could complete the circuit. The counselor had told her that some people simply didn't have that kind of mentality. They couldn't plan for disasters because they couldn't imagine having them happen.

"Key." She held the spare out to her ex-husband. "And don't forget to lock the door when you leave."

"Yes, ma'am," he said, winking at Dwight.

The spurt of anger she felt at the gesture was ridiculous. She acknowledged that, but she couldn't do anything about the fact that she'd felt it.

"Are you going or staying?" she asked the boy, her voice impatient where Dan's had been teasing.

Why would he want to go? Who would possibly want to be with you when there's any other option on the face of the earth?

"Going," Dwight said promptly, as if there had never

been any doubt. He picked up the ball, and then waited, hovering over Toby.

He wants to hold the leash, Sarah realized. He had asked her if he could, and she'd never answered him. Instead of just reaching down to take it as Danny might have, he was waiting for permission.

"He's pretty strong," she warned.

"So am I," Dwight said, tucking the ball under one arm and bending the other upward at the elbow to make a muscle.

He looked down at his triceps, hidden under the thin jacket, and then cut his eyes up at her. There was a trace of amusement in them, as if he knew what a joke that was, but still hoped she'd enjoy it with him.

"I'll take the ball," she said. "Don't let him pull you down the stairs. I don't want to have to explain to your mother how my dog broke your leg."

"I'll be careful."

Another of those phrases he had probably repeated a thousand times. It was a promise she'd required often enough. She had thrown that admonition at Danny every morning when she'd let him out of the car in front of school. Or even if he were just going into Louise's house.

Be careful.

I will.

And yet, despite all her warnings and precautions—

"Have fun," Dan said as they started down the stairs.

She didn't look back. And she didn't glance down to see if the boy had either.

Seven

"Sounds unlikely," Daryl Johnson said, "but you've got to remember he's riding high right now. This guy already thought he was smarter than God and that the police were too stupid to catch him."

"Then there we go, proving him right," Mac said.

Mac had been bothered by the message left on Sarah Patterson's answering machine last night. Uncomfortable enough about the possibilities it represented to touch base with his contact at the FBI. In doing so, he'd conveniently failed to mention his suspension.

"Everybody makes mistakes." Johnson's voice was carefully nonjudgmental.

"Even you guys?" Mac asked.

There was a pause before Johnson said, "Occasionally. You think I'm making one now?"

"You're the expert. I'm just a cop with a bunch of dead kids on his hands. Trying to figure out if this bastard is stupid enough to go after the mother of one of them."

Another few seconds of silence before Johnson responded. "He likes little boys because they're easy to control. Could it be that he thinks this woman would be, too?"

"He'd be wrong," Mac said unequivocally.

The image of Sarah's face as she'd held out that big gun, pointed straight at Tate, was in his mind's eye. There was no doubt in his mind that if he hadn't stopped her, she would have shot the son of a bitch. At that range, she wouldn't have missed.

At that range… Close enough to look Tate in the face. Close enough for Tate to look into her eyes. Close enough for him to know that she damn well intended to blow him away?

"What about other than the easy-to-control business? I mean…this guy kills little boys because he gets off on boys, right?"

"He kills because he likes killing people. He likes controlling them. Hurting them. Humiliating them. That's the sexual payoff for him. But yeah…to answer your question, he prefers boys. Sexually, I mean. His version of sexually isn't what you and I mean by that, however."

"So he wouldn't be interested in a woman?"

"Not in the usual way."

"Would he be interested in killing her?"

The pause was even longer this time. Mac wasn't sure he liked that. He knew he didn't like having to wait through it.

"Contrary to popular belief, there are indiscriminate serial killers. Maybe we should call them equal opportunity killers. Anybody who crosses their path is fair game. I could give you half a dozen names you'd recognize, but…I don't think that's what we're dealing with in Tate. In my opinion—and remember, that's all any of this is—it's more likely that whoever left that message was pursuing an agenda other than the one Tate's embarked on."

"Like what?"

"Borrowing some of Tate's notoriety. Maybe this guy figured the cops would go public with the threat. His little moment in the limelight, even if it's only reflected from Tate's crimes."

"You think he'll lie low for a while? Since we know who he is?"

"Tate, you mean? I think he'll move on. Relocate. He's probably already done that. If you're asking if I think he's through killing… Not until he's dead. There's no AA for this. And the only twelve steps that will do these guys any good are those that lead to the chair."

"We don't use the chair down here. Too inhumane," Mac mocked. "But if I could, I'd pull the switch on this bastard myself."

From what he'd read in Sarah Patterson's eyes that morning, so would she.

"You got to catch him first, Mac."

"And you think we've blown our chance."

"I think he's going to become someone else's headache now," Johnson said. And then, his tone brisker, more businesslike, "Be sure you get everything you have into the database. Maybe whoever ends up dealing with him next will pick up the pattern a little sooner. Otherwise… These guys get better with every murder. They learn what works and what doesn't. And Tate really is smart, which makes him very good at what he does."

There was a part of Mac that wanted to celebrate the idea of this guy moving on. Looking at the photographs they'd pinned to the board in the task force room had been bad enough. Meeting Sarah Patterson, learning the effect her son's death had had on her life, had made all those pictures even more real. He didn't want to have to put up photographs of some other kid's mutilated body.

At the same time, perversely, he hated to admit failure. This was his town. His job. Maybe it hadn't been his mistake that had let Tate walk, but it was also his department.

Besides all that, he wanted Tate. He wanted to be the one to put him away. He didn't want him moving on to some other unsuspecting city, where the cops would have to learn all about him, murder by murder, just as they had here.

"But…a phone call?" Johnson went on, pulling him back into the conversation. "Doesn't sound like something he'd be interested in. Not now."

"So I can tell her to relax."

"I didn't say that," Johnson denied quickly. "Believe me, Mac, I would never advise *anybody* to relax while someone like Samuel Tate is out there."

They hadn't made it back from the park until after dark. Sarah hadn't had the heart to cut short Toby and

Dwight's game until the last possible second. Then, to make sure that he didn't get into trouble because he was late, she had walked Dwight to the door of his street-level apartment.

He wouldn't let her ring the bell. In case his grandmother was asleep, he'd said. He had a key on a chain like the military used for dog tags around his neck.

"Are you sure your mom won't be upset that we're late?"

He looked up from his farewell hug of Toby to smile at her. "As long as I'm with you, it'll be all right."

Despite her doubts, Sarah had left it at that. She'd waited until he was safely inside and she'd heard the night latch engage before she turned away from the door, congratulating herself that she hadn't had to talk to Dwight's mother.

That would come later, she supposed, because, of course, she hadn't found a way to tell him not to wait beside her door again. At least she had escaped meeting Mrs. Ingersoll tonight.

On top of that good fortune, when she'd reached her apartment, she discovered that Dan had remembered to lock her door. She seemed to be batting a thousand.

Minor triumphs, maybe, but even the excursion to the park had been nothing like she'd been dreading, she admitted as she inserted her key. She had thought that seeing Dwight play with Toby would bring back painful memories. But this child was so different from Danny—different in every possible way—that she had been able to watch him with an emotional detachment she wouldn't have believed possible.

She pushed open the door and loosened her grip on Toby's leash. "Dan?"

As she waited for an answer, the dog trotted across the living room, headed for the kitchen. After a few seconds she heard him slurping water from his bowl.

"Dan? You still here?"

There was no answer. Relieved, she turned back to throw the dead bolt. When she had, she leaned forward, putting her forehead against the cool, smooth wood of the door.

The sense of sanctuary, which she had been afraid might be destroyed by Dan's or the child's presence within the apartment, settled comfortingly around her. That fear had been stronger somehow than the sense of violation she'd felt listening to the message last night.

Prompted by the memory, she glanced at the light on the answering machine. The small red eye was pulsing on and off like a toothache. The feeling of homecoming she had just celebrated disappeared in a bowel-clenching rush of adrenaline.

Please, God, no, she prayed, tears pricking behind her eyes.

She closed them, denying the moisture, again telling herself this could be anyone. Dan. Dwight's mother. Detective Cochran. The restaurant. Every phone call she received for the rest of her life wasn't going to be like the one last night.

As she stood there, paralyzed by dread, she heard Toby return. She opened her eyes to find him standing in the kitchen doorway, watching her. His head was cocked, as if he were wondering why she hadn't joined him. After that unaccustomed bout of exercise, he was probably ready for his supper.

Feed Toby, she told herself. Then she could worry about whatever was on the machine. She didn't have to listen to it now. There would be plenty of time to do that after she'd tended to the dog.

Whatever the message was, it was only a voice. Only the recording of a voice, she amended, deliberately distancing herself from what was on that tape. Someone's idea of a joke. She grasped at Cochran's explanation, the same one she had angrily rejected last night.

She crossed the room, giving the phone a wide berth. When she reached the kitchen, it was as if she had made it through some kind of emotional gauntlet. She didn't have to look at that blinking light. She didn't have to think about it. Not until she wanted to. Not until she was ready.

She took a can of dog food off the shelf and stuck it under the arm of the opener without looking at the label. Toby would be hungry enough to eat whatever she put in front of him. She dumped its contents into his bowl and turned to pitch the can into the trash. Sitting on the counter beside the sink was a glass.

Maybe Dan had remembered to lock the door, but in some ways nothing had changed. Tonight that was almost comforting.

When she'd disposed of the can, from force of habit she walked over to the sink and turned on the hot water. She rinsed the glass out before she set it down beside her mug and bowl.

Behind her, she could hear Toby snuffling around hungrily in his dish. Whatever it was she'd given him tonight apparently met with his approval.

She took a deep breath, releasing more of her tension with the slow exhalation. The blinking light was not necessarily anything bad, she told herself again. Not necessarily a repetition of last night's message.

Don't borrow trouble. Louise had said that to her over and over again during her marriage. At least she had before Danny died.

Tiredly Sarah lifted both arms and used her fingers to comb her hair away from her face. The smell of grease from the restaurant's kitchen, which always permeated the fabric of her cuffs, made her slightly nauseated.

She'd feel better if she got out of these clothes and took a bath. Maybe feel more like eating, although right now she couldn't think of anything that seemed the least bit appetizing.

Toby was pushing his bowl across the floor as he tried to get at the last of the gravy. The dish made a series of bump and scrape noises against the tile. Familiar. Known. Dear.

Her lips curved at the memory of the big lummox chasing that silly ball. He had played like an overgrown puppy.

Just feeding him every night wasn't really taking care of him. He needed exercise. Companionship. Dan was even better at that than she was.

Of course, Toby had always had a preference for masculine company. He'd trailed after Dan or Danny wherever they went. He had tolerated her, yet ironically, she was the one who had ended up with him.

To try to hold on to some part of Danny?

Whatever her reasons for taking the dog, he was now her responsibility. And she needed to do better by him. It was an obligation. A duty. She was the one who was supposed to be so damn good at those.

She put her hands on the edge of the counter, pushing away from it in order to head to the bathroom. Toby lifted his head as if he might follow her.

He wasn't totally sure, however, that he'd removed every particle of food from his dish. Before she left the kitchen, he was back at it. The sound of that bump and scrape followed her across the living room, where she again ignored the light on the answering machine.

Mac Donovan glanced at the address he'd jotted on the back of an envelope. He'd had Sonny read it to him over the phone off the complaint form Mrs. Patterson had filled out last night. With the information, his partner had included an unsolicited warning that Morel wasn't going to like Mac butting into the case.

As if this isn't my case, Mac thought, his resentment of what Morel had done boiling up again as he pulled his car up to the curb.

His eyes examined the dilapidated building whose numbers matched those he'd been given. It didn't fit with the impression he'd formed of Sarah Patterson.

Of course, he'd just met her, under circumstances no one could consider social. And his opinion had been influenced by his admiration of what she had tried to do, misguided or not. As one of the cops who had spent the last couple of years trying to catch Tate, he wasn't exactly unbiased. Still…

The place where she lived had been a private dwelling at one time. If it had followed the normal route most of these big Victorian houses had taken, it had gradually been carved up into apartments, each generation of them growing smaller and less attractive than the previous one.

That happened a lot in New Orleans, especially in neighborhoods like this. Not historic enough to attract preservation money or civic interest, the houses were simply allowed to slowly deteriorate.

He laid the envelope on the dash and opened the door on a post-twilight darkness. Someone had shot out the street lamp, but the lights on either side of the building's entryway, encased in mesh cages, survived. And there were lights on inside both of the ground-floor apartments.

As he studied the sagging porch over the front door, the curtain that obscured the window of the street-level apartment on his right was pushed aside. A child's face, ghostly white in the dimness, was pressed against the dark glass.

As he got out of the car, the kid waved. Mac glanced at the street behind him to see if that greeting had been intended for someone else.

There was no one there, so he lifted his hand and self-consciously twisted his wrist a couple of times. The kid's wave became more vigorous.

Not the usual reception a representative of the

N.O.P.D. could expect down here, he thought cynically. Turning back to the car, he pressed the auto-lock and then slammed the door, taking the beat cop's habitual survey of his surroundings as he did.

It was too cold for the inhabitants of the neighboring houses to be out on their porches and stoops as they probably would have been at any other time of the year. Tonight, they were all inside, trying to stay warm.

When he finally turned back to face the house, the child at the window had disappeared, probably called away to do homework or eat supper. As if in reaction to the thought, Mac's stomach growled.

Since he had eaten a late lunch, this was more likely a protest over the heaviness of that meal rather than anticipation of supper. He wondered if Sarah Patterson had already eaten dinner. A little surprised that he would even think to question that, he pushed the idea to the back of his mind and started up the sidewalk.

According to the address on the form, she lived in 3B. He considered the house again, counting stories. Unless the roofline hid an attic apartment, she was at the top. In the cheap seats.

Sonny had said she was a waitress. In this town that could mean very good money. Of course, you had to work your way up to the older, more established places that attracted the heavy tippers. Since she'd been divorced less than a year, maybe Sarah hadn't had time to do that. Or maybe she was just crummy at the job. She didn't seem to have the personality required for that perky servitude.

And how the hell would you know that? he wondered as he followed the sidewalk up to the entry.

He stopped to study the array of buzzers. Half of them were unmarked, bearing neither a name nor a number. Since the door was propped open with a narrow wedge of wood, designed to prevent the lock from engaging, he supposed it didn't matter if the residents were unidentified.

So much for security.

He pushed the door open, wondering how many customers he would lock out if he kicked the wedge out of the way. But that was none of his business. At least not right now.

Of course, neither was the woman on the third floor, but Mac didn't let that realization stop him from entering the building, letting the front door close against the block of wood.

The hall that led to the bedroom was dark, but Sarah didn't bother with the light. She walked into the bathroom, flipping on the one over the lavatory. As she began unbuttoning her vest, she closed her eyes, rolling her neck from side to side to work out the stiffness.

When she opened them, her gaze fell on the toilet. The seat was up, and when she saw it, an unwanted nostalgia crowded her throat.

That was another of the endless things she had nagged them about. All those nights when she'd stumbled into the bathroom in the dark, trying not to wake anyone, and had sat down on the cold rim of the john.

Just assume it's going to be up, Dan had said. *There's more of us than there are of you.*

There always had been. A masculine conspiracy.

She stepped across the narrow bathroom and, bending down, turned on the water to begin filling the claw-footed tub. Although there were rust stains from spigot to drain, the tub had been one of the selling points of the apartment. She had had to look pretty hard to find something charming about the place, but this big, old-fashioned bathtub had definitely qualified.

She heard Toby click down the hall as she walked over to the clothes hamper to drop her vest inside. He was heading back to the bedroom to take a nap on her bed. He'd finally learned that when the bathroom door was closed, the room was off limits.

Danny, on the other hand, had never understood why she would ever need to be alone, for any reason. She realized with a small jolt that she was smiling at the memory.

Just as she had smiled as she'd watched the dog and the boy play in the park this afternoon. Dwight ran with a gait that was almost girlish, as if he hadn't done much running, but that wasn't why she had smiled. It had been because of their pure, unadulterated joy in what they were doing.

She couldn't remember the last time she had felt like that. Maybe you had to be a child to feel it, and God knew there was nothing childlike left within her.

There was a noise in the hall, drawing her eyes to the closed door. She waited, listening for the sound to be repeated so she could identify it. When it was, she realized Toby was out there, sniffing along the bottom of the door.

Trying to get in? He hadn't done that in a long time.

The dog whined a couple of times, and then he barked, the tone sharp and demanding.

"Go take a nap," she said, as if he could understand the instruction.

When she began to turn back toward the tub, she caught a glimpse of her reflection in the mirror above the lavatory. The effects of a sleepless night followed by the long day were evident in her face. Her eyes were rimmed with red, the shadows under them pronounced.

She had begun to turn away from that depressing image when she noticed a smear on the shower curtain behind her, which was also reflected in the mirror. She completed the motion, her eyes searching for whatever she had seen in the glass. She found it, high on the edge, as if someone with dirty hands had pushed the curtain back to reveal the tub.

Dan? she wondered, taking a step to the side in order to examine the spot more carefully.

The smear wasn't dirt. Dan must have cut his finger and then come in here to find a Band-Aid or to wash the cut out with soap and water.

In the bathtub rather than at the lavatory?

Her gaze dropped to the water filling the tub. Surely when she'd bent down to turn the handles, she would have noticed if there had been droplets of blood on the white porcelain.

Toby barked again, still demanding, and then he began pawing at the door, his nails moving rapidly against the wood as if he were digging a hole. Still puzzling over the stain on the curtain, she strode over to the door and jerked it open. The dog was shocked enough by the abruptness of its movement to back up a step or two, his eyes red in the darkness.

"What the hell's the matter with you?" With her first word, he pushed by her, barreling into the bathroom.

"Oh, no, you don't." She tried to block his entrance with her knee, but it didn't work. He skidded across the ceramic tile, taking refuge behind the toilet.

As far away from her as he could get. As if he thought she was going to beat him or something. Her mouth opened to yell at him, but no sound came out.

The dog had left behind him a trail of paw prints on the white tile. Their edges were blurred and indistinct, softened by the thick fur around his pads, but there was no doubt about the medium with which they had been imprinted. The only way the damn dog could have gotten that much blood on his feet…

Then, her breath slowly congealing to ice in her chest, Sarah turned, looking out into the dark hallway.

Eight

As Mac stepped into the foyer, the accumulated smells of age and mildew were thick. An unpleasant contrast to the winter-tinged crispness of the outside air.

He stood in the fetid dimness a moment, getting a feel for the building. Somewhere, a baby cried faintly in long, sirenlike wails. A television blared unintelligibly from the apartment to his left. There was no sound at all from the one to the right, where he'd seen the kid.

His eyes tracked up the staircase that centered the hall. Its banisters had been intricately tooled from what appeared to be mahogany. A few of the individual balusters were missing, but it still managed to echo the elegance of the era during which the house had been built. Judging by the grime that virtually obscured the swirling arabesques of its pattern, the carpet that covered the tread probably dated from that period as well.

Third floor. He started up the stairs, realizing as he

approached the second story that this was where the baby lived.

Its hysteria seemed to be increasing. Surely somebody would shove a pacifier or a bottle into its mouth pretty soon. The noise was beginning to grate, and he'd only been here a couple of minutes.

As he continued to climb, he became conscious of the heat that increased with each step. The baby was whooping now, with no pauses between the shrieks, so that he wondered where the kid was getting the air necessary to fuel the sound.

As he climbed up the final flight, both the temperature and the discomfort increased, but at least the noise from the lower levels faded away. In contrast to the clamor below, the third floor seemed deserted. No sounds of televisions or radios. No signs of life.

Wild goose chase? he wondered, verifying that the door of 3B was to the right of the top of the stairs, separated from them by a narrow hallway. The heat here was stifling, although the window at the end of the hall had been left open, its sash raised a few inches.

He resisted the urge to take off his sports coat. After all these years on the job, he felt naked if he didn't slip on the shoulder holster as he dressed in the morning. From force of habit he'd done that today.

He walked over to the door of Sarah's apartment. Instead of knocking, he listened, his ear pressed against the wood. No sounds emanated from inside. Either she was an exceptionally quiet tenant, especially for this place, or she wasn't home.

After climbing three flights of stairs, he sure as hell

wasn't going away without trying. He pushed the bell, listening to it chime somewhere distantly inside. Then he again leaned forward, putting his ear against the door.

Almost immediately he heard footsteps. As they approached, more rapidly than he'd expected, he stepped back, positioning himself cooperatively in front of the peephole.

When she saw who it was, Danny Patterson's mother might not be willing to open the door. Mac knew that was a chance he'd have to take. With the message she'd gotten last night, she certainly wasn't going to open her door if she didn't have a clear view of whoever was out here.

The footsteps stopped, and he assumed she was looking through the peephole. After a few seconds, he lifted his hand to knock. Before he could bring it down, he heard the distinctive snick of a dead bolt being turned. His fist, poised to strike, hesitated in midair.

When the door swung inward, Sarah's face appeared in the crack. Her features were drained of blood, making her eyes unnaturally dark, wide and almost stark.

Maybe from years of seeing this same look in other victims' eyes, Mac recognized her terror even before she opened her mouth. "What's wrong?"

"There's blood on my dog."

"Your dog's hurt?"

"No. I don't think so. My ex-husband was here earlier."

Mac examined the non sequitur, still trying to figure out what the hell was going on to make her look like this. "You think your ex-husband hurt your dog?"

"Not the dog," she said. "It's not the dog that's hurt. I was going to go back there, back to the bedroom, to see what was going on, and then...you rang the bell."

"You think your ex-husband is hurt?" Mac was beginning to put the bits and pieces of her disjointed narrative together.

"I don't know." Her eyes seemed more rational now. Almost focused. "When I saw the blood, I thought—"

"What did you think, Mrs. Patterson?"

She shook her head again, not so much in denial of what he'd asked, as of what she had been thinking. "Would you come back there with me, please? When I saw the blood, I panicked. Because of that message last night. But...Dan may be hurt. If you could just go with me into the bedroom—"

By that time, Mac had figured most of it out. After last night's message, when she'd seen blood in her apartment, she'd jumped to the conclusion that the two things might be connected.

Given the kind of creature Samuel Tate was, Mac couldn't blame her for panicking a little. Not even if there was a perfectly reasonable explanation for what was going on.

Mac reached inside his coat and slipped his .38 out of its holster. The weight of the weapon settled into his hand with a familiarity that was comforting. "Stay here."

"My dog's back there. In the bathroom."

Was that supposed to be a warning? "Does he bite?"

For a fraction of a second there was a flash of something in her eyes. Shock or amusement. Maybe both. And then she shook her head.

"He's terrified. I tried to get him to come with me to the door, but he's hiding behind the toilet. He wouldn't budge."

"And he's bleeding?"

She shook her head again, the amusement he had seen in her eyes only seconds before disappearing. "He must have stepped in it. Or walked through it. There's a lot of blood. Too much for just a cut."

"A cut?"

"When I first got home, I noticed blood on the shower curtain. I thought Dan had cut his finger, but... There's too much for that."

"Okay." Mac deliberately kept his voice low and calm. "Is there anybody else inside the apartment?"

"I called Dan's name when I got home from work, but he didn't answer. I thought that meant he'd already gone, but now..."

"The dog in the bathroom and maybe your ex-husband. And you think he might be the one who's bleeding?"

He realized that he was letting her anxiety get to him. Why the hell would Tate want to hurt Sarah Patterson's ex?

"I don't know. I just saw the blood, and nobody else has been here."

Mac recognized her growing frustration with his questions, but if there was anything a policeman hated, it was going into a situation where you didn't know what to expect. It was always the unexpected that got you killed.

"You stay here—" he said again, only to be interrupted.

"I'm not staying out in the hall," she said, her voice determined. "Not until I know what's going on."

She was beginning to get her equilibrium back, maybe because she was no longer alone. There was a tinge of color along her cheekbones. Awareness in her eyes. The shock had worn off, to be replaced by a need to know.

Mac couldn't blame her for that. This was all probably much ado about nothing. The dog had cut his foot on something. With everything that had happened the last couple of days, she'd seen the blood and gone off the deep end.

"Then stay behind me and stay close. And don't touch anything."

He stepped past her, moving inside the apartment. He scanned the living room, but there was nothing out of the ordinary going on in here.

Through the open door to his left he could see into a small kitchen. The light over the sink was on, rendering the glass of the windows behind it opaque.

He glanced at her over his shoulder and then tilted his head to the right, questioning the location of the bedroom. She nodded, her eyes darting in that direction.

A light shone out into the hall, although the hallway itself was dark. He headed toward the light, moving cautiously across the living room, aware that she was right behind him.

As they neared the doorway, he spotted the switch on the wall to his left. Before he stepped through, he reached out, flipping it up and flooding the hall with light.

Nothing unexpected here. The soft gleam of worn wood. Walls a dirty, rental-property beige. An open door to the left, the source of the light he'd noticed earlier. A closed one on the right, which he assumed to be a closet. Dead ahead was the open door of the bedroom.

He stepped forward far enough to peer into the bathroom. A trail of bloody paw prints, fading in intensity, led across the tile to the dog, who was huddled in the corner. He looked up at Mac, his mouth open and panting. He was trembling, and he didn't offer to move from behind what he obviously considered to be the safety of the toilet.

Mac checked out the rest of the room, but there was nothing else of interest. He turned off the water, which had filled the tub, steam drifting upward from it. The shower curtain had been pulled back, so he couldn't see much of it from where he was standing. What was visible didn't show any blood.

The only other item in the room was a wicker clothes hamper. No place an intruder could hide.

He moved further down the hall, stopping in front of the door on the right-hand side. The one he assumed was a linen or utility closet. He jerked open its door to be confronted by neatly organized shelves holding sheets and towels and cleaning supplies.

Nowhere to hide here either. Deciding to err on the side of caution, Mac bent, looking under the bottom shelf.

Not even if he's a midget.

Which left the bedroom. His eyes shifted to its waiting darkness. As they did, he realized Sarah Patterson had been right.

The blood her dog had tracked had come from somewhere inside that room. The prints were out here in the hallway as well, although against the age-darkened wooden floor, they were harder to see than on the bathroom tile. Once Mac picked up the pattern, it was obvious they led back into the bedroom.

Son of a bitch, Mac thought, as the adrenaline began to pump.

He would normally be calling for backup right now. Except nothing about this particular situation was normal.

He was on suspension. He had no department-sanctioned reason to be calling on Sarah Patterson. And no right to be checking out her apartment with his weapon drawn.

Despite the fact that the hair on the back of his neck had begun to lift, as far as he knew nothing criminal had taken place here. There could be a dozen explanations for the blood he saw, including the one she'd mentioned.

Her ex-husband could have had an accident. He might be bleeding to death while Mac wasted time checking out an empty linen closet. Looking for a bogeyman who'd left a message on her answering machine.

There was no reason to believe Samuel Tate was, or ever had been, in that bedroom. No reason, according to the experts at the FBI, to think Tate had anything to do with this at all.

Influenced by all those months of frustration, Mac had bought into Sarah Patterson's panic. *Wishful thinking, old buddy.*

He moved, stepping back to the left-hand side of the hall and motioning her to close the distance between them. She obeyed, glancing into the bathroom as she passed the open door. He heard the dog whine when it saw her, but thankfully the mutt didn't seem inclined to follow.

Mac edged along the hall, conscious that she was right behind him. When he was as close to the bedroom doorway as he could get without revealing himself, he stopped to listen, his back against the wall. Other than Sarah's breathing, and his own, he could hear nothing. He turned his head toward her, putting out his right hand, palm up and facing her. Again, she nodded her understanding.

Transferring the .38 to his right hand, he reached out with the left, feeling around the frame of the door for the switch inside. He located it and then, taking a deep breath, pushed the switch up.

The light came on, but nothing else happened. No shot fired at the door. No sound of anybody reacting to that sudden blaze of illumination.

Taking another breath and settling his left hand under his right, he edged far enough into the doorway to see inside the room. Nobody was standing. No indication of danger. Not in his initial scan.

The second verified the impressions of the first. The closet was open, revealing a row of hanging clothes and some shoes neatly arranged in a line on the floor. The bed had been made, although the coverlet was subtly disordered, pulled up on the side facing the door, exposing the dark space beneath it.

And the bloody prints, more distinct than they had been on the floor of the hall, led from the far side of the bed across the pale blue throw rug at its foot. Whatever the source of the blood the dog had found, it was on the other side of that bed.

Mac considered the closet again. The door was one of those cheap sliding deals, where one panel slipped behind the other to allow access to either side. Which meant there was enough room for someone to be hiding inside, despite the fact that nothing in there appeared to have been disturbed.

His eyes on the far side of the bed, he walked over to the closet, moving as silently as he could. Using his left hand, he reached out and pushed both of the sliding panels to the other side of the opening. He moved in front of the closet at the same time, leading with his weapon.

More clothes. Undisturbed. The same precise line of shoes continued on the side he'd just exposed. Nothing else.

It took him only a couple of seconds to verify the closet was empty. He turned back to the bed, his eyes examining the space under it, exposed by the disordered bedspread. Nothing was moving there, either.

Truth or dare, he thought, putting his left hand back under the right. Then he took a couple of quick strides, which brought him to the foot of the bed. The blood on the throw rug was thick, matted into the fibers.

And he could smell it now. Along with that scent was the distinctive miasma that often accompanies violent death. The powerful sphincter muscles relax as life leaves the body. As do those of the bladder.

Not a kid. Dear God, let this be anything—anybody—but don't let it be another kid.

He took the final step that would bring him around the end of the bed, prepared, he believed, for what he would find.

He wasn't. He couldn't have been.

He turned his head, swallowing against the bile that had risen to burn the back of his throat. And he realized Sarah was right beside him, near enough to see what had sickened him.

"Dan," she said softly. "Oh, God, Dan."

"That's your ex?"

She nodded. And then, as he watched, she put the fingers of both hands over her mouth. She retched once before she turned and ran across the room.

He forced his eyes back to the body, which lay sprawled between the bed and the wall. There was probably no good way to die, and it was always possible that what he was looking at had been done postmortem. With this much blood, however…

Whoever had killed Danny Patterson's father didn't seem to have taken much time with it. Nothing like the slow, sadistic tortures Samuel Tate enjoyed inflicting.

This death had been relatively quick by virtue of the violence with which it had been delivered. Dan Patterson's throat had been slashed from ear to ear, cut deeply enough that he'd almost been decapitated.

And then, just for good measure it seemed, the blade that had been used to accomplish that had been shoved halfway down its length into one of the still-opened eyes.

Nine

"So you were gone…what? Maybe forty, forty-five minutes at the most?"

Sonny Cochran was asking the questions and being as patient as it was in his nature to be. They were all sitting in Sarah's living room, while the crime scene technicians worked up the bedroom and bath.

"About that." Sarah's voice sounded relatively steady, given the situation.

Other than those first few seconds, she hadn't seemed on the verge of fainting. And judging from the sounds he'd listened to after she'd left the bedroom, she wasn't going to be sick again. There wasn't anything left to come up.

Mac could see the dog from where he was sitting. One of the techs had gotten him out from behind the john, and then they'd tied him to the leg of the kitchen table.

His leash was long enough to allow him to reach the doorway. For a while, he had gotten up expectantly whenever someone arrived. Now he'd given up on being released, lying forlornly in the opening, his muzzle propped on his front feet.

Forlorn. That fit everything here, Mac thought. The decaying neighborhood. The building. That poor, terrified dog. And right now, even the woman Sonny was questioning.

"You didn't notice nothing out of the ordinary when you got back to the apartment?"

"There was a glass on the counter."

"A glass?" Sonny's tone betrayed his interest. Or at least it did to Mac, who knew every nuance of his partner's voice.

"I knew I hadn't used it. I figured Dan had. While he was working."

"Still there?"

"In the sink. But I rinsed it off. I didn't know…"

She didn't finish the sentence, but it was obvious what she was thinking. She'd had no way of knowing then that the glass might have significance to a crime. Fingerprints, for example, although that would have been a fluke. They didn't usually get that lucky.

"And in the bathroom…" she began again.

"You saw something in the bathroom?" Sonny prodded when she hesitated.

"There was blood on the shower curtain. Up high. Like someone had pushed it back to get to the tub."

"That's why you thought your husband had cut his hand," Mac added, making the clarification for his partner's benefit.

Nobody had attempted to throw him out. He was

letting Sonny take the lead, staying in the background, especially when anyone else was around.

As long as Morel didn't decide to show up—and there was a snowball's chance in hell of that—there shouldn't be any problem with him being here. Even with the efficiency of the department grapevine, he doubted the techs would know about his suspension.

"Dan's always smashing or nicking a finger. He's a contractor."

Present tense, Mac noted. None of this had sunk in. The shock was too great. Which was, perversely enough, why she was handling it as well as she was.

"The shower curtain had been pushed aside," Sonny said, bringing her back to her narrative. "Why would they do that, you think?"

"I thought Dan had washed off the cut in the bathtub. At the time I thought it was strange he hadn't used the lavatory."

"Need to check that drain," Sonny said to Mac, making a note.

"Tub's full," Mac warned, putting a quick end to the idea that they were going to get a blood sample there.

"I was going to take a bath." Sarah's tone was slightly defensive.

"Just make sure they get the curtain," Mac advised his partner.

"This was Tate," Sarah said unexpectedly. "I told you it was Tate on the answering machine last night."

"It's too early in the investigation to try to determine—" Sonny began.

"What do *you* think happened, Detective Cochran?"

Her animosity was obvious. "You think somebody just waltzed in off the street and killed Dan?"

"That's possible," Sonny said evenly. "Right now, just about anything's possible."

"The outer door of the building was unlocked when I got here. Security seems pretty lax." As he said that, Mac remembered the kid at the window.

He had thought at the time that he'd looked out in response to the sound of a car pulling up to the curb or maybe to the headlights. But it could be that the kid kept an eye out for any kind of movement out front. If so, he might have seen something that could be useful.

"They prop it open," Sarah said.

"Who does?" Sonny asked.

"I don't know. I always assumed it was somebody on the ground floor, but…I really don't know for sure."

"So anyone can get into the building without buzzing one of the tenants." Sonny was obviously thinking about the possibilities that presented. "You get a lot of traffic in and out here?"

"Not on the third floor," she said flatly. "Look, the idea that this was someone who wandered in off the street was supposed to be a joke—"

"What about the kid on the ground floor?" Mac asked.

For the first time during the course of the interview, Sarah turned her head to look at him directly. "What about him?"

Her tone was definitely unfriendly, and Mac couldn't help but wonder why. "He was looking out the window when I pulled up. I wondered if that was a regular thing."

Sarah's eyes continued to consider his face, the thoughts moving almost visibly behind them. "You're thinking he might have seen whoever came into the building this afternoon."

"He saw me."

"He was in the park then."

Then?

"You mean when the murder took place?" Sonny asked.

She nodded.

"How do you know that, Mrs. Patterson?" Mac asked.

"Because he was with me. We went to walk the dog while Dan was working in here."

"You said your ex-husband came to put in a security system."

"That's right. Actually, he was going to do that tomorrow. I gave him—" She stopped, her eyes widening.

"Ma'am?"

"I just remembered that I gave Dan my extra key."

"So he could get in tomorrow while you were at work?"

"Do you think they could look for it?" she asked without answering Mac's question.

"For the key?"

Sonny seemed puzzled by the request, but as soon as she had said the word *key*, Mac knew what she was thinking. Whoever killed her ex-husband might have gone through his pockets. If that key was missing—

"We'll get them to look," Mac promised. "So you're saying the kid wouldn't have been at that window while your ex was in the apartment."

"Dwight—that's his name—was waiting in the hall outside my door when I got home from work. Dan showed up a few minutes later. I took Toby and the boy to the park. It was after dark when we got back. I saw Dwight inside his apartment, and then I came upstairs."

"That's when you called your ex-husband's name and got no response," Mac said, helping the story along with the information she'd given him before.

"I thought he'd done what he needed to do and left. Dwight couldn't have seen anything. Not anyone coming in or leaving. Whoever this was must have come up here after we left for the park."

Was she trying to steer them away from questioning the kid? Mac wondered. He put the question in the back of his mind, because what she had just said opened up another, more intriguing possibility. "Unless he was already here."

There was a small silence before she spoke again. "What does that mean?"

"You go into the bedroom before you left to walk the dog?"

"You think he could have been back there waiting for me to get home?" Her voice was tinged with a new horror.

"Did you go into the bedroom?"

She shook her head, her eyes focusing on the door to the hall. "I went to the kitchen for the key. I came in here to pick up Toby's leash first. I didn't go in the back at all. But if he was already here waiting for me…"

Then this wasn't a burglary gone wrong. That was what Mac had been thinking as well. The knife in the eyeball hadn't seemed to fit with somebody getting caught in the act of robbing the place. Not even some crackhead.

"There's no reason to think he was waiting for you, Mrs. Patterson," Sonny broke in. His eyes said he didn't like what Mac had just suggested. "No reason to think any of this was directed at you."

"Except that it happened in my apartment."

"If he was waiting for you, then he would still have been here when you got back from the park. He was gone, which indicates he wasn't interested in you personally."

Mac knew they'd all like to believe this couldn't be Tate, considering it was the department's mistakes that had put him back on the street. "Or it could indicate he had a reason to leave before she arrived."

A flush of color began to spread upward into his partner's jowls. Mac wasn't supposed to be throwing a monkey wrench into the works. He was here on sufferance, which meant he shouldn't keep bringing up things the department didn't want brought up.

"A reason like what?" Sonny's question was derisive.

Mac stood up and walked across to the answering machine. He'd noticed the blinking light earlier, but he hadn't figured it was important. Now, however…

"I ain't sure they've dusted that," Sonny warned as he reached out to push the play button.

"If he'd touched this, it wouldn't still be blinking," Mac said, without looking up. He completed the motion, and the recorder kicked in almost immediately.

His voice. His message.

"Mrs. Patterson, this is Detective Donovan. I wondered if I could come by to talk to you for a few minutes. I'm in the neighborhood, so maybe if I stopped by say…around five-thirty, five-forty-five, I could ask you a couple of questions about the message that was left on your machine last night."

Then the mechanical voice of the recorder stated the date and time. Five-seventeen.

Mac hadn't intended to give Sarah much warning. And he hadn't left his cell number, making it as hard as he could for her to keep him from showing up. He had figured he'd deal with getting her to let him in after he arrived.

"I'm betting that when you get the time of death, it's going to be close," he said. "I figure my call came in while the guy was here."

"You think that's why he left?" Sonny asked. "Because he heard your message?"

Mac could tell his partner was considering the idea. Did that make it more likely this wasn't a random killing? More likely that either Tate or someone set off by the publicity surrounding Sarah Patterson's attempt to bring her son's murderer to justice had been waiting for her to come home?

"I think it's possible," Mac said. "Especially if Mrs. Patterson doesn't find anything missing. That would pretty much rule out the burglary theory."

Nothing appeared to be out of place in the apartment. It hadn't been tossed by someone looking for money or valuables to pawn. Maybe they hadn't had time, but Mac felt in his gut this hadn't been a robbery gone wrong.

"You notice anything missing?" Sonny asked her. "Anything of value?"

"I don't *have* anything of value," Sarah said.

"Would your dog have let somebody come into the apartment with you not here?" Sonny asked.

"He's not a watchdog. When we got him, we thought maybe he'd be some protection, but..." She shook her head. "He turned out to be pretty much worthless for that."

"So what you're saying is that somebody could have gotten in, and the dog wouldn't have put up a fuss?"

"How would they get in? The door was locked."

"Locks keep out the honest people, Ms. Patterson. Somebody wants in your place, they'll find a way. Fire escape off the bedroom?" Sonny asked.

"Yes."

"You keep that window locked?"

"Of course."

"I didn't notice any broken glass," Mac volunteered.

He hadn't been looking for any. He hadn't been looking at much of anything except the blood and the grotesque positioning of that knife.

"Could have used a suction cup. Cut the piece out and then reach inside and open her up."

They were back to the burglary theory. The department would love for that one to work, only Mac didn't believe it. Not any more. And he was beginning to think Sonny didn't either.

"Was that your knife in the bedroom?" he asked.

"What?" Obviously she hadn't thought about the possibility before. "I think... I think it might be," she said softly. From what was in her eyes, she had allowed the image of the body to reform in her head as she tried to come up with an answer.

Mac glanced at Sonny, who nodded permission. "Could you check, please?"

"In there?" Her eyes considered the door to the hall.

"Wherever you keep the knives," Mac explained.

She rose and, with Mac following, walked into the kitchen and over to the drawer beside the sink. She reached out to grasp the pull, but Mac put his hand around her wrist. The bones felt as delicate as a child's under his fingers.

She looked up, eyes widened. Maybe she didn't like to be touched. Or maybe she didn't understand why he didn't want her to grasp the handle.

"There might be prints."

He inserted his ballpoint inside the old-fashioned open chrome handle, being careful not to touch the center. He lowered the pen until there was as much below as above the pull. Then using both hands, he slid the drawer out.

It stuck a couple of times, as wooden drawers tended to in this climate. Eventually he eased it far enough out that they could see the contents. There was a silverware tray with a few case knives, forks and spoons. To its side were a couple of longer, sharper knives.

"The big one isn't there," Sarah said, her voice very low.

Tate carried his own tools. The patrolman had discovered the suitcase containing them in his van after the accident.

Mac wondered if it had been given back to him when the judge released him. It seemed that even a system so flawed that it could put a killer back on the streets wouldn't return his implements of torture to him.

Suddenly, Sarah seemed to waver, swaying slightly so that Mac quickly put his hand under her elbow. "You okay?"

"Somehow that makes it worse."

He nodded as if that made sense. Personally, he didn't see how it could be any worse, no matter what the murderer had used or where he'd gotten it.

"Will this be on the news?" she asked, looking up into his eyes. "Will they give out his name?"

The fact that Dan Patterson was the father of one of the victims and that he had been killed almost as soon as Tate was released would have been enough to guarantee a media frenzy. With his wife having just tried to shoot Tate—.

"I don't want Dan's mother to hear about it from the TV," she went on. "She's not well. This is going to be so hard for her. She lives with him."

"You want me to send one of the uniforms to break it to her?"

He could tell the idea was tempting. After a moment, she shook her head.

"I should do it. I should be the one. I owe her that much. After Danny died…"

"I'll take you."

Mac had surprised himself with that offer. Morel wouldn't want him within a hundred yards of Sarah Patterson, much less driving her around. Especially not considering the insanity that was about to break over their heads when the press got hold of this.

Besides that, the protective urge he'd felt since he'd seen her standing below him on the courthouse steps that morning hadn't lessened. If anything, it had increased. In his situation—

"Thank you. Do you think we can we do it soon?"

"Anytime you're ready."

Sonny wasn't going to like this, but he could handle his partner. They had no legitimate reason to detain Mrs. Patterson. No one had suggested she might be a suspect.

If what she'd told them about the kid and the park was true, she had an alibi. She'd been with the boy during the killer's brief window of opportunity.

That was something else he had wanted to do, he remembered. Talk to that kid. It might go better if she was with him when he approached the boy.

The kid knew her, and the parents apparently trusted her enough to let her take him to the park. They might not want their son talking to the police, but with Mrs. Patterson there—

"I just realized that I'll have to take Toby," she said. "Is that all right? I can't leave him here. Not with…" She tilted her head toward the back of the apartment. "Besides, he's terrified."

Mac hesitated, thinking about the interview he'd been planning to sneak in on their way out.

"He's no trouble," she added, trying to convince him. "He'll lie down on the back seat and go to sleep. He loves to ride. He doesn't get to do that much anymore."

"So you're going to stay at your mother-in-law's tonight?" Mac asked. She wouldn't want to come back here, of course, but apparently she realized that only with his question.

"I hadn't thought. I guess I could."

"She'll be okay with the dog?"

"I can tie him up somewhere," she said. "I just can't leave him here."

"You want to get some things. Pack a bag, maybe."

Her eyes went to the open door, and he knew she was thinking about having to go back into that bedroom.

"I could do it for you," he said, again surprising himself. Her gaze came back to his face. "Nightgown? Toothbrush? Change of clothes?"

He didn't say change of underwear, but he thought it. And then, the mental question automatic, he wondered what kind she wore.

Which made him pretty much of a sick bastard himself, since it was her husband lying back there dead. Ex-husband, he corrected. Now very ex.

After a moment she shook her head. "I can borrow something from Louise. Right now I just need to get out of here."

"Why don't you get the dog and a jacket? I'll tell Detective Cochran about the knife."

She nodded, looking around the kitchen, almost as if she were disoriented. "That's the glass I found." She lifted her chin toward the sink.

"I'll tell him that, too. You go get your stuff."

He didn't want to leave her alone in the kitchen. The whole apartment was a crime scene, and this time they couldn't afford any mistakes. He put his hand in the center of her back, gently directing her away from the drawer where the knives were stored and the glass in the sink.

"Tell him this was Tate," she begged, her eyes on his face.

He nodded, and only with his agreement did she move. Not to the door, but to the dog.

The mutt sat up, expectant again, as she bent to unfasten his leash. And then, without releasing him, she knelt, burying her face in his thick coat.

Mac didn't understand what was going on until her shoulders began to shake. She didn't make any sound. There was just that small jerking movement of her body.

The dog leaned against her, relishing the human contact. When "we" got him, she had said. And belatedly Mac realized this must have been her son's dog.

Everybody had a breaking point. He would have thought Sarah Patterson had reached hers long ago, but seemingly, through everything, she had managed to hold on. Hold down a job. Keep a roof over her head. Take care of her murdered child's mutt.

Tonight she had come home to the life she'd had to rebuild, hour by hour, maybe even minute by minute, to find her ex-husband slaughtered like an animal in her own bedroom.

She was entitled to cry. And she was entitled to shed those tears in private, crime scene or not.

Ten

"I'm going to take her to give her mother-in-law the bad news. You got any objections?"

Sonny looked over his shoulder, his attention reluctantly pulled away from the removal of the shower curtain.

"Morel ain't gonna like it."

"Screw Morel. She doesn't want his mother to hear it from the TV. You aren't planning on taking her downtown, not tonight anyway. And she sure as hell can't sleep here."

Sonny delayed answering until the tech carrying the curtain had pushed past Mac, leaving them alone in the bathroom. "So what do you think?"

"I think you got a public relations nightmare on your hands."

"Jesus, Mac, you're starting to sound like Morel."

"I've been taking lessons."

"I meant about who did this."

"She says Tate."

"I know what she says. I want to know what you say. You were gonna talk to the FBI."

"They don't think he'd be leaving messages, but they can't rule it out."

"That's a shitload of help."

"The knife came out of the kitchen drawer," Mac told him.

"And Tate carries his own."

"You know what happened to his kit? The one the rookie took out of the van."

"Beats me. We're probably still holding it. That don't mean he's gonna come unprepared. He never has."

Tate was what the FBI classified as an organized killer, which meant every step was carefully planned and prepared for. Despite the mutilations he inflicted on his victims, that meticulous nature carried throughout the course of the crime.

There was no bloodlust frenzy that made him lose control. According to the profilers, control was what he was all about.

"If this *is* Tate—" Mac began.

"It ain't. This is somebody who saw what Ms. Patterson tried to do and wanted in on the action. Her ex just happened to end up in the wrong place at the wrong time."

"You need to think about that before you put it out, Sonny. Tell Morel to think about it. People aren't going to be comforted if you're telling them that we've got two killers out there."

"Almost any night you want to choose, we got a homicide around here. This one ain't any different."

"The hell it isn't. You don't think somebody's going to put this together?"

"Maybe," Sonny said. "But we're gonna keep 'em from doing that for as long as we can. By the time they do, we'll have caught the guy."

Mac knew Sonny didn't believe that any more than he did. "Call me tomorrow," he said.

"Getting involved ain't a good idea," his partner warned again before he could move out of the doorway. "That's friend-to-friend advice."

"Low profile," Mac promised.

"I don't mean involved with the case. This ain't no time to go tilting at windmills, Mac."

"The guy who did that was nuts."

"That's what I'm talking about."

"She's been through a lot."

"Which means she'll be ripe for the picking. That ain't your style, Mac."

Ripe for the picking. Vulnerable. She was. Maybe more than any of them had understood before.

"You think that's why I'm doing this? Why I'm taking her to her mother-in-law's?"

"I'm just saying now isn't such a good time to make a move on her."

Rage washed through Mac in a wave, out of proportion to the accusation. Because the accusation had come from Sonny, who ought to know him better than that? Or because it had come too close to the truth?

"Screw you."

Mac turned and walked back to the living room. Sarah was standing by the door, wearing her jacket.

She was obviously waiting for him, the dog's leash in her hand.

"Something wrong?" she asked, reading either his face or the stiffness of his posture.

"Not a thing."

Nothing beyond being on the outside of my own case while everybody else seems determined to botch it. And then getting accused of having ulterior motives when all I'm trying to do is help somebody out.

"You ready?" He managed, only because he was working at it, to sound slightly less belligerent.

She studied his face a few seconds more before she nodded. "Do they need the number where I'll be?"

"If they do, they can look it up."

Without thinking, he put his hand against the base of her spine, turning her and then urging her toward the door. Again, as she moved beside him, he was aware of how small she was. Vulnerable.

And no matter what Sonny thought...

He took a breath, fighting a renewed surge of resentment, as he opened the door and watched the dog pull her toward the stairs. No matter what Sonny thought, acting on his attraction to Sarah Patterson wasn't what this offer had been about.

That was the last thing Sarah Patterson needed right now. And it would make him the kind of predatory jerk he had always despised. All he was doing was giving her a ride to her mother-in-law's. He doubted he'd see her again after tonight.

Maybe, he admitted to himself, that wouldn't be a bad thing.

* * *

"Why couldn't you just leave it alone?" Dan Patterson's mother said. "Why couldn't you let the police handle it? It's their job. Not yours."

"Louise, I'm so sorry, but...the police don't believe this had anything to do with what I did." Sarah's tone was conciliatory, but she was clearly thrown by her mother-in-law's reaction.

Of course, this wasn't what Mac had been expecting either, considering Sarah's worries about the older woman's health. Louise Patterson's anger was probably as much a product of her grief and shock as Sarah's unnatural calmness had been. The old woman's face had crumpled as she'd listened to the news of her son's death, but her tears had almost immediately given way to recriminations.

"I told you," Louise said, ignoring the hurt in Sarah's voice. "I told you that you had to let it go. I told you that more than two years ago, Sarah, but you wouldn't. Now see what you've done."

"Mrs. Patterson, what happened to your son tonight isn't your daughter-in-law's fault," Mac intervened, feeling that Sarah had been emotionally beaten up enough.

The faded blue eyes cut to his face, remaining there only a second or two before they returned to Sarah's as her harangue continued unabated.

"It wasn't enough that we had to lose Danny. Now he's killed Dan, too, and all because of you. Taking a gun to the courthouse like you had the right to shoot that man."

"I had the right." Sarah's anger finally broke through.

"That bastard murdered my son, and they just let him get away with it."

"And now he's killed *my* son. Now they're both dead. Or is that what you wanted all along?"

"Mrs. Patterson—" Mac said again.

"You know it's not," Sarah interrupted, her words stronger than his attempted mediation. "I *never* wanted anything to happen to Dan. You know that."

"I know you broke his heart. And I know he's dead. They're both dead. I hope you're happy, Sarah. You wanted to punish Dan for Danny's death. Well, maybe now—finally—you'll feel like he's been punished enough."

"I'm going to call your sister." Sarah's voice had gone flat, wiped clean of the animation that had been there only a moment ago. "I'll tell her to come over and stay with you tonight."

She stood, and without looking at either of them, picked her jacket up off the back of the couch where Mac was sitting. She shrugged into it as she walked toward the foyer, every motion abrupt, conveying anger where her voice had not.

When she opened the front door, the outside air swept through, penetrating the front room of the thirties-style bungalow. She slammed it closed behind her, leaving Mac alone with Dan Patterson's mother.

The old woman lowered her head, putting her hands over her face. She didn't look at Mac again.

He sat there for a couple of minutes, unsure which of them needed whatever comfort he could offer the most. Finally he stood, feeling incredibly awkward to have been a witness to this. The noise he made getting up off the vinyl couch was enough that Mrs. Patterson had to have heard it although she never lifted her head.

"Will you be okay until your sister gets here?"

No response.

"Mrs. Patterson?"

No movement from the huddled figure in the chair before the blaze of the cheerfully artificial gas fire.

"I'm going to go outside and check on your daughter-in-law. Somebody will be here with you soon," he added as a sop to his conscience.

She still didn't look up, and in a way, he was relieved. All he wanted was an excuse to get out of here. Away from the overheated room and its faintly unpleasant odor that was probably equal parts old age and loneliness.

He headed toward the door Sarah had just banged shut, but once he reached it, he was unable to stop himself from looking back. Dan Patterson's mother sat unmoving, shoulders hunched, both hands over her face. She was still sitting that way when Mac closed the door behind him.

"She's wrong, you know," Mac said.

Sarah turned from her unthinking contemplation of the occasional lights they passed, shining out into the darkness from houses scattered haphazardly along the rural two-lane.

She supposed they were headed back into the city, although they hadn't discussed a destination. Actually, she didn't think they'd spoken since she'd asked him if she could use his cell to call Dan's aunt Pauline.

"You aren't responsible for what some madman does," he went on.

"Not even if I goaded him into doing it?"

"You can't know that. You don't even know if your ex-husband's death has anything to do with what you did."

She turned back to the window, her eyes studying the black emptiness, broken now only by the mile markers that measured their progress. Progress to where? she wondered. Where the hell did she go from here?

"She'll figure that out eventually," he said.

"She's in the beginning stages of dementia. So…she probably won't. It doesn't matter."

Nothing seemed to matter now. Not even Tate.

She would feel better if she could find some spark of the anger that had driven her to take Dan's gun that morning and seek out Danny's murderer. It seemed there was nothing that vital left inside her now.

There was, instead, an overwhelming sense of despair. Sadness. And an exhaustion that seemed to have drained the life force out of her as surely as—

She took a breath, forcing her mind away from that comparison. She'd become very good at doing that during the last three years. Very accomplished at not thinking about the things that didn't bear thinking about, until it seemed there was nothing left she *could* think about.

"Alzheimer's?" Donovan asked.

He meant Dan's mother, she realized.

"They can't really tell, but…probably. It happens so gradually. I haven't been to see her in a long time. Too long," she added, confessing the other guilt she was feeling right now. “She always wanted to talk about Danny. Or to ask when Dan and I were going to start living together again. It just all got to be too hard. Finally I stopped going.”

“You have to take her condition into consideration.”

He meant about what Louise had said. And of course, he was right. Except…

“Except that’s what I did.”

There was a long pause. She was aware that during part of it he had turned his head, looking toward her instead of at the highway.

“What *you* did?”

“About Danny’s death. I blamed Dan. I did the same thing Louise did tonight because I needed someone to blame. Someone I could make hurt like I was hurting. I *wanted* to hurt somebody.” She had known what she was doing, intellectually at least, but it hadn’t prevented her from spewing forth her anger and bitterness. “I picked Dan. So…what she said tonight is only fair.”

“This isn’t about fairness or wanting to hurt people or even about placing blame, Mrs. Patterson. All it’s about is the crazies out there. No matter what your mother-in-law says, you aren’t responsible for your husband’s death. The only person responsible for that is the one who took that knife out of your kitchen drawer and used it on him.”

“Do *you* believe it was some stranger? A burglar?”

The silence before he answered was long enough that she had begun to think maybe he did. Or that he didn’t want to tell her if he didn’t.

“Sonny’s right. At this stage, it could be anybody. It

could be somebody looking to jump on Tate's bandwagon."

"Or..." She had heard that in his voice. A lack of conviction.

"Or Tate sees you as a danger."

"He should. I'd kill him in a heartbeat."

She wondered if he was thinking, as she was, about the morning he'd stopped her from doing that. She'd been furious at him then.

She should be even more angry at him now if she truly believed Tate had killed Dan. That meant another person was dead. Another person who had, at one time, belonged to her. A person who wouldn't be gone if Mac Donovan hadn't kept her from shooting Tate.

Yet right now she couldn't seem to work up any anger at all. Maybe she was just too tired. Or maybe Detective Donovan's solicitousness had confused her. Defused her. All she knew was that she was in the car with the cop who had protected her son's killer, and she didn't have enough energy to hate him.

Actually, she just didn't want to think about this anymore. She wanted to close her eyes and forget it had happened. If she could, she would erase the last few days, from the time she'd pulled Dan's gun out of her purse until now.

Because no matter whose version of Dan's murder you believed, Louise was right. If she hadn't stood on the courthouse steps that morning and tried to shoot Samuel Tate, none of this would have happened.

Eleven

"I've been thinking," Mac said.

Sarah turned away from the window in response, but it took him several seconds to work up nerve enough to tell her *what* he'd been thinking.

"You can't go back to your apartment." He didn't mention that it was just as obvious she wasn't going to be spending the night with her mother-in-law. "You want to think about a motel? With the dog, that could get complicated."

There was a long pause before she answered. "I don't have a credit card for a motel. And I'm not sure how much cash I have on me. I didn't take time to count it up this afternoon because I was hurrying home to meet Dan, but…I doubt it's enough for that."

Who the hell doesn't have a credit card these days? Mac wondered.

"How about a friend? Somebody from work?" he said aloud.

There was a pause. "No," she said simply. No explanation.

"Okay. Then… I've got a couch."

The words were in his mouth before he'd had time to rethink the wisdom of making the offer that had just occurred to him. But it made sense, anyway you looked at it.

He couldn't put her out on the street. There were several shelters in the city, of course, but she was not only a material witness in a murder investigation, she was also a potential victim.

The whole time he was working out that justification, what Sonny said echoed unpleasantly in his head. Just because his partner had accused him of trying to take advantage of her didn't mean he didn't have some kind of obligation here, he reasoned. After all, if he hadn't prevented her from shooting Tate—

"Are you offering to let me stay with you?"

He couldn't hear any emotion in her question. Not shock or gratitude or disgust.

"If you want to. Strictly…" Strictly *what?* he wondered, searching for some word that would work. Business? Professional? What? When he couldn't find anything that approached what he wanted to say, he changed the sentence. "Just until you figure out where you go from here."

She didn't answer, but he could feel her eyes on him.

He turned his head, meeting them. And then wished he hadn't.

She looked lost. Beaten. *Vulnerable*.

"Are you sure that...?" Her search for the appropriate word was no more successful than his. "Are you sure it will be all right?"

"It'll be fine."

"You're not married."

He didn't know how she'd gotten to that from what he'd said. Or maybe she hadn't. Maybe she was just curious.

"Divorced. Law enforcement officers have one of the highest divorce rates of any profession."

Another of those things he'd read somewhere that had stuck in his head. Maybe it had helped to think that's what had happened with him and Karen.

"Any children?"

"No. Thank God," he added, and then wondered, belatedly, if she'd take offense. She had lost her son, and here he was claiming to be glad he didn't have any. "Divorce is hard on kids."

"Your wife didn't like you being a detective?"

He thought about whether Karen had liked it or not, but it wasn't really that he was a detective. Not just that.

"She didn't like the hours. The pay. The lack of respect. I don't know. In the end she didn't like much of anything."

Another silence. Of course, there wasn't much she could comment on in that litany of woes.

"I don't have any clothes," she said finally.

"I can find something for you to sleep in."

"And you're sure...?" The question faded.

He wasn't, but he didn't see anything else he could do. Even if he didn't believe somebody from the department should be keeping an eye on her, no shelter was going to take her with the dog. At least he didn't think they would.

"I sleep on that couch half the time anyway."

"Why?"

"I go to sleep watching the news. Too lazy to get up and go to bed, I guess."

And the noise from the television keeps me from figuring out how empty the place is. How empty the bed is.

Neither of those were reasons he'd ever before acknowledged, not even mentally. Which wasn't to say they weren't valid. Or that he hadn't been aware of them.

"I really appreciate this," she said.

"You need me to stop at a drugstore or something? Pick up a toothbrush? Something for the dog to eat?"

"He's been fed tonight, but...I usually give him a can in the morning."

"We can stop. You probably need a few things. I'll get some doughnuts. For the morning."

"Is that what you eat for breakfast?"

"I eat coffee for breakfast. I figured you'd need something. You have anything to eat tonight?"

If she'd had time to feed the dog, maybe she'd made a sandwich or something before she'd gone to take her bath.

"I'm not hungry."

"You need to eat."

Despite the platitude, he couldn't blame her for the loss of appetite, but he didn't want her passing out on him. He heard her sigh and expected another denial.

She said instead, "I'll eat one of the doughnuts if you get them."

"Okay."

"Did you ask me to stay with you because you really think Tate was waiting for me this afternoon?"

There had been a small jolt of anxiety when she'd begun that question, but its finish was nothing like he'd been expecting.

He should have been. He'd seen her bounce back from shock to asking the hard questions before. She'd done it when Sonny was interrogating her.

He thought about lying. There were certainly other valid reasons for the offer he'd made, including that he didn't know where he'd take her if not to his place.

But she deserved to know the truth about what he'd been feeling in his gut since Sonny had told him about that message. He still believed it, despite Johnson's opinion. Despite the change in methodology used in Dan Patterson's murder.

"I think he might have been."

"And you feel responsible."

He hadn't. Not until she put it into words. Now that she had…

"I'm a cop, Mrs. Patterson. Protecting people is what I do. You just happen to be the one who needs that right now."

He hadn't meant for that to sound as unfeeling as it probably had. Or as dismissive.

She said nothing in response. After a moment, she turned her head, again looking out the window at the passing night.

* * *

What he felt against his face was cold. Wet. And unfamiliar enough to bring him out of a sleep so deep he was groggy with it.

He put his hand up, brushing at whatever had touched him and encountered something solid. Something that moved when he touched it. Something—

"What the hell?"

He had finally come awake enough to recognize that the dog was nosing his face. He pushed him away, but apparently not strongly enough to discourage him. The mutt came back, licking his chin before Mac could lift onto his elbow to put his face out of range.

"He's always been partial to men."

The voice came from across the room. Like his identification of the dog's nose against his face, it took him a couple of seconds to place it. A couple more to remember why Sarah Patterson and her dog were in his apartment.

"Come here, Tobe." She made a ticking sound with her tongue that the dog ignored.

Following that noise, Mac located her. She was sitting on the floor, leaning back against the wall.

She was wearing the T-shirt he'd given her to sleep in. He could see its white shape in the light provided by security lamps in the parking lot outside.

Her face was little more than a pale blur, but he could see the dark spot that represented her mouth open when she spoke again. "I'm sorry he woke you."

The dog made another attempt to sniff him, but by

now Mac was alert enough to deflect it. He managed to make the reflexive push a halfhearted caress, mostly because he felt sorry for the animal.

The dog had clearly been confused by what was going on. The long ride. Ending up in some strange place, where nothing was familiar except the woman who watched them from across the room.

Mac's eyes considered the window through which the glow from the halogens was seeping into the room. It was definitely still night. The way he felt, it had to be, but since Sarah was up, he had needed to verify his physical evaluation of how many hours' sleep he'd really had.

"What are you doing in here?"

"I couldn't sleep."

That was hardly surprising. Even so, most people would have stayed in the bedroom. Turned on the light and read maybe.

"You okay?"

He eased up a little more to try and evaluate that. He'd been pretty insistent about sleeping on the couch last night because he thought she might feel better about the situation if she had a door she could close and lock between them.

There had been a few moments of uneasiness after they'd gotten here. The awkward discussion of where each of them should sleep. His retrieval of something from his dresser for her to wear. Deciding together what to do with the dog.

Mac had been the one who'd opted not to tie him up. He'd kept seeing that hangdog expression after the tech had tethered him to the table leg. He'd figured, ridiculously he supposed, that the dog had been almost as traumatized as the woman, so he'd left him in the kitchen with a bowl of water and one of the cans of dog food they'd picked up on the way home.

Home. For some reason the word resonated more strongly than usual. Maybe it was having someone else here. Someone else breathing in the quiet darkness.

"I just…" She strengthened her voice to try again. "I slept out, I guess."

"You have a nightmare?"

That would explain her reluctance to be alone. As if that needed any explanation other than what they'd discovered in her bedroom tonight.

"Things seemed to keep running through my head. I can't shut them off."

He nodded, and then realized she probably couldn't see him. Not any better than he could see her.

"It's hard to put traumatic events out of your mind."

"I did this after Danny's death. After I found out what he'd done."

She meant Tate. After she'd found out what he'd done to her son.

Living with those pictures in the task force room all these months, Mac had fought those reoccurring images himself. And he didn't even know those kids. He couldn't imagine what it would be like to know those things had been done to someone you loved.

"You want some coffee?" He finally pushed up to a sitting position.

When he'd rummaged in his drawers for the T-shirt

and sweatpants he'd given her to sleep in, he'd grabbed a pair of the latter for himself. It wasn't his usual sleeping attire, but then this wasn't the usual night.

"Are you ready to get up?"

"Why not? I don't think either of us is going to sleep anymore."

"I could say that I didn't mean to wake you, but… that wouldn't be true."

"You sic Toby on me?" Mac reached down to ruffle the fur behind the dog's ears.

She laughed, the sound reassuring somehow coming out of the darkness. "I didn't stop him. I probably woke him up."

"It's okay. I don't take much sleep. That's something else you learn early in this profession."

"Not to need sleep?"

"To sleep when you can. Where you can. To go without when you have to."

"When do you have to?"

"Probably the same times you do. When you can't get stuff out of your head."

"You do that?"

"Not as often as I used to. When I first started—"

He stopped, thinking about those days. He'd thrown up at the sight of the first floater he'd been sent out on. Mostly that had been the stench, but not all of it. This was a climate that wasn't kind to bodies that had been dumped. Too much moisture. Too much heat. Insects. And plenty of wildlife.

That was one reason Tate had been successful so

long at hiding what he was doing. And none of what Mac was thinking right now was anything he was going to share with Danny Patterson's mother.

"When I first started," he went on, "I couldn't get any of it out of my head. You don't last long if you don't find ways to cope."

"And you did?"

"Eventually."

She didn't ask how. And he couldn't have told her if she had. You just learned not to think about certain things. Not to let the images in. Or maybe you learned not to think about what you had seen as being real people.

That was something he didn't like to consider, but he didn't deny it was a possibility. Maybe that's why the kids had been so tough. He hadn't been able to do that as well as he usually did.

After his sentence, there was silence between them a long time. It should have been uncomfortable, but it wasn't. It was almost companionable. And that was as strange as anything else that had happened tonight.

"I think I'd like that coffee," she said finally. "If you're sure you're ready to get up. If not..."

"I'm okay," he lied.

He felt like he'd taken a beating, but he knew from experience that that would pass. It was amazing what massive amounts of caffeine could accomplish. He had already started the process of inching himself off the couch when her voice stopped him.

"I don't know why you're doing what you're doing," she said. "Coming by the apartment tonight. Taking me to Louise's. Offering to let me sleep here. Maybe it's guilt. I don't know. But I do know it's above and beyond the call of whatever your official duties are, so…" Again there was a hesitation, expanding far beyond the length of the first. "I should say thank you. I know a lot of people are trying to catch Tate and put him away. I know that, no matter what I say. Nobody can want him to do what he does ever again."

"No," Mac agreed.

None of them did. None of the cops who'd worked on these cases, despite the mistakes or the delay in figuring out what was going on that the press took such delight in pointing out. Especially not the poor rookie who had screwed up the search of Tate's van. If anything, that had been the result of an overzealousness on his part to get this bastard off the streets.

"So…thank you," she finished.

This wasn't a town or a populace that looked on the police as the good guys. Mac could count on the fingers of one hand the number of times somebody had said thank you to him. Not that it was anything he ever expected. Maybe back when he was puking his guts out over a decaying body in some bayou, but not now.

He couldn't explain why hearing this particular woman say it—her voice expressionless, her face unseen—had such an impact. It tightened his throat, forcing him to swallow against an unexpected knot of emotion.

"I'll go make that coffee," he said, pushing up out of the deep, soft cushions.

He heard the dog's nails click against the floor as he

followed him into the kitchen. It was a long time before Danny Patterson's mother joined them there.

Given what Mac had felt when she'd expressed her gratitude, that, too, was a damn good thing.

Twelve

Sarah took a deep breath, holding it a second before she turned the key. Then she pushed the door of her apartment open. Instead of rushing inside and heading toward the kitchen and his bowls as was customary after any outing, Toby hung behind her. Despite how prepared she had thought she was, Sarah, too, hesitated on the threshold.

Without saying a word, Mac pushed past her, turning when he reached the center of the small living area.

"If you tell me where to look, I can round up whatever you need. You don't have to go into the back, but I think, considering the building security, you should come inside."

Before they'd come over, Mac had called the detective who'd interviewed her last night. After he hung up, he'd assured her that the "crime scene" processing had been done. She supposed that meant everything the police felt might have any bearing on Dan's murder had been removed.

What she hadn't been prepared for was the emotional barrier opening this door again had produced. She prided herself on the mental toughness Danny's death had forced upon her. Now, as she hovered in the hall outside her own apartment, she acknowledged what a farce that was.

"Sarah?"

Mac's voice broke the spell that her cowardice had created. She stepped inside, pulling the door shut behind her. From force of habit she threw the dead bolt and then turned to look at him.

One corner of his mouth lifted, the same movement she'd noticed that night on the stairs of the precinct. Then, she had identified it as self-deprecation. Now it looked suspiciously like parental pride. Or maybe congratulations.

"So what do you need and where do I find it?" he asked.

"I'll do it." She held Toby's leash out to him.

She was determined not to let what had happened here spook her again. After all, Tate wasn't hiding in the bedroom closet.

But he might have been yesterday. And if you'd been the one to go back there instead of Dan…

Mac took the lead from her hand, dragging Toby back to the kitchen and tethering him again to the table leg. "Lead the way," he said as he reentered the living room.

She thought about telling him that he didn't need to accompany her. Instead, she did what he'd suggested.

She didn't glance into the open bathroom as she passed by. She had watched the technicians take out the bloodstained shower curtain last night. She had just as soon not know if they'd confiscated anything else.

When she reached the bedroom, she saw that the closet doors were closed. Without allowing herself to hesitate, she walked over to them and pushed one sliding panel behind the other. Standing on tiptoe, she stretched upward to retrieve the small cloth suitcase she kept on the top shelf.

Before she could snag its handle, Mac moved behind her. As he reached over her head, she was once more aware of him physically. Of his size. That he was male. And of the clean scent of soap and shampoo that surrounded him, the same fragrances that had filled the small bathroom of his apartment after her shower this morning.

He lifted the bag off the shelf and crossed the room to lay it on her bed. She turned in time to see him unzip and then throw back its top.

For some reason she had a flash of memory of Dan's hand bringing his cigarette up to his mouth on the restaurant's patio yesterday. She deliberately destroyed it, concentrating on the here and now.

Mac had brought her back to the apartment so she could pick up some things she'd need for the next few days. Underwear and a couple of changes of clothes, including her uniform for work.

She'd called her boss this morning, explaining the situation and asking for a few days off. At least until the funeral. Although he'd told her to take as much time as she needed, she couldn't afford to stay out long. It would be too easy for him to find someone to replace her.

"I think I'll take a look around while you're packing. You sure you're okay back here?"

"I'm fine, but... What exactly are you looking for?"

"I don't know. Anything the techs might have missed."

He'd suggested last night that Tate might have been waiting for her to come home and had been interrupted by Dan's arrival. If that had been the case, there might be some indication of how the killer had gotten in or where he'd hidden.

With that thought she was again conscious of the double closet behind her. And aware that unless she protested, she was about to be left in this room alone.

"Call me if you need me," Mac added. "For getting things down, I mean."

She nodded, but waited until he was out of the room before she walked over to the chest. She began methodically to take items out of the drawers and to place them in the suitcase. When she finished with the folded clothes, she added a couple of outfits from the closet.

She could hear Mac in the front of the apartment as she moved into the bathroom to gather up her toiletries. She avoided looking into the mirror over the lavatory, mostly so her eyes wouldn't focus on the area where the shower curtain was missing, but also because she didn't particularly want to see on her face the results of the last few days. The mirror over Mac's counter had documented them quite clearly this morning.

She was zipping her makeup bag closed when the doorbell rang. Her hands froze, her eyes lifting automatically. In the glass she saw Mac lean into the open doorway.

"Expecting somebody?"

Mouth dry, she shook her head.

He disappeared down the hall before she could ask what he intended to do. She laid the bag down on the counter and followed.

When she reached the living room, she saw that Mac had his eye to the peephole, his gun out again. He turned to her and shook his head, apparently unable to see whoever had rung the bell.

She tapped her chest with one finger, indicating that she should be the one to answer. If this was someone from the media, they'd have a field day with the fact that Mac was here. It would only add to the speculation that had erupted after the scene on the courthouse steps. And it would certainly not make it any easier for him to get his job back.

Maybe realizing some of what she was thinking, Mac nodded before he stepped to the side of the door, where he'd be hidden when she opened it. She walked across the room, reaching for the knob just as the bell sounded again.

"Who is it?"

"I saw you come home."

Dwight. Her recognition was part relief and part exasperation.

"Can I say hello to Toby? I saw him come home, too."

"Not right now, Dwight. I'm kind of busy."

"Aren't you going to walk him? I brought his ball."

"The kid from downstairs?" Mac asked as he pushed his weapon back into the shoulder holster.

She nodded. Before she could protest, Mac reached out and threw the lock, opening the door.

Surprised, Dwight's gaze moved from one grownup to the other. "I'm Dwight David Ingersoll."

"Mac Donovan." Mac held out his hand, which swallowed the small one Dwight offered in return. "You see all the excitement yesterday?"

"Some of it. I saw *you*."

"You were at the window downstairs. You waved at me, didn't you?"

Dwight nodded, pleased at being recognized.

"You wave at everybody who comes up the walk?"

"Just people who look like they're nice."

Mac's lips twitched again, but he managed to keep a straight face. "Thanks for the compliment. I think you look nice, too."

"Are *you* going to take Toby out to walk?"

"Why don't we all do that," Mac suggested.

She knew he had wanted to talk to the boy yesterday, but surely he understood her reluctance to have any further dealings with the child. Dan was dead, for no other reason than his association with her. Why put Dwight at risk on the off chance he might have seen something that could shed some light on what had happened up here yesterday?

"I don't think we have time for that," she said.

"I don't see why not." Mac raised his brows, as if trying to clue her in.

Exasperated, Sarah ditched the subtlety. Let Dwight think what he would.

"I told you he wasn't here yesterday. He couldn't have seen anything. He was in the park with me."

"For the first time?"

"What?"

"Was that the first time he'd gone with you to the park?"

"I had to ask my mother," Dwight said. "I used to just go to the corner with Toby."

"If he's watching you," Mac said, ignoring the boy, "then he's already seen you together."

"Who?" Dwight's eyes again tracked from one to the other.

"Nobody," Sarah said automatically.

"A man who sometimes comes to this building." Mac's words came on top of her denial. "You think you can remember everybody you've seen coming up the walk in the last few days?"

"I'm not here all the time. I go to school. To Davidson Elementary. My teacher is—"

"If you're determined to talk to him, at least do it inside the apartment," Sarah urged.

The thought that someone might be watching them gave her chills. Sadly, however, Mac was right. If Tate *had* been following her the last couple of days, he was already aware of her association with Dwight Ingersoll.

"And those are the only white men you've seen here lately?"

"You aren't supposed to notice whether people are black or white," Dwight said. "My teacher says that doesn't matter."

Except your teacher isn't looking for a serial killer, Mac thought. A *white* serial killer.

"The man I need to find is white. So in this case, it *does* make a difference," Mac explained patiently.

"Those I told you about are the only ones I saw."

The boy lifted the last of the package of peanut butter crackers Sarah had given him to his mouth, delicately nibbling along its last untouched edge. He'd eaten all of them that way, from the outside in, turning them carefully while Mac questioned him.

Mac knew he should have put it together sooner, starting with the way the kid looked. His complete obsession with Sarah and the dog. Even his waving last night. Watching him eat those crackers had simply confirmed what he should have gathered from all the other clues. There was something wrong with Dwight Ingersoll.

Which meant that even if he'd provided them with any kind of information about Tate being here, his testimony wouldn't have a snowball's chance in hell of standing up in court. Not with a defense attorney who was worth a damn.

"Okay, then." Mac decided to cut his losses. "I think that will do it. You've been really helpful."

The boy beamed, basking in what Mac would bet was unaccustomed praise. Sarah shifted in her chair, her eyes meeting his.

At first she'd left him alone with the kid to ask his questions. After about ten minutes, she'd returned, bringing the suitcase he'd taken off the closet shelf with her. She'd taken the seat nearest the back hall, and she hadn't said anything during the rest of the interview.

"I think Toby would like to go out now." Dwight's gaze again moved hopefully from one to the other. "He gets tired of being cooped up inside all day."

A statement which would apply to the boy as well, Mac guessed. He looked at Sarah, brows raised, seeking permission.

"Not today," she said to Dwight. "I'm going to be away for a few days. When I get back, we'll go to the park again and play ball. I know Toby is going to miss doing that with you."

The kid's face fell, his disappointment palpable. For a moment Mac was afraid he was going to cry, but it seemed Dwight Ingersoll was better at dealing with setbacks than most children his age. Or maybe he was more experienced with them.

"We'll walk down with you," Sarah went on. "I need to talk to your mother."

"You aren't going to tell her I'm bothering you, are you? She doesn't like for me to bother people."

"Of course I'm not going to tell her that. You aren't bothering me, Dwight, but I just can't use your help with Toby for a while. Not until I get back."

"I could keep him for you. While you're away, I mean. I'd take real good care of him. I'd walk him every day. You could give me his bowls. And his food." The boy was almost stuttering in his eagerness to make those arrangements.

Sarah rose, bringing the dog, who'd been lying on the rug between them, to his feet as well. She walked across to put her hand on the back of Dwight's head, smiling down at him. "I know you would. I know you'd take very good care of him, but… I need him with me."

"Because you'd miss him?"

"Because I'd miss him. But thank you for the offer.

It was very kind." She lifted her eyes to Mac. "I think it's time we should go."

He couldn't see the harm in giving the kid the fifteen minutes outside that he wanted, but he didn't intend to argue. He knew Sarah was uncomfortable with the idea that she might bring the boy to Tate's attention. Considering her history—and Tate's—who could blame her?

He rose, too, sticking out his hand to the child. "Thanks again for all your help, Dwight. Think I could tag along the next time you take Toby to the park?"

"Sure. You can throw the ball for him, too. You can probably throw it farther than me, but I can throw it pretty far."

"Don't forget your ball," Sarah reminded.

"I won't," the boy said, picking it up from the floor where he'd placed it when she'd given him the crackers. "I'll put it in my special place until Toby and you get back."

"Thank you. Come on, Tobe." She bent, securing the leash to the dog's collar again. "Would you like to take him down the stairs?"

The kid nodded, pale eyes widening with excitement.

"Remember what I told you. Don't let him pull you down."

"I won't. He's a good dog, aren't you, Tobe. A very good dog." Dwight headed toward the door, the mutt trotting contentedly beside him.

"The mother?" Mac mouthed.

"She should know what's going on."

She meant Tate. And she was right. The more eyes watching out for him the better, as far as Mac was concerned.

Although Dwight wanted to use the key around his neck, Sarah insisted on ringing the bell. She wasn't sure she'd ever get to meet his mother otherwise.

There was no response until she'd pushed the button twice more, and when it came, it was only a disembodied voice. "Who's there?"

Sarah glanced at Dwight, who nodded. "Sarah Patterson, Mrs. Ingersoll. I live on the third floor. I want to talk to you about your son."

They waited again, the silence stretching uncomfortably long. Finally the door opened, but only as far as the chain lock would allow, giving them a truncated view of the woman inside.

"What's he done now?" And then when she spotted the child. "What have you been up to, Dwight?"

"He hasn't done anything. I'm sorry I didn't make that clear. I'm just a little concerned about him. Could we come in, please?"

The blue eye visible through the crack examined her and then moved to consider Mac. Whether he was the deciding factor or not, Sarah would never know, but after a moment Dwight's mother closed the door and removed the chain before she opened it again.

Mrs. Ingersoll wore a coral-colored chenille bathrobe, belted at the waist. She was barefoot, and her hair was disarrayed enough that Sarah wondered if she'd been sleeping.

“Okay, what exactly are you so concerned about?”

“May we come in?” Sarah asked again.

“Sorry. The place is a wreck. I didn’t have time to clean today.”

“We don’t mind. Inside would be more…private.”

“You need privacy to talk about my son? Maybe I’m missing something, but—”

“You saw the police here yesterday,” Mac interrupted.

“Yeah?”

“The incident that brought them is part of what we’re concerned about.”

“He do something wrong?” Dwight’s mother lifted her chin in the child’s direction.

“No, ma’am. We just wanted to make sure that you knew the building isn’t as safe as perhaps it once was.”

“Drug dealers. I know. But we don’t have anything to do with that. Have you been messing with those people, Dwight? I told you about that.”

“No, ma’am.” The excitement of bringing Toby downstairs had faded from the boy’s eyes. “I don’t have anything to do with them.”

“Dwight’s done nothing wrong,” Sarah said. “We just wanted to make you aware of an increased danger in the area. Especially for children.”

“What kind of danger?”

Sarah looked pointedly down at the child, still holding Toby’s leash, and then back up at his mother. “I’d rather not talk about this in front of him.”

Mrs. Ingersoll’s lips pursed slightly before she opened them again. “Go check on your Nana. See if she needs anything.”

Obediently, Dwight held the leash out to Mac, who smiled at the boy as he took it. "You can say goodbye to him if you want."

The child bent, putting his arms around the dog. "You be good while you're gone, you hear? I'll save your ball for you. I'll put it in my special place, and we'll play with it when you get home."

"Go on," Mrs. Ingersoll urged.

Dwight released the animal and slipped through the door past his mother. She waited until they could no longer hear his footsteps before she asked again, speaking directly to Mac, "What danger?"

"I'm sure you're aware that a serial killer of little boys has been operating in this area for the last few years. We have reason to believe he may have been here yesterday."

"*Here?* In the building? Is that who killed that man they carried out?"

"It's possible."

"And you think he may be interested in Dwight?" She sounded slightly surprised that anyone could be.

"We don't know that he's even aware of Dwight. But your son's the right age. And the right size. We thought we should warn you so you can keep a closer eye on him. Keep him inside."

"He's gotta go to school. I've been through all that. Him missing too many days, I mean."

Sarah suspected that in this neighborhood it would take a lot of absences before the authorities got involved. "Maybe you could walk him to school. Just for while."

"I got my mother here. I can't leave her alone. She's… She's not right in the head."

"You don't ever go out?"

"For groceries." Mrs. Ingersoll's tone was defensive again. "Necessities. If I do, then Dwight's here. We take turns. Nobody can take this twenty-four hours a day. Wait a minute. I know you. I seen you on TV. You're the woman—" She stopped, obviously putting together the news stories on Sarah with the warning they'd just issued.

"Maybe you can just be more watchful of Dwight," Mac interjected. "Now that you know the situation. If you see anything suspicious..." He held out one of his business cards, "Anything at all, you can reach me at that number."

Dwight's mother nodded as she reached out to take the card, slipping it into the pocket of her robe. Her still-fascinated eyes considered Sarah again, as if she were a rock star or some other celebrity, before she asked Mac, "Is that all?"

"Unless you have any questions."

"Are you leaving?" she asked Sarah.

"For a few days."

"Must be nice to be able to get away from this place." Mrs. Ingersoll's eyes lifted to Mac's face, and her smile widened.

"It was good to have met you," Sarah said briskly. "You have a fine, sweet little boy. You're a very lucky woman."

The woman laughed again, but by that time Sarah had already turned away. She knew if she didn't, she wouldn't be able to hide what she was thinking.

A sweet little boy you don't deserve. A little boy who is alive, and if you aren't very careful—

"Take care," Mac said behind her. "And take care of Dwight. If he were mine, I wouldn't let him out of my sight. At least not for the time being."

"I won't. And thanks. I'll be sure to call you if I see anything out of the ordinary. Oh, and my name is Beverly. Bev to my friends."

As the flirtation played out behind her, Sarah pushed the foyer door open, inhaling a long draught of cold air as soon as she stepped outside. She was trying to banish the stale closeness emanating from inside the Ingersoll apartment.

She wasn't sure she'd accomplished anything with her warning to Dwight's mother. If not, at least she'd tried.

"Well, that explained a lot." Mac had stopped beside her on the stoop.

"Like Dwight's hunger for some attention?"

"Among other things. Poor little guy."

"You think she'll watch him?"

"I doubt she knows he's there half the time."

"Why not? Obviously she doesn't work. Did you wonder what those 'necessities' she mentioned might encompass? Maybe that's how she supports them."

"Probably on welfare. Her mother would get Social Security. She could even be collecting child support from Dwight's father. Of course, none of that rules out her involvement in something less legal."

Like prostitution? Or dealing drugs herself? Sarah wasn't sure which of those Mac had meant by that remark, but she didn't pursue it.

She had learned more about Dwight Ingersoll's situation than she wanted to know. And far, far more than she had ever intended to find out.

Thirteen

Sarah had suggested they stop somewhere on the way back to his apartment to let the dog run. As a result, Mac was sitting on one of the benches overlooking the river, watching Toby tear from one bush to the next, apparently looking for squirrels or birds.

Sarah trailed him, his leash in her hand. The breeze touched her hair, so that she occasionally reached up to push a strand off her face. Despite the fleece jacket she wore, its collar turned up against the cold, she looked slim and athletic. Hardly old enough to have had an eleven-year-old son. Much less to have lost one.

She hadn't invited him to join the romp. In all honesty, he'd gotten the feeling that she'd rather he didn't, but despite that, he'd been thinking about it. Before he could, his cell rang.

He fished it out of his inside pocket, glancing at the caller ID before he flipped the case open. "Hey."

"Hey, yourself," Sonny said. "So how's the man of leisure?"

"At leisure."

"How's the lady with the mouth."

"Walking her dog."

"She's still with you?"

The disapproval that had been in his partner's voice yesterday was there again. Mac didn't like it any more now than he had then.

"Until I figure out what's going on."

"Probably not a bad idea," Sonny said.

"That's a switch."

"You remember the key she asked us to look for?"

The spare Sarah said she'd given her ex-husband. And now Mac knew where this was going.

"I remember."

"We didn't find it. That don't mean whoever killed the guy took it, but…"

"But you wouldn't sleep in that apartment tonight."

"Not without changing the locks," Sonny admitted.

"Can you get somebody to do that? Say the scene needs to be protected or something?"

"Why don't you all just get it done?"

"I doubt she's got the money. And I doubt she'd let me pay. Besides, if that *was* Tate who did her ex, it seems to me the department owes her at least the cost of a locksmith."

"Speaking of which…"

Mac could tell he wasn't going to like this one, either. "Yeah?"

"Nobody here is thinking it was Tate."

Mac laughed. "Then who do they think it was?"

"Whoever left that message maybe. That ain't to say he's not dangerous, of course. We just don't think it's Tate."

"That's a stretch, even for the department."

"Dan Patterson's murder was nothing like Tate's MO. Nothing. Patterson was an adult. He was killed relatively swiftly. And it was not done on neutral territory."

Tate had never, as far as they knew, entered the homes of his victims. He always picked them up somewhere else. Their bodies were always found in some secluded rural area, usually by accident, and usually long after the crime.

The one victim they'd discovered before the predators and insects made much headway had told them all any of them wanted to know about his methodology. Sonny was right about that, too. What he did wasn't designed to be quick.

"That's because he didn't *intend* to kill Patterson." Mac wasn't sure why he was bothering to make these arguments again. Sonny was simply repeating the party line. "He was forced into doing that by the ex's unexpected presence in Sarah's apartment. Then, when I called and said I was coming over, he knew he had to get out of there. None of your arguments guarantee this wasn't Tate."

"None of yours guarantees it was. It ain't gonna fly, Mac. They aren't even giving this one to the task force."

"How the hell can they make that decision? He called her, for God's sake."

Sonny said nothing because they both knew the

answer to that, too. The department didn't believe the phone call had been made by Tate. And if not, there was no reason to tie the serial killer to the murder of Dan Patterson. It would become just one more unsolved homicide in a city that had a lot of those.

"I'll try to get her locks changed," his partner said finally. "Other than that..."

"Other than that, you can all kiss my ass." Mac closed the cell with a snap, more furious than he had any right to be.

He shut his eyes, trying to block the image of Dwight Ingersoll and that ridiculous pink ball. When he was unsuccessful at that, he opened the phone again, punched up Sonny's name, and hit Send.

"Cochran."

"No matter what they tell you about Patterson's murder, Sonny, I'm telling you that you need to put somebody on the building. Full time."

"You know we don't have enough manpower to—"

"He may not know she's gone. If he doesn't, he'll be back."

"There's no reason for him—"

"He wasn't there for Patterson. He was there for her. And once he's made up his mind, our boy doesn't like being denied."

"Our *boy,* according to the Bureau, is probably a thousand miles away from here right now."

"*Or* he's watching that apartment. Waiting for her to come back. I get that you can't admit to the possibility that Tate did Dan Patterson, but what are you gonna do when the next kid goes missing? And by the way, there's one living right there. Bottom apartment, to the right as you face the entry. Nine years old. Perfect age, wouldn't you say? Something happens to him, and you aren't going to be able to keep the public from making the connection between Tate and the murder that took place in that building yesterday. One in which the victim's name was the same as the woman who a few days ago tried to shoot Samuel Tate."

There was a long silence, which Mac waited through.

"I'll see what I can do," his partner said grudgingly.

"Thanks."

"I ain't making you no promises, you understand, but I'll do my best."

"And the locks?"

"I'll tell them we've got a crime scene to protect. It should be done in a couple of days."

"Thanks."

"She being civil to you?"

At the reminder Mac glanced up, eyes searching the area where Sarah and Toby had been when he'd begun this conversation. She was coming toward him, maybe ten feet away from the bench where he was sitting.

Toby was back on his leash. His tongue hung out, but he seemed to be getting back to normal after yesterday's trauma. Tail wagging, he literally dragged his mistress toward Mac.

Her cheeks held a touch of color from the cold or from her exertions in recapturing the dog. Her hair, which he'd thought was brown, was touched with red and gold highlights. Windblown, it tangled around the clear, pale oval of her face. Without makeup to hide them, a spatter of freckles was visible across the high-bridged nose.

Not for the first time, Mac acknowledged the validity of Sonny's doubts about his motives. Sarah Patterson was a beautiful woman.

"Yeah," he said into the phone. "Not a problem. I'll talk to you tomorrow, okay?"

"She there? I get it. Don't do nothing I wouldn't do, good buddy."

"Don't worry." Mac closed the phone, pushing it back into his pocket. By that time the dog was leaning against his leg, once more attempting to lick his face. He stood, reaching down to scratch behind the mutt's ears. "Have a good run?"

"Toby did. I had a good drag. Who were you talking to?"

"Cochran. My partner. Ex-partner right now, I guess."

"What did he want?"

Mac hesitated, wondering if there were any good way to break the news. If he didn't tell her though, she'd eventually ask. Just as soon as she was ready to go back home.

"They didn't find your spare key."

Her face changed, the lines of tension that had marred it until the last half hour there again. "That means he has it."

"Not necessarily," Mac began and then knew he couldn't lie to her about this. "But yeah, that's what we're thinking."

"Then they *do* believe it was Tate."

"That isn't the official version, but I suspect most of them wonder."

"The *official* version?"

"That's not the story that will be given to the press. If they're interested enough to pursue it."

"Why wouldn't they be? They were pretty damn interested in pursuing me. You, too, for that matter."

"Which might be the only reason they'd be interested in what the department is going to classify as another unsolved murder in a part of town that sees a lot of them."

"And the fact that he was my ex-husband…?"

Mac shrugged.

"God. And yet they don't think this has anything to do with Tate." She shook her head. "Maybe somebody should clue the papers in to the connection."

Mac could imagine Morel's reaction if someone did. And if his boss had any idea Sarah Patterson was staying at his apartment… "You aren't thinking about doing that, are you?"

"Why not? Why not let the city know that murdering son of a bitch is still out there. Only now, it's not just little boys he's after. Now no one is safe. I wonder how the police would like that."

Not worth a damn. And as much as Mac would like to see Morel try to talk his way out of that reality when the press confronted him, going to the media wasn't a good idea. Not in his situation.

"The public knows we let Tate go. The papers have certainly been willing to play that up. And in actuality, the department's right. Nothing about the particulars of your ex-husband's murder ties Tate to it."

"Nothing but me," Sarah said. "You don't think the press would be interested in that?"

"About as interested as they were when you tried to shoot Tate."

Some of the media frenzy from that was dying down. As soon as the connection between her ex-husband's death and Tate was made—and there was no doubt in Mac's mind that eventually it would be—Sarah would be right back in the spotlight.

If the press also discovered that she was living with him, then so would he. And that was something that was bound to get Morel's back up even more than it was now.

"Why don't you give it a couple of days?" he suggested. "Some of the evidence they took from the apartment may definitively put Tate there. After all, with his arrest we've now got his prints and DNA."

Even if Tate had been unwilling to give the department a sample, they would have obtained one from something he'd used during those few days before his hearing.

"Why wait?" she asked. "Why shouldn't the cops have to explain that convoluted reasoning to the public?"

"Because for one thing, it will turn your ex-husband's funeral into a media circus. It seems to me it would be easier for your mother-in-law if that didn't happen."

And easier for you if her accusations aren't spread out on the front page of every newspaper in the state.

He didn't bother to express that thought. If he read Sarah Patterson right, she wouldn't take any shortcuts in what she saw as the right thing to do. If she thought what she was doing would help Patterson's mother cope with his death, then maybe she'd be willing to wait a couple of days before going public with her accusation.

"I need to find out when that will be. Do you know how long they'll hold his body?" She brushed a tendril of hair away from her cheek, tucking it behind her ear.

"An autopsy usually takes a couple of days. The body will be released to the family as soon as that's done."

"In this case, released to Louise."

"Yeah."

"I don't know whether she's capable of handling the arrangements."

"She the only family he's got?"

"Pauline, who's in her seventies. I think there are some cousins, but not here. Do you think they'd let me do that? I mean would they release the body to me?"

"Officially, his mother's the next of kin."

"And I'm the *ex*-wife."

"That's about it."

"Danny was buried in their family plot. I imagine Dan will be, too."

"In Madisonville."

She nodded.

That might make it easier to keep a lid on the connection, which is what the department would prefer. For right now, that was what would be best for him as well.

If the cemetery was in keeping with the size of the town, it would also make it easier to identify the mourners. Not that he expected Tate to show up for the funeral.

Still, checking out who did was something the cops did as a matter of course.

All Mac knew was that no matter who made the arrangements for Dan Patterson's funeral, he would be in attendance.

Fourteen

The ease she'd felt drinking coffee with Mac Donovan this morning had been lost during the course of the day they'd spent together. Maybe part of that was due to her worry about Dwight. Or Mac's reaction to his department's decision that Tate hadn't been involved in Dan's death. Whatever had caused the increased tension between them, she had become more aware of it as they neared the reality of spending another night together.

She had managed to swallow a couple of pieces of the pizza he'd ordered for dinner, more out of recognition that she needed to eat something than because she was hungry. Mac had stoically finished the rest, but then, judging by the friendliness of the delivery guy, he ate a lot of the stuff. Or he was a very good tipper.

"More wine?" He held the bottle over her glass.

"Not for me, thanks."

"Pretty bad, huh? Somebody gave it to me last Christmas. I hadn't had an occasion to open it since."

Sarah wasn't sure how this qualified as an occasion, and although she was no expert, she had had far worse than the inexpensive merlot. "It's fine. I'm just not much of a drinker. Maybe because of what I do."

"Waitress, right?"

"Since the divorce."

"And before?"

"I helped Dan with his business. He's a contractor. Was a contractor."

"I would think that with all the construction, somebody would be looking to hire."

"Me? Probably. I haven't asked."

"I've heard the money waiting tables here can be really good. Especially in some of the places in the Quarter."

"I haven't asked there, either."

He took a sip of the wine he'd added to his glass, letting the subject drop. Normally she would have been more than willing to do the same. For some reason she felt an obligation to try and explain her life since Danny's death.

"I guess that in employment, like in everything else, I've followed the path of least resistance. I make enough to pay the rent and to feed me and Toby. There's been no incentive to do anything else."

She realized she had just used the past tense. As if something had changed.

"It's an easy trap to fall into." Mac looked at her over the rim of his glass.

"I couldn't figure out why I should do anything else."

"Divorce is always hard. Divorce on top of the rest…"

"Did it affect you like that? Your divorce."

"The death of my marriage was so gradual I think the only emotion both of us felt when it was over was relief that we didn't have to go on pretending."

"That's sad."

"Yeah. That, too."

"Sorry. If anyone should know better than to ask personal questions it's me."

"It happened three years ago. And what you asked wasn't all that personal."

"She still live here?"

"She remarried less than a year later. An insurance salesman from Mobile. They've got a house there and another on the Gulf. He comes home nights."

"And she knows he always will."

"I'm not sure she was worried about me not coming home so much as she was tired of being shut out. At least that's what she told the therapist. That I never talked to her about what I was working on. I figured who the hell would want to hear me talk about the stuff we deal with every day. Most of it isn't exactly dinner conversation."

Stuff like Danny's murder.

"I'll do the dishes." She pushed up from the table to collect their plates. "Then I think I'd better take Toby out again. Is there a park or a public green within walking distance?"

"The dishwasher's empty. We can just stick them in there. And although this neighborhood may be safer than the one you're used to, I wouldn't call it risk free. I'll walk him for you."

"Thanks, but I could use the fresh air. And you're

right. This is considerably safer than the area where we normally walk."

"Look, I know you don't want me tagging along, but under the circumstances, I really don't think it's smart for you to go out on your own."

"What gave you the impression I didn't want company?"

"I don't know. Maybe because you seemed to enjoy the run so much this afternoon when it was just you and him."

"Toby likes you. Which means he might actually mind you. And I don't. Mind having you along, that is."

She carried the dishes over to the sink to rinse them off before she inserted them into the dishwasher. Mac brought the glasses, finishing the wine in his while she loaded the plates and silverware.

"I'll get my jacket and the beast," he said as he set the empty goblet down on the counter.

They had locked the dog in the bedroom while they ate. Otherwise he would have watched every bite either of them took, hoping for a handout.

"If only he were," she said.

"A beast?"

"I might feel better about going back to my apartment if Toby were more protective."

"Toby's a lover not a fighter," Mac agreed.

"When we got him and discovered what a wuss he is, I was actually relieved. No matter how friendly a dog seems, you can never know his temperament until he's lived with you a while and you've watched him interact with people."

"Good dog for a kid."

"Yes, he was," she said, relieved that the overwhelming feelings of grief and anger Tate's release had revived seemed to be fading. Or rather to have become hidden again under the commonplaces of human interaction.

"I'll bring your jacket," Mac said. "The one you wore today?"

"That's fine. I'm going to finish up in here."

"Don't worry too much. The maid comes tomorrow."

"Should I do something with my things?"

"She's the maid, not my mother," Mac reassured. "She wouldn't care if the Mongol Horde was staying here, as long as they weren't too messy."

He disappeared through the kitchen doorway. Sarah leaned back against the counter, wondering how the hell she'd ended up living with a divorced cop and worrying about becoming gossip fodder for his maid. As if any of that mattered.

There was, as Mac had said, nothing personal about any of this. Even if there had been, it was no one's business but theirs. They were consenting adults, with no ties to anyone else.

Consenting adults. The phrase, and all its implications, echoed in her head.

"Ready?"

She looked up to find Mac back in the doorway, her jacket in one hand and the end of Toby's leash in the other. The big dog was weaving in and out around his legs, his eagerness to be outside plain.

"Ready if you are."

And once more a phrase that seemed to have a dozen

possible connotations reverberated inside her mind as she followed Mac out of the apartment.

Mac wasn't sure what awakened him. Only that it was not the cold, wet nose of the dog this time.

This was something more subtle. Something that had brought him awake without imprinting itself on his consciousness.

Normally he'd have turned over, pushed his pillow into a more comfortable shape, and gone back to sleep. Not this week, he thought, easing up off the couch. He brought the .38 he'd slid under the couch cushion with him.

He visually checked the front door. In the dim light from the halogens in the parking lot, he could see that the chain was engaged.

He turned, surveying what he could see of the kitchen. Before he had completed that scan, he heard the noise that had probably awakened him.

From the bedroom, he realized, adrenaline already flooding through his system. On bare feet he sprinted across the room to press his ear against the cheap, hollow-core door.

Nothing. He reached out with his left hand and turned the knob until the catch released. Then, leading with his weapon, he pushed the door open with his shoulder.

The halogens that had illuminated the living room provided enough light for him to see into the room. The bed was empty, its covers thrown back. And the door to the adjoining bath was closed.

Was that what he'd heard? Sarah getting up to go to the bathroom? Closing its door behind her?

Except neither seemed to jibe with the noises that had sent him here, weapon in hand.

"Sarah? You okay?"

No response. He crossed the room, gun extended in front of him in both hands, and put his ear against the second door.

From inside the bathroom came a sound he recognized. The water was on in the shower, and beneath its familiar pulse was the unidentifiable something that had dragged him from sleep.

His blood ran cold. He forced himself to open the door, using the same approach he'd taken in entering the bedroom. The light was off, but he could see the cloud of steam rushing out toward him.

"Sarah?"

Still no answer. He stepped inside the small room, the sound of rushing water growing louder. Again he heard the noise that had brought him here. A whooping intake as if someone were gasping for air.

Mac jerked the sliding door of the shower open, but all he could see was a black shape against the white tile. He reached behind him to flick on the overhead light.

Momentarily dazzled by its brightness, he lifted his left arm to shield his eyes until they could adjust. When they had, he knew he'd made a terrible error of judgment.

Sarah was huddled in the corner of the enclosure, her forearms crossed over her head, which was lowered so that he couldn't see her face. The sound she made was like no crying he'd ever heard. Deep and guttural, the force of her sobs shook her entire body.

"Sarah." As he said her name, he reached out and touched her shoulder.

Her head came up to reveal bloodshot eyes. She looked like a drowned kitten, her hair plastered to her skull from the incessant beat of the shower.

Mac laid his weapon on the counter behind him and reached back into the enclosure to turn off the water. In the sudden silence he could hear her breathing, small ratcheting breaths she seemed unable to control.

He almost asked what was wrong, but realized that question would be insane. What the hell was right in Sarah Patterson's life? She had buried her eleven-year-old son. And she was about to bury her ex-husband, for whose death she blamed herself.

Instead of badgering her with stupid questions, he did the only thing he could think of. He grabbed the out-sized bath cloth he'd put out for her last night off the towel rack and carried it over to where she crouched against the wall.

"Come on." He reached down to take her elbow and pull her up.

She didn't resist, standing and letting him wrap the towel around her. When he had her covered, he urged her to step out of the shower and onto the mat.

He thought about drying her off and then getting her into something warm. That would be the logical thing to do. Some rational solution to offer a woman who'd obviously reached the end of her resources.

Instead, motivated by the same vulnerability that

had touched him from the start, he picked her up as he would a child. Holding her in his arms, he sat down on the closed john and cradled her against the warmth of his body.

After a few minutes, the tremors that had racked her frame began to lessen until there was only the occasional shiver. Even then he didn't release her, rocking her slightly and saying the same inane, ridiculous phrases over and over.

"It's all right. Everything's going to be all right."

He lost all track of time, but after what seemed an eternity, she shifted within his arms, pushing away from him to try and sit up.

"Sorry," she whispered.

"For what? You've got nothing to be sorry for."

"I can't even remember the last time I cried like that."

"Then maybe you ought to do it more often."

She nodded as if that made sense. "I dreamed about Dwight. Once I started…" She took a breath, her head moving from side to side.

"You've had a lot to deal with. Not just in the last few days."

"But I *had* dealt with it. I thought I had holding it together down to a science. Then tonight—" She laughed, the sound full of disbelief.

"I've seen grown men, cops, react the same way. And with less provocation." When she made no response to that lie, he asked, "You want to talk about the dream?"

She shook her head again.

"You want to go back to bed? Try and get some sleep. I'll sit in there with you."

Her eyes searched his face, which he tried to keep as expressionless as possible. After a moment she shook her head again.

"Coffee?" he suggested, remembering last night.

"Come with me."

In context those words made no sense. Then suddenly, looking down into her eyes, they did.

Ripe for the picking.

Sonny's words. Sonny's fear.

Not one he'd shared. Not then.

He pushed the words through a throat gone dry. "I think you need to tell me exactly what that means."

"Come to bed with me."

"I don't think that would be a good idea."

"Why?"

"Because I'm not a eunuch. And because, frankly, it's been a while."

"More than a year."

He started to correct her and then realized she wasn't talking about him. Until a year ago, she and her ex had been trying to make their marriage work.

"I got mad at Sonny because he insinuated I intended to take advantage of you."

Her lips curved, almost a smile. "Did you?"

"No. But…that would be."

"You didn't start this, Mac. I did."

"While you were coming off a crying jag."

"There's an expression I haven't heard in a while."

"Okay. How about while you were feeling emotionally battered. Vulnerable. Or a half dozen other terms Sonny would gladly supply."

"You always care so much what he thinks?"

"He usually thinks pretty highly of me."

"Then why would it surprise you that I do, too?"

"Is that what this is about? Thinking highly of me?"

"Partly. It's also about need. And loneliness. And nightmares."

"I told you I'd sit with you until you go to sleep."

"That takes care of the last two."

He could feel himself beginning to react to the thought of taking her to bed. Feeling that elegant body move beneath his. Having those slim, beautiful legs wrap around him as he drove deeper and deeper into the sweet, wet heat of her.

"There are a thousand men—"

"And I didn't invite any of them into my bed. *Your* bed," she amended, her lips curving again.

He began to shake his head, more in self-denial than in rejection of what she'd offered.

"Whatever you're thinking about my motives," she said, "you're probably wrong. I think somewhere inside I've known I was going to ask you for a while now. I wasn't consciously thinking it, but everything was in place for this to happen. Then I watched your hands tonight as you poured the wine, and I wanted them moving over my body."

Not to respond to her admission would take a self-control he didn't possess. Besides, every response he was making was of the physiological variety, the kind few men, even at his age, had a whole hell of a lot of choice about.

The curve of her lips deepened. And something

happened in her eyes. Something even more inviting than her words.

"You have very nice hands, Mac."

She raised one of hers to lay it against the side of his face. With her thumb, she brushed over the fullness of his bottom lip.

"And whatever you're worried about," she went on, "don't. I know what I'm doing. You aren't coercing me. You aren't taking advantage of me. You aren't doing a single thing that's wrong or immoral. You offered me your strength when I cried. Your warmth when I was cold. This is no different, Mac. Except this time, I have something to offer *you*."

Fifteen

It was strange that, after being celibate so long, she'd had no doubts about the rightness of this. No second thoughts, not even now. And no regrets. The only thing that had given her pause was the way Mac had responded.

She had expected his initial reservations, of course. After all, he was a decent man, and anyone with any sort of moral compass would have thought that any decision she made right now would be influenced by her emotional state. What she hadn't expected was the way he had gone about making love to her once he'd made up his mind.

Making love…

That was exactly what this felt like. As if he were making love to her. And taking the time to do it right.

When he'd carried her out of the bathroom and laid her on the disordered bed, she'd expected some cursory foreplay, quickly followed by the main attraction. In all honesty, that's what she'd been hoping for when she'd issued her invitation.

It hadn't played out that way, despite the fact that he had been as physically ready as she had. Instead, when he'd stripped off his T-shirt and sweatpants, and then slipped into bed beside her, he'd begun a slow seduction.

Not that she had objected to his attention to detail. It was simply something she hadn't required. Because of that, it had taken her a few minutes to readjust her expectations.

Once she had, his patiently experienced approach had dissolved the few remaining tendrils of tension, allowing her not only to relax, but to become a willing participant in what promised to be a mutually satisfying endeavor.

Right now, his lips tracked along her jawline and then down her throat. Occasionally on that journey, they had hesitated, seeming to make a more detailed examination of some particular spot before they moved on, leaving a trail of moisture in their path.

She closed her eyes, giving herself over to the sensations building within her lower body. Almost unfamiliar after so long an abstinence, they seemed more powerful than they ever had before.

Because Mac was unfamiliar? An unknown element? After all, wasn't that one of the romantic fantasies every woman supposedly harbored—making love to a stranger?

As that thought formed, Mac's mouth strayed lower. His fingers, slightly callused and totally masculine, cupped along the outside of her breast, urging its fullness inward toward his lips. They closed around her nipple, suckling gently at first and then becoming increasingly demanding.

Then—again unexpectedly—he began to tease the tautening bud with his teeth, nipping and then releasing it, to again caress with his tongue. Myriad nerve endings, placed in that area by a generous nature, reveled in the contrast.

Pleasure ran outward, like ripples across a pond, spreading from the epicenter of those sensations. Then gradually, so gradually that for a few heartbeats she wasn't sure what was happening, the feeling induced by his teeth and the pressure of his mouth changed, edging toward that fine line between enjoyment and pain.

Perhaps she made some sound. A gasp or a whimper. Maybe he simply sensed her tension. Or perhaps, and she was willing to concede the point, he was a master of the delicate cat-and-mouse game he was playing.

For whatever reason, he immediately deserted the small peak he'd aroused, turning his attention to the other breast. There he began the process all over again, as painstakingly as before.

His tongue circled the areola, causing the skin of her nipple to lift, seeking the caress of his lips. This time, when that was accompanied by the light pressure of his teeth, desire began to run molten through her veins, seeming to seep, like liquid fire, into every cell of her body.

Once more, just when she feared the sensation had grown too demanding, he moved again, his tongue drawing an arrow of wet heat between her breasts and then lower. He stopped briefly to explore her navel, delving inside its small concavity before circling the rim with an exquisite slowness.

Then his mouth, still trailing fire, trailed lower still.

His tongue grazed her belly, moving inexorably toward that secret, most intimate part of her anatomy.

She resisted an almost physiological urge to deny him. After all, he was a stranger, and it had been so long…

Then his body moved over hers, putting an end to any thought of protest. Hands on her ankles, he forced her knees up and apart, increasing her vulnerability.

And she, who had lost—or so she thought—all ability to trust, no longer considered refusal. Her hips arched upward with the first stroke of his tongue.

Her eyes opened to the ceiling of the darkened bedroom above them. Her lips parted, as one sighing breath escaped, followed quickly by another. The pressure inside her body now was vastly different from that which had gone before.

This was relentless. Undeniable. A force of nature, like a storm or a flood. Or a wildfire, out of control and threatening to burn everything in its path.

His mouth shifted, following the pattern of pleasure followed by demand that he had employed before. Despite her familiarity now with the concept, she was again unprepared for the consequences.

Like summer lightning, flickers sparked by the caress of his lips and tongue set fire to the rest of her body and then finally to her brain. Pleasure became a living entity, controlling and dominating.

This was what she had sought. This mindless fullness. Loss of control. The spiraling blackness, stealing from her the ability to think. To plan. To know.

The conflagration had begun, and there was nothing she could do to stop it. Even if she had wanted to.

On some level she was aware when he shifted positions again, looming above her for a few seconds before he drove into the heart of the maelstrom he'd created. Becoming one with it. One with her.

Together they labored, unaware of the effort. Aware only of the fulfillment that lay just beyond their reach.

Then, suddenly, she was there. Her breathing was suspended as wave after wave of heat shimmered through her body.

Awareness of time and place disappeared. She welcomed its loss as he continued to move above her in the darkness.

After an eternity, she became aware again of his weight. Of the feel of his body, sweat-slick and heated above hers.

She waited until his breathing eased, and the hammering rhythm of his heart had slowed to something approaching normal. He shifted, easing the pressure against her breasts as he rolled to one side to prop above her.

He bent to touch her forehead with his lips before he straightened again. "Okay?"

She smiled to hear the concern in his voice. "Why wouldn't I be?"

"That was..." He hesitated and then shook his head.

She agreed that all the normal descriptions seemed trite. Overused. Silly.

"Good," she suggested.

His answering laughter was only a breath. Had he laughed because he had been as surprised by this as she had been?

"I expected good. What I *didn't* expect—"

"I know," she said quickly.

She didn't want to talk about what had just happened. She didn't want him to talk about it either.

All she had wanted was the physical release usually afforded by sex, whether it was great, good, or indifferent. But there was no denying this had been the first.

"Are you sure—"

"Shut up, Mac. Just shut the hell up and go to sleep."

"I thought you were supposed to get all pissed off if I did that."

"Only if I were looking for all of the things I'm *not* looking for."

"Care to list those?"

"Not particularly. It seems to me this could be to our mutual advantage."

"What does that mean?"

"You said it had been a long time."

"Yeah?"

"I'm just saying we've got nothing invested here. No relationship to maintain. We just happened to be occupying the same space at the same time. And apparently it has been a long time for both of us."

"Mutual advantage?"

"I'm using you, Donovan. I hated to have to spell that out, but everybody knows about cops."

He laughed again, a real one this time, the sound of it satisfying in the darkness. She couldn't remember the last time she'd been this relaxed.

Because you can't remember the last time sex was this good? Or this uncomplicated? Now if she could only keep it this way....

"What does everyone know about cops?"

"You know you don't want to hear my opinion of cops. Present company excepted, of course."

"Thank you."

"You're welcome."

At some point he had eased his body down beside hers, no longer propped on his elbow above her. His right arm lay over her stomach, his hand wrapped around her forearm.

His thumb moved up and down against her skin, its motion hypnotic. Soothing.

So much so that she couldn't even remember the dream that had sent her into the shower enclosure. The details hadn't been all that clear, not even immediately after she'd awakened. Or maybe she had blocked those that had lingered in her consciousness. All she knew was there had been a feeling of loss. And of helplessness. And that it had involved Dwight.

Now, in the peaceful gloom of Mac Donovan's bedroom, the movement of his thumb lulling her into a sense of security, she allowed even those remnants to fade into the void that had swallowed the rest.

She turned her head, so that her cheek was against the softness of his hair. The scent of his shampoo was again in her nostrils. Familiar. Welcome. Safe.

Other thoughts drifted in and out of her consciousness as she lay beside him, sated and exhausted, from both her emotional meltdown and from their lovemaking. None of those stayed in her head long enough to become worrisome.

After a long time, Mac's breathing settled into a

rhythmic inhalation and release that represented sleep. She listened, allowing its regularity to lull her into a deeper relaxation.

There was nothing she needed to take care of tonight. Nothing to worry or wonder about.

All she needed to do was close her eyes and match her slow breaths to his. In and then out. Erase the thoughts as they occurred from the blackboard of her mind until it literally became a blank slate. And when she had…

When she had, there would be nothing there. Nothing but the forgetfulness she had sought when she'd begun this.

She had told Mac she had something to offer, but she knew that the memory she would carry in her heart from tonight was the gift he had given her. And the unexpected tenderness in which he'd wrapped it.

Sixteen

The last person Mac had wanted to see today was almost the first he saw as he helped Sarah out of the car at the Mt. Pilgrim Cemetery. He met Sonny's eyes, nodding slightly to acknowledge his partner's presence.

Police presence, he amended. There was no doubt in his mind that Sonny was here because the department had wondered, just as he had, if Tate would be bold enough to show up for Dan Patterson's funeral.

"You want to sit with the family?" He bent so that the words were for Sarah's ear alone.

She glanced up at him to shake her head before she looked again toward the tent that had been set up over the newly dug grave. He took her arm, guiding her across the uneven ground to the small group of mourners gathered around it.

He recognized Louise Patterson, who was already seated in the middle of the row of folding chairs lined up under the awning. She was conferring with someone

Mac assumed to be either the funeral director or the minister. As the man finished the conversation and moved to stand at one end of the raw hole in the ground, Louise's eyes came up, spotting his and Sarah's approach. Her face changed, grief replaced by fury.

Sarah hesitated, seeming to literally shrink from that unspoken rage. Instinctively, Mac put his hand on the small of her back as a gesture of support.

He wondered if, in her dementia, Dan's mother would actually make a scene at her son's funeral. Then he wondered how he could protect the woman beside him if she did.

Something about Sarah Patterson had evoked his every protective instinct from the moment he'd noticed her on the courthouse steps. Now that their relationship had evolved into something very different from what it had been that day, those feelings had also evolved, becoming stronger. Fiercer.

"This is close enough." Sarah stopped on the edge of the small crowd, as far away from the casket and her former mother-in-law as she could manage and still hear the service.

Mac stopped, too, but his eyes continued to scan the area around the gravesite. Century-old oaks, their branches swathed with Spanish moss, dotted the churchyard. There were perhaps a hundred tombstones, some old enough that their inscriptions had virtually been obliterated by the thick growth of algae and erosion.

There was literally no place to hide here. If Tate intended to witness Dan Patterson's interment, he would have to be among those gathered at the edge of the artificial grass that surrounded the grave.

With that realization, Mac turned his attention to the crowd, his gaze moving consideringly from one to the other. Even though with some he could see only the backs of their heads, he was confident that Tate wasn't here.

He looked for Sonny again, finding him on the other end of the back row of mourners. His partner met his eyes and shrugged.

Long shot. They had both known that, but they had also understood that the possibility Tate might show up was something they couldn't afford to ignore.

Now all he had to do was listen to whatever the preacher wanted to say about Dan Patterson and then get Sarah away from there before the animosity he'd seen in Louise's eyes came roaring out.

A car door slammed out on the dirt road that skirted the cemetery, drawing his attention. Not a car, he realized. A van. A big white one with the call letters of the television station that had gotten him suspended blazoned on its side. Emerging from it were the same anchor and cameraman with whom he'd had the run-in over the tape.

Mac turned his face away from them and removed his hand from where it still rested against Sarah's back. He tried to think if there was anything he could do to prevent what he knew was about to happen.

He again caught Sonny's eye, giving a quick tilt of his head toward the road. His partner's gaze followed his direction.

Mac could tell by Sonny's face when he'd made the

identification. Mac raised his brows, but his partner deliberately ignored him, looking back at the minister, who'd begun reading the 23rd Psalm.

As the words, familiar since childhood, washed over him, Mac tried to focus on the ceremony. He had known that the media would eventually make the connection between the woman who'd tried to kill Tate and Dan Patterson's murder. What he hadn't anticipated was that they'd choose what should be a private expression of grief to make that relationship public.

He glanced to his right, looking over Sarah's bowed head. Apparently she wasn't yet aware that the service was being filmed. He hoped for her sake that they could get through whatever eulogy had been prepared before she noticed the camera.

Then, as soon as all the tributes to her ex-husband had been made, he would get her out of here and past the reporters. And they'd damn well better not stick a microphone in her face.

Struggling for calm, Mac took a deep breath, once more attempting to concentrate on the scriptures rather than on the presence of the video crew.

After he had finished reading the psalm, the minister moved on to his prepared remarks. Unfortunately, he made reference to the death of Dan's son as well as to the fact that he had himself been murdered, eliciting another bout of sobbing from the front row.

Mac cut his eyes down toward Sarah, trying to gauge her reaction to that outpouring of grief. Her head was still bowed, the handkerchief she'd asked to borrow before they'd left the apartment clutched tightly in her hand.

He was aware again of how small she was. Fragile enough that it seemed a strong wind would blow her away.

And then the image of her standing on those steps, that big semiautomatic held out in both hands, was in his head. However vulnerable she looked, he needed to remember there was steel at her core.

Drawing in another breath, he released it between pursed lips in an attempt to ease his growing tension. Sarah looked up, her eyes questioning. He shook his head, the movement slight, and turned his gaze back to the preacher.

At a gesture from the minister, a young girl in a long black dress had stepped onto the carpet of artificial grass. A guitar that looked too heavy for her to hold, much less play, hung from a strap around her neck. She strummed a few chords and then, her voice clear as birdsong, she began to sing "The Old Rugged Cross." Mac hadn't heard the hymn since childhood Sundays spent in a country church, but the words were all there in his head before she sang them.

On some level he was aware that the cameraman from the television station filmed the performance. Aware also of the muffled crying of the female mourners.

The woman at his side remained stoically silent throughout it all, her head bowed until the last notes of the solo faded away into the cold afternoon air. As soon as they had, the preacher advanced toward the folding chairs, shaking hands with those seated there.

Mac put his hand under Sarah's elbow. "Let's go."

"Is it over?" she whispered back.

He nodded, urging her toward the road.

"I should say something to Louise."

Before he could stop her, she stepped forward, skirting the edge of the small crowd. Mac followed, trying to decide how to avert her arrival at her intended destination without causing a scene. Her mother-in-law was still talking to the minister, her eyes locked on his face.

"Let it go," he said, catching Sarah's elbow. "She isn't going to listen—"

She pulled her arm from his clasp, pushing her way between the casket, already in position above the grave, and the row of chairs. She moved into position at the minister's side, but Louise didn't look at her until he had gone on to speak to the next person in the row. At that point, Sarah either said something to her or her mother-in-law simply lifted her eyes, assuming she was someone else waiting to talk to her.

"Are you happy now that you finally got what you wanted?" Mrs. Patterson made no effort to lower her voice.

Since the others standing near the coffin were waiting in respectful silence until she could acknowledge their condolences, Louise's words seemed to ring out as loudly as the minister's. Her expression conveyed her disdain of her daughter-in-law in case anyone might have been in doubt of her meaning.

Sarah's reply was so soft even Mac couldn't hear it, although by now he was again reaching for her arm. Louise's was clearly intended to be heard by everyone within earshot.

"You blamed Dan for Danny's death, although

you're the one who never had time to tend to your own son. I raised that baby because you were too busy. Then you blamed his daddy for what happened to him. Dan was finally making a new life for himself, with a woman who loved him. He was moving on, putting everything behind him, until you stirred it all up again by trying to take the law into your own hands. This is your fault, Sarah. All of it. You have no right to be here acting like you ever cared about him. No right at all."

Unable to listen to any more, Mac took Sarah's arm and physically turned her away from the tirade. He didn't look at her face, instead almost dragging her back to where he'd parked the car.

The TV crew had moved closer to the tent, perhaps in response to Mrs. Patterson's vitriol. Although they continued filming as he drew Sarah past them, Mac ignored them, his only consideration now to get her out of here. If those ghouls had nothing better to show on their broadcast tonight than the ravings of a demented old woman—

Once more Sarah pulled her elbow out of his hold. He stopped, unsure what was happening.

"Did you film that?" she demanded of the cameraman, who continued to hold the video cam on her face.

"Your mother-in-law seems to blame you for your ex-husband's murder, Mrs. Patterson. Would you care to comment about her accusations?"

"Would you like to know who *I* blame for my ex-husband's death?"

Sensing that she might be onto something that would make for a dramatic segment on the local news, the anchor nodded, holding the microphone out to catch every word.

"Sarah." Mac tried again to intervene, but was ignored.

"You might want to talk to the N.O.P.D. about screwing up the arrest of a serial killer. Or why don't you ask the judge who let him go on a technicality if she feels any responsibility for Dan's death? I seem to be the only person in New Orleans who's willing to say that Samuel Tate shouldn't be allowed to draw another breath—"

Mac put his arm around her body, physically forcing her to move forward and away from the camera. He was sure the crew continued to film as he took her to the car and pushed her inside.

He waited until they were back on the county two-lane before he looked over at Sarah, who was once more looking out the window on her side. "What the hell did you think you were doing?"

"Answering their questions." She kept her head averted.

"You do realize that little tirade will be on the news tonight as well as in the headlines tomorrow?"

"Good."

"You think drawing Tate's attention back to you is good?"

"Why not? As long as he's concentrating on me, he'll have less time to molest and murder some other child."

"I'm not sure it works that way."

Even as he said it, he wondered if it could. Did Tate's quest for revenge for what Sarah had tried to do supersede his homicidal impulses? If so, could they possibly use that to lure him out of hiding?

Except no one in authority believed Tate was still in the area. Or that he was the one who'd murdered Dan Patterson. And until they did…

"Why am I not surprised?" Sarah said.

"What the hell does that mean?"

"You haven't been *sure* how Tate works all along, have you? He's just been one big mystery to the police department since he started his rampage here."

"Hey. I'm on your side, remember."

Her lips closed as she swallowed, the movement visible down the line of her throat. "I know. I'm sorry. It's just… He had no reason to come after Dan. Maybe me, but not Dan. But it was an accident. Something nobody could have foreseen. He was in the wrong place at the wrong time. I had no way of knowing Tate was going to be there that afternoon. No way to prevent—"

"You aren't buying into his mother's crap, are you? It's no more valid than the rest of the garbage she spewed."

She said nothing in response, again turning to look out her window. He thought maybe she would let it go, but the accusations had apparently cut too deep.

"She did look after Danny a lot. Maybe—"

"So? You were working. Women work because they have to. You weren't buying furs and jewelry with what you made. You were buying a future for your son."

The words, meant to comfort, were out of his mouth before he realized their unintended cruelty. Danny Patterson would never enjoy the future both his parents had struggled to provide for him.

"What happened wasn't your fault. None of it. Only one person is to blame for Danny's death. The same person who also murdered your husband. If you try to take the blame for his actions, then he wins."

"He's already won," she said, her voice low and bitter.

"No, he hasn't. Because this isn't over yet." Although Mac was aware she had turned to look at him, he didn't meet her eyes.

"You think he's still here." Not a question, but a statement of fact.

He did. He couldn't have justified his absolute conviction about that, but it was there.

Samuel Tate was still in New Orleans. Because whatever was going on, this wasn't over for him, either.

Mac had hesitated to push his luck with the FBI profiler who'd worked with them on Tate. For one thing, he didn't know what Daryl Johnson's reaction to his suspension might be. For another, he was pretty sure how Morel would view any contact between them.

Still, the more he thought about Sonny's reaction to his request for surveillance on Sarah's apartment building, the more he'd wanted to run some things by someone who knew more about the killer's tendencies than he did.

Which was why, in the end, he'd been willing to take a chance on this call. Because he hadn't read anything negative in Johnson's greeting, he'd gotten right to the point.

"I know you don't think Tate had anything to do with the message left on Mrs. Patterson's phone or with her husband's death." Johnson had already told him the former, and if he believed what Sonny said, the profiler had also come down on the side of those who thought Dan's death was unrelated to the serial killer. "I have what I guess is a hypothetical question."

"In that case I'll give you a hypothetical answer."

"Fair enough. Let's say Tate did leave that message. And let's say that he was responsible for Patterson's death although that was tangential to his intent."

"Tangential?"

"In that it wasn't what he was there for."

"There in Mrs. Patterson's apartment?"

"Yeah."

"Okay."

"Does Patterson's death restart the clock?"

Sarah had said on the way home from the funeral yesterday that if Tate were concentrating on her, he'd have less time to be hunting little boys. Mac had started to wonder whether Dan Patterson's death would satisfy whatever urges drove Tate to kill children.

"You're asking me if Tate is still in the area, will you have some time before he starts hunting again?"

"We think that's what he was doing when he was arrested. The timing was right. But now that he's killed again…"

"I really wish I could tell you what you want to hear. For all our sakes."

"And you can't."

"There's a ritual involved in what Tate does. Actually, with the organized ones there's a process. Procedures that they always follow. For most of them the act isn't complete unless the ritual is also complete."

"So if he were interrupted or if he had to kill on the spur of the moment—"

"If, say, in case he were surprised by someone who *wasn't* his intended victim and had to kill to protect himself?"

"You're saying that murder wouldn't satisfy him."

"That's right," Johnson said. "As strange as it sounds, he probably would be annoyed that he'd had to kill someone that way. It wouldn't feel 'proper' to him."

"So if we're right, and he *was* out hunting before—"

"Then he's going to be out hunting again. It's been—what?—since your last murder? Five months?"

"About that."

"Then I'd say he's due. *If* he were there," Johnson added carefully.

"I appreciate your time. It was just a thought. Something I'd wondered about."

"No more messages?"

"What?"

"Has Mrs. Patterson received any more messages?"

"No. No, she hasn't."

Of course, Sarah hadn't been back to her apartment either. Not since the afternoon he'd gone with her to pick up her personal items.

"That's a good sign it wasn't Tate. If it *had* been, I doubt he would have given up so soon. Once he chose to communicate with her, I would have been willing to bet he'd continue to do so. The fact that he hasn't seems all the more reason to discount him as the source of the original message. Besides being totally out of the pattern for him, I can't think of anything he might get out of doing something like that. It just doesn't make sense."

"Yeah. Well, as I said, this was strictly hypothetical. Once I thought about the possibility, I thought it couldn't hurt to check. Thanks."

"Anytime, Mac. Just be glad Tate is somebody else's headache now, and you all can get back to concentrating on the ordinary, garden-variety criminal."

"I don't think we grow those down here."

"Thank your lucky stars that you don't grow a lot of the Samuel Tate variety."

"You guys track down anything from his prints? I know they weren't a match to anything in AFIS—"

"We're still looking. Trying to find anything that will lead us anywhere. I understand you guys are pretty sure he was a Southerner?"

"That was everyone's impression, based on talking to him. There are always traces of an accent that are hard to erase."

"Maybe we'll get lucky."

"If he pops up somewhere else and you guys get wind of it, could you give me a call?"

"You got it, Mac. You've lived with this guy so long, I think you're seeing him in every shadow."

"You may be right. I'd just like to know something definitive about his whereabouts. We'd all sleep better at night."

"I understand. We're putting out another alert on his methodology. Maybe when he surfaces the next time, whoever is in charge of the investigation will recognize something about the murders."

"Good luck."

"Lots of times, no matter how diligent we are, that's what it boils down to. Luck. Or a screw up on their part. We gratefully accept either."

So would I, Mac thought, as he hung up the phone. *So would I.*

Seventeen

Sarah had ordered Chinese delivery, which she was portioning onto their plates when Mac's cell rang. Their eyes met across the table, just as hers and Dan's had so often in those terrible weeks after Danny disappeared. They'd been frantic to hear something, anything, but also dreading what that might be.

"You *could* ignore it," she suggested.

The media had been all over her confrontation with Louise. They'd made so much of the fact that Mac had escorted her that day that she knew he was worried about his job.

Instead of following her suggestion, Mac dug the phone out of his pocket and looked at the caller ID. When he flipped open the case, she assumed the call was from Sonny or someone else he felt he couldn't afford to ignore and went back to spooning food on the plates.

"Hello." He listened for several seconds before he

said, "Okay, slow down and say that again. I'm not sure I understand."

Her eyes lifted once more, watching him. She could sense how hard he was concentrating on whatever he was being told.

"And you're sure that's all she can tell you?"

Another pause.

"Yeah. Yeah, I do remember that. Have you called the police?" He put his hand over the mouthpiece, whispering to her, "It's Mrs. Ingersoll."

With that knowledge, Sarah replayed the conversation up to now. If Mac was telling Dwight's mother she should call the police, this must have something to do with an occurrence at the apartment building.

Or with Dwight himself?

She took a breath, fighting the rush of absolute terror that thought evoked. Had something happened to Dwight?

But if so, surely the woman would already have called the police. Why call Mac instead of dialing 9-1-1?

"We'll be right there." Mac closed the phone, finally looking up at her.

"What?"

"Dwight apparently went out this afternoon while he was supposed to be staying with his grandmother. He isn't back. His mother wasn't particularly worried until it got dark, but now—"

"Went out where?"

He hesitated before he told her. "From what his mother can piece together, based on the grandmother's version of events, you understand, Dwight was going to the park to walk with you and your dog."

The cold knot of fear that had formed in her stomach exploded, clogging her lungs with ice. "That's… I mean I haven't been over there in days. You *told* her to keep an eye on him. Not to let him out of the house—"

"This is the grandmother's story, Sarah. Mrs. Ingersoll told us the woman isn't all there. We really have no way of knowing what happened—"

"So what you're saying is Dwight could be *anywhere*. Somebody could have come to their door and dragged him out of the apartment, and those two wouldn't know anything about it."

Without answering, Mac opened his phone again, running through his contacts list before selecting one of them. As he waited through the rings, he refused to meet her eyes.

Without any preliminaries or explanation, he asked whoever he'd called, "Did you put somebody on that apartment building like I asked you to?"

"Sonny?" Sarah questioned, reading between the lines. "Is that Sonny?"

Mac ignored her. "Damn it, why didn't you, Sonny? I told you a kid lives there and that he—" Mac stopped, listening to whatever his partner was saying. "Screw the manpower issues. And screw you, too. The kid's disappeared, and nobody knows where. The mother says she called the precinct and got the runaround. What the hell is wrong with you people? That building is the only connection we've got to Tate, and you clowns blow it again."

Once more Mac listened, his face hardening. After

a couple of seconds, he closed the phone with a twist of his wrist.

"Get your coat."

She didn't waste time with questions. She grabbed up the containers she hadn't opened, almost throwing them into the fridge before she headed to the front closet where she'd hung her jacket. When she had it on, she grabbed Mac's, looking around to find him fastening the leash onto Toby's collar.

"What are you doing?"

"I thought maybe we could get something of the kid's from his mother. See if Toby could pick up his scent from that."

"Toby?" She shook her head, thinking how far from a bloodhound or any other kind of working dog Danny's mutt was. "I don't think Toby's ever—"

"It can't hurt," Mac snapped, cutting off her objection. "And right now… Right now, we don't seem to have all that many options."

"Dwight? Are you out here?"

Sarah's voice had grown hoarse in the half hour or so they'd been out in the park. Although she was less hopeful now than when she and Mac had started their search, she didn't know where else to look.

A couple of policemen had arrived at the Ingersoll apartment before they'd managed to get away from Dwight's mother. Dressed in that same bedraggled bathrobe, she hadn't offered to join them in scouring the park, pleading her need to give the policemen the information they would have to have to put an official search for her missing son into motion.

She had supplied them with the bottoms of a pair of pajamas, which she said Dwight had worn the night before. Although Toby had dutifully sniffed the garment, he'd been far more interested in his proximity to the familiar park and its trees. He'd almost pulled her arm out of the socket in his eagerness to get across the street and into it.

Once they'd reached the area where she and Dwight had played with the dog, Sarah let him off the leash in hopes that if allowed to run free, he might pick up the child's scent. Maybe look for him to play another game of catch.

For the first few minutes, as Toby ran from bush to bush, she had actually thought the dog might lead them somewhere. It soon became apparent that all the animal was doing was sniffing places where other dogs had done their business.

"Answer me, Dwight. I've got Toby. He's waiting for you to throw the ball for him."

"*If* he's here, Sarah, he would have answered you by now."

Mac sounded as dejected as she felt. Not only had Toby proven worthless as a tracker, she hadn't been able to tell from the grandmother's incoherent ramblings whether Dwight had even mentioned the park to her before he'd left this afternoon.

"If he's still able to answer."

She pulled the collar of her coat tight against her

throat. Its light weight wasn't providing much warmth against the cold, moisture-laden air off the river.

"There's no sense making yourself sick out here. If Dwight came to the park, it's obvious he's no longer here. It's time to give up. Let the professionals do their job."

"Like they have all along?"

"There's nothing more we can do," Mac said, ignoring the gibe. "And you need to get in out of this *cold*."

"Just quit, you mean? We should stop looking for Dwight because it's *cold?*"

"We don't even know if he came to the park. Besides, when the search teams start, they won't want us here."

"The *search* teams?" she mocked. "Are those the same ones who looked for Danny? The ones who didn't find his body for more than three months?"

"Sarah—" Mac reached for her arm, but she pulled away from him.

"You go on inside if you're cold. This is the only place I know to look. And if someone did lure him away by telling him something about Toby or me—"

As if he recognized his name, the dog began to bark. They both turned, trying to locate him in the darkness. Judging by sound, he had drifted farther away from where they were standing than either of them had been aware.

"Toby?" Sarah called.

The animal continued to bark, the sound insistent now. Determined.

"He's found something." She worked to keep her voice steady, trying to control the surge of hope recognition of that particular type barking gave her.

"He's probably treed a squirrel," Mac said. "Or cornered a possum. It doesn't mean—"

Ignoring him, Sarah started walking in the direction of the frenzied barking. "Toby? Where are you, boy?"

There was no response but a continuation of the sounds the dog had been making. Three or four sharp yaps and then a momentary silence.

As Sarah tried to gauge the direction they came from, she could hear Mac behind her, fighting his way, as she was having to, through the dense underbrush. They were nearing the center of the park now, an area almost totally overgrown because the commercial mowers the city used couldn't handle the terrain.

She pushed through a mass of tangled vines, hoping they weren't poison ivy. Although she couldn't see Toby, she was encouraged because his barking was clearer now. Closer.

And then, as she broke through the thickest vegetation she'd yet encountered, she spotted him, the white patches of his coat standing out against the darker shapes around him. He was standing at the base of one of the giant oaks that shaded the park in summer. Its low branches trailed Spanish moss, pale and ghostly against the dim light from the distant street lamps.

Squirrel, she thought. Just like Mac said.

As she walked toward the tree, Sarah took the leash out of her coat pocket. This insanity had gone on long enough.

"Toby, stop it. Hush, now. Hush, Tobe. That's enough."

At the sternness in her voice, the dog backed away from the trunk a step or two. He looked at her briefly, his eyes glowing red in the dimness.

Unfortunately, he wasn't disciplined enough to obey her command for long. Before she could get close enough to secure his collar, he was at it again. In addition to the annoying yaps, now there was the periodic low, rumbling growl.

As upset as Toby was, Sarah was afraid that she might have to drag him away by force. As the thought formed, she realized for the first time that the dog wasn't looking up into the tree that loomed above him.

He was focused instead on something beyond it. And the sounds he was making deep in his throat had become more threatening.

Sarah took a step back, trying to see around the oak's broad trunk to the area Toby was interested in. For a moment she couldn't distinguish anything in the dense undergrowth that might have set him off.

Then, a shape seemed to jump out at her. Something different from the surrounding sprawl of reaching vegetation.

Her gaze had already moved beyond the anomaly when it registered on her brain. She made another visual sweep of the same section.

Whatever she'd seen only a second before was no longer there. The image, however, of something straight and tall and man-shaped, seemed burned on her retinas.

"Mac? Is that you?"

She spoke his name tentatively. That's not where she'd expected him to be. Maybe he'd found an easier passage, she thought, wisely skirting the thicket she'd struggled through.

"Coming."

Mac's voice put him behind her. In the opposite direction of whatever—or whoever—she'd just seen.

She swallowed against the force of her fear, eyes again sweeping the spot where she'd seen someone standing. Watching Toby?

With that thought she once more became aware of the dog, who continued to growl menacingly. She turned her head to look down at him. His attention was still focused on the line of bushes where Sarah had seen the shape, the vapor from his breath as he barked visible in the cold air.

"Sarah? You find him?"

Mac was closer than he'd been before. And still behind her.

"Somebody's out here, Mac. That's what Toby's barking at."

"Some*body*?"

She turned, reassured by his nearness. She watched as he pushed his way through the tangled barrier that separated them.

"I saw him. Standing just beyond that tree."

Mac directed his flashlight toward the area she'd indicated. There was nothing there now but a maze of bare, arching branches.

"Are you sure?"

"I saw someone." She examined the memory, wondering if what she'd seen had been a trick of the shadows. Branches moving in the wind.

"Could be somebody from one of the search teams," Mac suggested.

"Then why didn't he say something?" she argued. "He had to have seen me. He certainly would have heard Toby."

"He probably thought you were just out walking your dog. The department isn't going to advertise that we've got another missing child. Not until they have to."

He took the leash from her hand as he moved past her, obviously intending to attach it to Toby's collar. As he began to stoop to accomplish that, Mac stopped, almost recoiling.

"Mac? What is it?"

"Nothing. Stay there, Sarah. Just... Just wait a minute, okay?"

She didn't believe it was nothing, but for some reason she obeyed. Whatever Mac had found, clearly he didn't want her to see.

She turned her head, eyes once more examining the dark area that had been the focus of Toby's hysteria. She knew someone had been standing there. Toby had seen him, too. Had sensed the threat he represented.

"Mac?" she called again. Whatever he'd found under the tree, the known would be less frightening than the unknown had become.

He didn't answer this time. He was balanced on the balls of his feet, studying the ground. As he slowly directed the flashlight around the foot of the tree, Sarah caught a glimpse of something terrifyingly identifiable.

At Mac's feet, highlighted against the blackness of rotting leaves, lay a small, worn white tennis shoe.

Eighteen

Mac moved the switch of the flashlight to the off position, even as he acknowledged the impossibility of protecting Sarah from this. He leaned forward, fumbling among the leaves that had been loosely piled over the body until he located first the head and then the neck.

He already knew the answer to his question by how cold the skin was. Still, as a matter of training, he sought the pulse of blood that should have been throbbing through the carotid artery. It wasn't there.

He brought his hand away, swallowing to deny the surge of bile into the back of his throat. He began to blow small puffs of air out through his mouth, a trick one of the older cops had taught him the day they'd pulled his first floater out of the river.

"Is that him? Is it Dwight?"

He heard Sarah start toward him. He got to his feet before she could arrive, grasping her shoulders and turning her. With his arm around her back, he propelled her away from the body.

"Don't."

"Is it Dwight?"

"I don't know. But… It's a child."

"Oh, my God. Oh, my God. Is he—"

"Yeah." In the background the dog continued to bark, the grating, insistent noise now part of the horror. "Can you get him out of here?"

"What?"

"Toby. Can you take him somewhere? Just…talk to him. Shut him up. Do something."

She nodded, but her eyes left his to track back to where the body lay. "You said you didn't know. Could you look? Could you make sure?"

Who the hell did she think this could be? Who had they been out here looking for the last forty-five minutes?

"I don't want to do anything that might destroy evidence." That wasn't exactly a lie, but it was close enough to one that he felt guilty for saying it.

The truth was he didn't want to shine that damn light down into those lifeless eyes. He didn't want to see the child's bloodless face.

More importantly, he didn't want her to see it. There were enough of those kinds of memories in Sarah Patterson's past already. She didn't need this one, too.

"*Evidence?* So you can lock whoever did this up? Why bother? They're just going to let him out again."

There was nothing to say in the face of that caustic bitterness.

"Just shut the damn dog up. I need to call. I need to get the techs out here."

When she nodded, he handed her the leash. He stuck the flashlight in his outside coat pocket. As he reached inside his jacket to fish out his cell, Sarah pushed by him on her way to the dog.

He'd be damned if he was going to call Sonny again. He'd told them they needed to watch the kid's building. He'd told them Tate was the one who'd killed Dan Patterson. Sarah told them he'd left the message on her machine. They had both told them everything they needed to know in order to prevent this. And nobody had listened.

Anger building, he punched in 9-1-1 and waited through the rings. The voice that answered was black, young, and disinterested, even when he told her about the boy's body. He wondered how many other homicides had been reported to this particular operator. Enough that she'd grown inured to hearing about death.

When he'd given as much information about the location as he could, he hung up to wait. Only then did he realize that Toby had finally stopped barking. An eerie stillness had settled instead over the area, so that he could hear condensation dripping off the leaves of the trees around him.

He turned, trying to locate Sarah. A light glowed faintly in the darkness.

Flashlight. *His* flashlight, he verified by patting his pocket. Sarah must have taken it as she'd brushed by him. Now she was bending down to play its beam over the body.

Mac watched, unable to prevent what was about to

happen, as she carefully removed the damp leaves from the face of the boy under the tree. He couldn't see the kid's features from this angle, but he didn't step forward to get a better look. He'd known all he needed to know from the time his fingers touched that cold, still flesh.

Sarah's body seemed to slowly fold inward. Her knees gave way until they rested against the ground. Then her head fell forward so that it was bowed on her chest.

The light went out, and Mac heard the sharp intake of breath he knew would precede her tears. He flinched from the sound. He didn't think he could stand to listen again as those merciless sobs racked her body.

And what choice do you have?

No matter what either of them had intended when this started, they were now irrevocably entangled in one another's lives. Emotionally as well as physically involved.

He could do nothing about the pain she felt, but he should be there for her as she suffered it. He shoved his phone into his outside pocket and took the four strides that would carry him to where she knelt.

He bent, putting his arm around her shoulder. He didn't try to lift her as he had that night in the shower. Instead, he held her hard and tight against his body.

She trembled, but the outburst he'd dreaded didn't come. After a moment she pushed away from him a little, putting her closed fist over her mouth.

"I'm so sorry," he whispered. "I didn't do enough. I told them they needed to watch him, but… I should have seen to it. I should have made sure—"

"It isn't him, Mac. It isn't Dwight."

It took a moment for the sense of her words to break through his litany of self-blame. Even when they had, he didn't believe her.

After all, how many dead kids had she seen? Did she realize how different a face could look with all the animation, all the life force, sucked out of it?

He reached down, taking the flashlight from her other hand. He held it out, directing the beam toward the features she'd exposed. And then he pushed its switch back on.

He had known this face would haunt him, just as all those others in the photographs on the task force's white board had. And it would.

But he also knew now that Sarah had been right. This face didn't belong to Dwight Ingersoll.

"You aren't going to try to tell me that isn't Tate's handiwork, are you?"

Sonny swiveled on the balls of his feet, looking up at him. "I'm not going to try to tell you anything, Mac. Not until we've processed the scene. The autopsy will verify whether or not—"

"Oh, for Christ's sake, Sonny. I'm not the media. You and I both know who killed that kid. By tomorrow everybody in New Orleans is gonna know it, too."

His partner stood, moving back from the body to allow the technicians to take over. He walked a few feet away, motioning for Mac to follow. When they were out of earshot of the rest, Sonny turned to face him.

"I do what I'm told, Mac. And I say what I'm told

to say. You ought to try it sometime. You might not be sitting on the sidelines for this if you did."

"That's good, Sonny. I seem to remember that you're the one who was gonna go to the Wal-Mart and get me a lighter."

"I'm not talking about that. You did what you needed to do with the tape. I'm not questioning that."

"Then what the hell was that little sermon all about."

"Morel. He don't like you. He never has. You know that, and you still go out of your way to alienate him."

"We got another dead kid on our hands and another one missing, and you're going to lecture me on Morel."

"Did it ever occur to you that we need you? That maybe you could eat a little humble pie and keep some other poor kid from ending up like this one?"

That wasn't a thought Mac wanted in his head. With the ease of long practice, he dismissed it from his mind as quickly as he could.

"What are you doing about Dwight Ingersoll?"

"We got a bulletin out. That's all we *can* do right now. Nobody saw him get snatched. As far as we know he went out to play and is late getting home."

"Yeah, so is he, I guess." Mac jerked his head toward the body behind them.

"We're doing what we can within the guidelines we've been given. You know that. You know how this works."

The problem was Mac did. He even understood the restraints. If they overused the alerts, putting them out for every kid who was a couple of hours late getting home, they would diminish their effectiveness.

"You know who he is yet?"

"We're looking for boys reported missing in the last couple of days. Got a couple of black kids, but nobody white who fits the age and size. I guess Tate could have taken him earlier or brought him back here from somewhere out of state, but..." Sonny shook his head.

"So you're admitting this is Tate?"

"Whaddaya think, Mac? You think I enjoy this? Enjoy you and me being on different sides? Enjoy finding dead kids?"

That was about as animated as Sonny ever got, so Mac knew this was all getting to him, too.

"I know you don't," he conceded, modifying his tone. "I'm just frustrated. I knew something else was gonna happen here. For some reason Tate broke his pattern. When he did, that meant all bets were off."

"When he got into her apartment?"

"Yeah. And I can't figure out why."

"How about because she tried to blow his head off?"

That's what he'd been thinking at the time. That Tate had been waiting there to kill Sarah, and Dan Patterson had surprised him. Then Tate had had to kill him in order to get out of the apartment before Mac arrived.

Only, if Sarah hadn't been back from the park to let Mac in, what possible threat was he going to be? Why hadn't Tate just waited for Mac to leave and waited for Sarah to return and then do what he'd intended to do? Even if Sarah had returned in time to let Mac in, there was no reason to believe he would have searched her apartment and discovered either the killer or the body.

It made no more sense than killing some boy and

leaving his body virtually across the street from where she lived. Maybe if this *had* been Dwight…

"Why put him here?" he asked aloud.

"The kid?"

"Tate usually dumps them where he thinks they won't be found. That's always been his pattern. The few that have been discovered before the body decomposed were lucky accidents. This one… I'll be real surprised if he's been dead more than four or five hours."

"I don't know, Mac, but I never look a gift horse in the mouth."

"What?"

"The kid. No predators. No insects. The cold. It hasn't rained. Hell, this one's gonna be like a gift for the forensics guys."

Like a gift…

The phrase stuck in his brain, strongly enough that Mac put it aside for further consideration. Sonny had turned to watch the photographer set up his lights to take pictures of the body and the surrounding area.

"Sarah said she saw somebody out here. Standing in the shadows beyond the tree."

"You see him?"

Mac shook his head. "She was pretty adamant, but conditions weren't exactly ideal. I thought you might want to get somebody to look in that direction. Maybe there are footprints."

"They'll check."

"And Sarah lifted some of the leaves off his face. She was careful, so I don't think she touched anything, but they should know."

Sonny nodded, seeming unconcerned about the possible contamination. "She back at her own place?"

Mac thought about lying, but despite his earlier anger, this was his partner. "Not yet."

"Motel?"

"Why are you asking?"

"I'm thinking we might need to put some surveillance on her." Sonny turned his head, looking him in the eye.

Mac could see the speculative gleam. "You think Tate's going to try for her again?"

"I think what you said before is right on."

"What I said before?"

"She's the only connection we've got to him now. And he doesn't seem to be able to let it go. That's why I was wondering where she's staying."

"She's at my apartment."

Sonny's lips pursed. "You mind if I tell the department that? If they're thinking what I'm thinking, then they're gonna want to know."

"I'm not going to let anything happen to her."

"Her ex would probably have told me the same thing."

"Her ex didn't know what we know now."

"Fair enough. You want me to put surveillance on your building?"

"So now we got the manpower for that?"

Sonny didn't respond, looking again to where the techs were working under the flood lights.

"I'm not going to let anything happen to her," Mac said again, his voice flat.

"Suit yourself, buddy."

"If we find Dwight Ingersoll alive, you can put somebody on his building. I think Tate knows the kid means something to Sarah."

Poor Dwight. He'd gotten involved in this insanity because he was lonely. Because Sarah had shown him some kindnesses. Because he wanted to be friends with her dog.

None of which should have put him in Tate's path of destruction. Of course, nobody deserved to be put in Tate's path.

"I'm going to go check with the Ingersolls," Mac said. "See if they've heard anything."

And check on Sarah.

He had finally been able to convince her she would be more help at Dwight's apartment telling the uniforms who were interviewing the mother everything she could remember about those afternoons she and Dwight had played in the park than she would be standing out here in the cold watching them process the body. He wasn't sure what good her memories would do, since they had searched those areas themselves, but at least it had gotten her inside. And, he acknowledged, she'd gone not because of any argument he'd made, but because she was aware that they'd done everything they could out here.

"Let me know if he shows up."

"I will. And Sonny..."

"Yeah?"

"It isn't what you think. With Sarah, I mean."

His partner turned his head to look at him again. "It ain't none of my business, Mac. I know that. I just hate to see you get mixed up in somebody else's grief, you know? There's plenty of women who come without the baggage this one is toting."

Mac nodded. Sonny was his friend. No matter how much he might disagree with what he was saying, he respected him for trying to say it.

In this case, his partner was probably right. Sarah Patterson had a lot of demons. He'd seen a few of them, but he'd probably only scratched the surface. In spite of that...

In spite of that, he was heading back across the street to make sure she was okay. And until she told him specifically not to, he suspected he was going to spend quite a bit of his time doing exactly that.

Nineteen

"They haven't identified the body yet," Mac said as he accepted the cup of coffee Sarah offered.

He figured she'd made it, since Mrs. Ingersoll was sitting in the exact same position at the kitchen table where she'd been when they'd come to get something that had belonged to Dwight. The ashtray in front of her was fuller than it had been then.

"They're checking for any boys reported missing in the last few days who fit the general age and size," he went on. "They should have an ID soon."

"That poor mother," Mrs. Ingersoll said. "And she doesn't even know it yet. You're sure—"

"Absolutely," Sarah assured her. "That child isn't Dwight."

Mrs. Ingersoll sighed and stubbed out her cigarette in the overflowing dish. "I don't know why everything takes so long."

"It's just the way these things work," Mac said.

"*When* they work," Sarah added under her breath.

She hadn't looked at him straight on since he'd come inside. He knew why, because he knew what she was thinking. The same thing he was. The only person who *didn't* seem to understand was Dwight's mother.

And his grandmother, of course. She was ensconced in her recliner in the living room, the television blaring away on some sitcom. He wasn't even sure she was aware now that Dwight was gone.

"Will the police call me or should I call them?"

"They'll call when they have something," Mac said.

This was the first time he'd been on the "other side" of this kind of situation. The waiting side.

He had to admit he'd never thought much about how the families of the missing spent these hours. He opened his mouth, about to attempt an explanation of the process the police were going through in trying to find Dwight, when Mrs. Ingersoll stood up, her eyes focused on something in the front room.

"Where the hell have you been?" she demanded angrily. "Do you know how much trouble you've caused?"

Sarah reacted before Mac could, pushing past him and hurrying out of the kitchen. "Dwight? Oh, my God, Dwight, where have you been?"

Mac and the boy's mother followed. Apparently the kid had let himself into the apartment using a key hanging around his neck.

He'd been in the process of dropping it back down into the neck of his sweater when they'd begun bombarding him with questions. Eyes wide, Dwight looked from one to the other, as if unsure who to answer first.

His cheeks were reddened from the cold as were his hands, their chapped knuckles curved around the key he still held. He wore the same jacket he'd worn the day Mac questioned him in Sarah's apartment and no hat.

His mother crossed the room faster than Mac had seen her move before. She took the boy's arm and shook him hard.

"You were supposed to be watching Nana. How the hell would you have felt if something had happened to her while you were out gallivanting around?"

Mac felt sorry for the kid, whose eyes were now shifting from his mother's furious features to his grandmother, who seemed oblivious to the commotion.

Finally they settled pleadingly on Sarah. "I did what you told me, but you didn't come."

"What *I* told you?" Sarah repeated, shaking her head. "I don't understand, Dwight."

"In the note you sent me. I went to the playground, and I waited and waited for you and Toby, but you never came. Did you lose him?" The boy leaned to the side to look around Sarah, obviously searching for the dog.

"No, he's fine. He's upstairs in my apartment, but… I didn't send you a note, Dwight."

"Are you lying?" his mother demanded, shaking his arm again. "You answer me right now, you hear. And don't you start trying to blame this on somebody else."

"But he gave me a note." Dwight dropped the key, and with the hand that had held it, he reached into the pocket of his jacket. From it he pulled out a folded piece of yellow paper. "He *said* it was from you."

Sarah reached for what he held out, but Mac pushed her arm away. Surprised, she looked at him questioningly.

"I need a plastic bag, Mrs. Ingersoll," Mac said. "One of the zipper kind, preferably."

The mother's eyes, widened in surprise, focused on his face, but she didn't release her son's arm. "What for?"

"Evidence," he said softly.

Sarah's mouth opened and then closed, but he could tell from her face that she, at least, knew what he was thinking.

"Could you get me a bag?" Mac repeated to the mother.

He walked forward and stooped in front of the child, so that they were approximately on eye level. "Just hold the note until your mom gets the bag to put it in, okay?"

The boy nodded, his arm still stretched out in front of him, the paper gripped between his thumb and forefinger.

"It's okay," Mac said. "We were worried because we didn't know where you were. Nobody's mad at you. Your mom's just scared. We were all afraid something had happened to you."

"I'm fine."

"I can see that." Mac smiled at him reassuringly, and the thin, hunched shoulders visibly relaxed. "I want you to do something for me, okay?"

Dwight nodded again, and then his eyes lifted to

watch his mother's approach. She held a sandwich bag out to Mac, her face still tight with anger.

"Thanks." He took the bag and opened it, allowing the boy to put the note inside. When he had, Mac closed the bag and then slipped it into his shirt pocket. "Now tell me about the man who gave you that."

The boy's gaze came back to his face, but his eyes flicked up to his mother once more before they moved on to Sarah. Mac assumed she smiled at him, because the corners of Dwight's mouth made an answering motion, transforming his pinched features.

"He said it was from her."

"From Sarah?"

"He said Miz Patterson who lives upstairs."

"Where was this, Dwight? Where he gave you the note."

"On my way home from school."

Mac felt Sarah stir behind him. At least she knew enough not to say anything.

"And after he gave it to you, where did you go?"

"Here."

"You came home?"

"I had to look after Nana 'til Mama got back from the store. This is coupon day."

"But you didn't tell your mother about the note?"

"I tried, but she was in a rush." His eyes again lifted to his mother's face. "I tried to tell you, Mama. Really I did."

"And after your mama left," Mac said hurriedly, hoping to avoid more recriminations from the mother, "you went out to meet Sarah."

"I tried to wait until she got back, but she was late, and it was gonna get dark soon. I didn't think Toby could find the ball so good in the dark."

"So you went out before your mother got home."

"I thought she'd be here in just a little while. She just went to the store, and Nana was watching her shows. I left her some cookies, and I made her promise that she wouldn't go anywhere. I thought Mama would be right back. That's what she told me when she left. 'I'll be right back.'"

"And then you went to the playground."

"The note said 4:30 p.m., but it was later than that when I got there. I thought maybe they were playing somewhere else, so I looked all over everywhere, but I couldn't find them. And then it was dark, and I thought I'd missed them because I'd come too late, so I came on home."

"Did you see the man who gave you the note?"

"On the way home from school?" It was clear from his voice that Dwight was confused by the question.

"I mean did you see him again. After you went to meet Sarah and Toby at the playground."

"Nobody was there. All of the kids had gone home and all the teachers, too."

"And that man wasn't there, either," Mac clarified.

Dwight shook his head.

"Can you tell me what he looked like?"

The boy's shoulders lifted, almost a shrug. "Nice. He looked nice."

"Nice? Like nicely dressed, Dwight? Neat and clean? Or nice like friendly."

"Just…nice. He *was* clean, though."

"What was he wearing?"

"A coat. And some pants. And he had on gloves. Black ones."

He would, Mac thought. And that meant there would be no fingerprints on the note.

Not that it mattered. There was no doubt in his mind who had lured Dwight Ingersoll out at twilight. What he didn't understand is why Tate had gone to all that trouble and then not taken the child.

Because he had already satisfied whatever drove him to kill with the boy in the park? Or because killing Dwight wasn't what this was about?

He likes control, Daryl Johnson had told him. Tate had certainly had that this afternoon. They'd all jumped sky-high when he'd yelled frog.

Especially him and Sarah.

"We may want you to look at some pictures and see if you recognize him," Mac went on, trying to clear his thinking of the distraction anger would provide. "Do you think you could do that?"

"I guess. Where are they?"

"I don't have them with me. Somebody may bring them over here for you to look at. Or they may want you to come down to the police station."

"Am I in trouble?"

"With the police? No, they'll just want you to tell them all about the man who gave you that note. Just tell them what you told me. And anything else about him that you can remember."

"Okay."

"Good boy." Mac stood, putting his hand on Dwight's shoulder and squeezing gently. "I'll bet you're hungry, aren't you?"

"A little." Again the pale, blue eyes darted to his mother's face.

"I'll call and let them know he's home," Mac said to Mrs. Ingersoll. "Why don't you fix him a sandwich or maybe some soup? Something to warm him up."

For a moment she looked as if she meant to refuse. Then, her reluctance obvious, she turned and headed back to the kitchen. Mac used his hand on Dwight's shoulder to move him in that direction.

The boy stopped when he got to Sarah. "I'm sorry I was late."

She glanced at Mac, as if wondering what to say. He lifted his brows, at as much of a loss as she was over how to get through to this child.

Finally, Sarah bent and put her arms around Dwight, hugging him quickly. The contact lasted only a second or two, but when she broke it, she put her hands on either side of Dwight's face, so that he would be forced to look into her eyes.

"I didn't send you that note, Dwight. Someone tricked you. Going out alone when it's almost dark is very dangerous. I would *never* ask you to do that. And in the future, if I want to give you a message, I'll come to you and tell you myself. I won't ever send someone else to do it, I promise. Do you understand?"

The boy nodded, his face moving up and down between her palms.

"Good." Sarah smiled at him encouragingly. "And now I want you to promise *me* something. Okay?"

He nodded again, more forcefully this time, eager to please her.

"I want you to promise me that you won't believe everything a stranger tells you. There are some very bad people in the world. People who..." She hesitated, and then started again, taking a different tack. "You can always trust your mom and whatever she tells you. And you can trust me. *But*—and this is very important—only if you hear something directly from our lips. You shouldn't trust someone who just tells you that we said something. Do you understand?"

The boy nodded. "He lied. That man."

"Yes, he did. And a *lot* of people lie. That's why you have to be careful who you believe."

"What about him?" Dwight glanced over at Mac.

"Detective Donovan? You can trust him, too. He helped me look for you tonight."

"Because he's your friend."

"Yes, he is," Sarah said without looking at Mac.

"And he's Toby's friend."

"He's Toby's friend, too," she agreed, smiling at him again. "Just like you are. But good friends are very rare. You always have to be careful who you choose for your friend. And you have to know someone a really long time before you can be sure they are your friend. Do you understand?"

Although the child nodded, Mac wondered how much of that little lecture would stick the next time someone offered him a chance to throw the ball for

Toby. In his innocence, Dwight Ingersoll was far too easy to manipulate.

Which brought him back to the questions he'd posed before. Why, when he'd had the perfect opportunity to take Dwight, had Tate chosen to kill another boy? And why leave that child's body where they might reasonably have been expected to look for Dwight's?

"I made that soup like you told me."

They turned to find Mrs. Ingersoll standing in the opening to the kitchen. It was obvious she'd been watching them talk to Dwight.

Sarah put her hand on the boy's back, encouraging him to go to her. "Tell your mother you're sorry for worrying her."

Obediently Dwight crossed the room, stopping in front of his mother. "I'm sorry, Mama, for going out when you didn't know where I was going. And I'm sorry for leaving Nana all alone. I won't do that again, no matter what anybody tells me."

Mrs. Ingersoll nodded, her mouth tight. Mac could sense the effort it took for her not to say something cutting to her son. "Go eat your dinner before it gets cold."

As Dwight disappeared into the kitchen, his mother crossed her arms over her chest. "He doesn't think," she offered, speaking directly to Mac. "He never has. I don't know why he's like he is...." She shook her head, apparently at a loss to explain the boy's behavior.

"You *do* understand that the man who gave him the note is very likely the man who murdered the other boy? The child we found in the park. That could just as easily have been Dwight. He was very lucky tonight."

"What is it they say? God looks out after fools and drunks."

"It is up to you to look out after your son, Mrs. Ingersoll," Sarah said, "because God isn't going to. Detective Donovan tried to warn you about this the other day. He told you to keep him inside. To keep a close eye on him. And to keep your doors locked."

"Is that what *you* did, Mrs. Patterson?" Dwight's mother lifted her chin as if she were challenging the suggestion that she might not have behaved properly. "Is that how *you* looked after *your* son?"

There was a long silence, broken only by the canned laughter coming from the television set in the living room.

"My son's dead, Mrs. Ingersoll. I suggest, if you don't want that to happen to yours, you follow Detective Donovan's advice."

Sarah turned, picking her jacket up off the chair she'd laid it on when they'd come in from the park. "I'll go get Toby from upstairs," she said to Mac. "I'll meet you at the car."

Twenty

Sarah grabbed Toby's collar as he shot out of the door of her apartment. Apparently the dog had been no more eager to spend time in there than she was. At some point she knew she'd have to, if for no other reason than to clear out her personal belongings, but she admitted that right now she wasn't up to it. Not yet.

With Toby secured with his leash, she leaned back against the door, trying to release the tensions that had built through the long hours of the evening. Tensions that had culminated in the thinly veiled accusation made by Dwight's mother.

She wasn't sure why what the woman had said bothered her so much. After all, no one in their right mind would take mothering advice—or criticism—from Beverly Ingersoll. It was certainly through no action of hers that Dwight had escaped Danny's fate tonight.

Actually, she amended, it was through no action on

anyone's part that Dwight had escaped. No one was responsible for that but Samuel Tate himself.

She heard Mac coming up the stairs. He was talking on his cell, probably notifying the police that Dwight was home, just as he'd promised Mrs. Ingersoll he'd do. She straightened away from the door, rubbing at the skin under her eyes to make sure none of the moisture that had welled in them as she'd made her way up here was visible.

As Mac reached the top of the stairs, he folded his phone and put it into his pocket. "You okay?"

"I make it a policy not to let the ravings of idiots get to me."

"Good. Hey, Tobe. You ready to get out of here?"

"He didn't like being cooped up in the apartment. I can't say that I blame him."

"You lock it?"

"Yeah."

"You need anything? More clothes? Cosmetics?"

"Not bad enough to go inside to get them."

Mac held out his hand, palm up. She looked down at it and then shook her head. "I'm good."

"You didn't even go in, did you?"

She hesitated, but there was no reason to lie about something so stupid. "I told you. I didn't have any reason to."

"Then give me the key, and I'll make sure they got things straightened up."

He meant cleaned up, Sarah realized. And he was talking about the blood. Dan's blood.

"You don't have to do that tonight. There's no hurry."

As the phrase came out of her mouth, she wondered. "Unless you're ready for me to move back here."

"What do you think?"

"I don't know."

"Yes, you do," he said. "Now give me the key. You can wait out here in the hall with Toby."

"I'm not a coward, Mac."

"No, you're not. And you don't have to prove it to me."

She fished the key out of the front pocket of her jeans and laid it in his palm. "Knock yourself out."

One corner of his mouth ticked upward, but he lowered his head to insert the key into the lock before she could tell if that movement developed into the grin she was growing to enjoy way too much.

"You think she'd care if I took Toby down to say hello to Dwight?" she asked.

"What do you care if she does?" He had pushed the door open, but turned back to ask the question before he stepped inside.

"Actually, I'd kind of like it if she *was* pissed."

"Then by all means, knock yourself out."

"I just thought Dwight might like to say good-night to Toby before we left."

"He's getting ready for bed." Dwight's mother hadn't taken the chain off the door, peering out at Sarah through the two or three inches it allowed.

Considering that the child had been eating supper less than five minutes ago, Sarah didn't believe her. And considering Mrs. Ingersoll's question about how she'd looked after Danny, she wasn't opposed to pushing the issue.

"That seems pretty early, even for a school night. Besides, it won't take a minute. He's very fond of Toby, you know. A feeling that's reciprocated. I thought visiting with him for a few minutes might relax him."

For a long moment Dwight's mother didn't answer. The sound of the television drifted out into the hall through the crack in the door.

"I'll get him," she said finally, "but please don't put ideas into his head."

"About what?" Sarah honestly didn't know what she meant.

"He's been after me to get a dog. Says he'll take care of it. Says the super must not mind them because he let you have Toby here."

"He let me have Toby because I paid a pet deposit. I'll explain that to Dwight."

"I can't afford that. Or food for an animal. Explain that to him, too, while you're at it. I don't seem to have much success *explaining* things to him."

"Of course," Sarah said, keeping her tone carefully neutral.

Instead of inviting her to come in, Mrs. Ingersoll closed the door in her face. Sarah released a long, slow breath, telling herself she was doing this for Dwight, who had little enough to look forward to. If she could manage to add any joy to his sad existence—

The boy stepped out into the hall, pulling the door almost closed behind him. Without saying a word to Sarah, he bent, putting his arms around Toby and burying his face in his thick fur. After a moment, he turned his head so that his cheek lay against the dog's neck.

"I miss you so much." The soft words were obviously intended for the animal.

Although Toby could by no stretch of the imagination be classified as calm in temperament, he sat perfectly still while the little boy hugged him. Finally Dwight looked up at Sarah, his eyes shining.

"I think he missed me."

"I think he did."

"Can we go throw the ball for him? Just for a minute or two. I think my mother would let me as long as I'm with you."

Remembering the scene in the park, Sarah shook her head, softening the denial with a smile. And a promise she hadn't meant to give. "I'll bring him back, and we'll go to the park another afternoon. Is it all right if Detective Donovan comes with us?"

No matter what Tate had intended to convey by what he'd done tonight, he'd made one thing perfectly clear. He knew about Dwight. And he knew about her connection to him.

"Sure. You said he was Toby's friend, too. We can share him."

"I think there's enough of Toby to go around." She lowered her voice. "Don't tell Detective Donovan, but I'm pretty sure Toby likes you better."

"I know he does," Mac said as he descended the last of the stairs. "He told me so."

"Toby doesn't talk. Dogs can't talk." Dwight's smile indicated his pride in knowing that was a joke.

"Well, if he *did*," Mac said, "that's what he'd say. And now he needs to say, 'Good night.' It's past his bedtime."

"And yours." Just as she'd been unable to resist the quick hug she'd given him, Sarah put her hand on Dwight's head, tousling the badly cut hair. "Sleep tight. And have very sweet dreams."

"Good night, Toby." The boy again wrapped his arms around the dog's neck. "See you soon."

"You remember what I told you, Dwight. Okay?"

"I'll remember."

"Tell your mother to lock up," Mac reminded.

"She will. She doesn't like those people on the second floor."

The boy opened the door, and then he stopped, turning back to look at Sarah. "I forgot to ask you."

"Ask me what?"

"What that man said for me to ask you."

The cold that had knotted her stomach when Mac told her the boy was missing was suddenly there again. The only man she and Dwight had discussed tonight—

"You mean the one who gave you the note?"

Dwight nodded. "He said that when I saw you to be sure and ask you whether you liked what he did for you."

For a few long heartbeats neither she nor Mac said anything. Maybe he was doing what she was doing—trying to figure out exactly what Tate's question meant. And trying to figure out how to answer Dwight.

"What he did for Sarah?" Mac repeated. "Are you sure that's what he said, Dwight?"

"I'm sure. He made me say it back to him. Ask her whether she liked what I did for her."

"What did you think he meant?"

The boy shrugged. "Giving me the note, I guess."

"Then the answer is I didn't like it at all," Sarah said. "Because he lied to you. I didn't send you that note, Dwight. He shouldn't have told you I did. And *because* he told you that, you went out when you shouldn't have and got into trouble."

"Then if he asks me again, I should tell him you didn't like it at all?"

"If you see him again, Dwight, you shouldn't talk to him. He's not a good man. You should run away very fast if you see him."

"Never talk to strangers." The boy repeated the phrase like a mantra.

"That's right," Mac said. "And even though you've talked to him before, he's still a stranger. And he's still a bad man. You understand?"

The boy nodded, blue eyes moving from one of them to the other.

"Now you go on back inside and get ready for bed," Sarah said. "We'll come back another day and play ball."

"Tomorrow?"

"If not tomorrow, then soon. I promise."

"Okay, then. Good night. Good night, Toby."

He slipped inside the apartment. Sarah waited until she heard the lock turn and the chain being put into place before she turned to Mac.

"Was Tate talking about Dwight? About taking the other boy and not him?"

"I don't know." Mac took her arm, leading her toward the outside door. "Whatever he was talking about," he said as he opened it for her, "I don't like the idea of that bastard asking you anything."

As soon as they were outside, he turned and removed the wedge that was used to keep the front door to the building open. Then he took his phone out and flipped the case open again.

"Who are you calling?"

"Sonny. He needs to hear this."

Sarah used the leash to hold Toby close to her although he had begun his "go to the park" countdown. Standing on the stoop, she realized it had grown even colder while they'd been inside.

She looked across the street, trying to see if the floodlights the police had used were still in the park, but she couldn't tell from here. She glanced at Mac, but he was still waiting for someone to pick up.

"Can you call from inside the car?" To emphasize her point, she hunched inside her jacket.

"He's not answering anyway." Mac closed his cell, sticking it back in his pocket. He took her arm and started down the steps. "We need to walk him again?"

"Force of habit. We come out that door, he thinks he has to pee. He'll be okay until we get to your place."

"Still cold?"

"Cold. Tired. Hungry. Angry."

"Angry?"

"He's playing with me, and he's using Dwight to do it. And there's nothing I can do about it."

She had had her chance, and she'd blown it. It was all well and good to blame Mac, but there had been time to pull the trigger before he reached her. Dan hadn't been right about many things in his life, but he'd been right about that one. *Shoot, don't talk.* If she had—

"Maybe there is."

"Like what?"

He didn't answer, opening the back door to put Toby into the car instead. Then he opened hers, waiting for her to slide into its relative warmth before he closed the door and walked around the front.

He stopped before he opened the driver's side, scanning the area. When he finally got in, he turned the key in the ignition and began fiddling with the heater.

"Like what?" she repeated.

"I need to talk to some people first." He pulled away from the curb, easing the car into the street.

"What people? What does that mean?"

"The FBI. There's a profiler there who's been working with the task force. I need to ask him some things."

"Concerning what I can do about Tate?" She must have missed something because the conversation seemed to have jumped the track.

"Concerning what *we* can do about him."

"I don't understand."

He turned to meet her eyes. "I don't think he's ever done anything like that before. It's another break in the pattern. That has to be significant."

"Anything like what? Like talking to Dwight? Like the note?"

"That. And the rest. Your ex-husband. Leaving the message on your answering machine. It's all aberrant behavior for him."

She laughed, the sound bitter. "As opposed to his normal behavior of murdering little boys."

"Exactly."

Mac had obviously missed her sarcasm. Or maybe she was missing his.

"*That's* aberrant behavior, Mac."

"Not for him. *This* is. He's made some kind of connection to you. I said that to Sonny before, but I didn't understand then how far this went. He wanted to give you a message, and he chose Dwight as the medium of conversation."

"He wanted to taunt me."

"Maybe. But…he was willing to forego killing Dwight to do it. Doesn't that argue he feels some pretty powerful connection to you? Some…I don't know, fascination maybe."

"Fascination?" The thought made her physically ill.

"I don't mean that kind. Although it's something to ask Johnson about."

"The profiler?"

"Yeah. Tate clearly isn't into women, so I'm betting he isn't attracted to you in that way, but there is *something* there."

"I tried to kill him, Mac. *That's* what's there. I tried to blow his goddamn head off."

Maybe he finally recognized the anger in her voice. Or maybe he just realized that she'd had enough for one night.

He glanced over at her, but whatever he saw in her face made him turn back to the road. And he didn't attempt to share any more of whatever theory he'd devised to explain what Tate had done tonight.

Sarah eased a breath, trying to gather the control that had frayed badly in the last few minutes. Mac wasn't the enemy. Trying to help her had already cost him a great deal. Why would she want to alienate the one person who seemed to be on her side?

"I'm sorry."

"Don't be. I go off half-cocked sometimes. We'll figure this out. We'll figure him out. I'm going to make Sonny put somebody on surveillance of the building. They can drive Dwight to and from school, too."

"Will they do that?"

"They will because, as of tonight, he's a material witness in a murder case."

Because Tate had talked to him, she realized. And because the most incriminating statement he had made was the question he'd asked Dwight to convey to her.

Twenty-One

They were walking the dog on the strip of dead grass adjacent to the convenience store on his corner when Mac's cell rang. He took it out of his pocket, glanced at the caller ID, and then opened it. "Yeah."

"Sorry I missed your call," his partner said. "I was in a meeting."

Mac would have put money on what it was about. The sad part was they were probably more concerned about the fact this latest death was going to be another PR disaster for the department than they were about the dead kid in the park.

"Hope this one was more productive than the average."

"Maybe," Sonny said. "For you, anyway. Morel wants to see you."

"Now?"

"What do you think? The sooner, the better, Mac."

"He pissed?"

"No more than he has been for the last week. The media's already got hold of this."

"The kid in the park? How?"

"You talk to them?"

"Of course not."

His denial was more emphatic than it probably should have been. He hadn't been the one who'd alerted the press, but he'd thought about it. Especially if the department didn't admit very soon that the most recent victim was Tate's handiwork.

In all honesty, he hadn't expected them to. Not as long as they thought they could get away with delaying the announcement.

After all, the boy in the park was proof absolute the department had been wrong about Tate leaving the area. Now he'd killed another child, and the city would be outraged anew at the justice system for having let him go.

Other than the fact that it had taken the death of another child to force that realization on the populace, Mac couldn't be sorry the charade the N.O.P.D. had tried to carry out was at an end. He just couldn't figure out why that would make Morel call him back in tonight.

"Good. Because if you play your cards right, I think you got a shot at getting in on this one."

"Play my cards right? As in apologize to Morel?"

Mac wondered if he were willing to do that. They were the ones who'd been wrong. About everything. Maybe he should be looking for an apology from them.

"I don't think he's expecting that. He knows he's got a problem."

"Damn straight."

"So, do I tell him you're coming?"

"Mrs. Patterson's with me. With what happened tonight, I don't want to leave her alone."

That was true for several reasons. Since he and Sonny had already talked about the need to protect Sarah, Mac was hoping that was the interpretation his partner would put on the stipulation.

"I don't think anybody would mind if you brought her. It might even be helpful."

Mac wasn't sure he liked the sound of that, but if he was going in tonight, then Sarah was coming with him. She could corroborate what he wanted to tell them about Tate's behavior. She could also help plead the case for surveillance for Dwight and his family.

"We're on our way." Mac closed his phone, turning around to look for Sarah.

After he'd stopped to take the call, she'd apparently continued to walk Toby. They were following the privet hedge that had been planted between the store and the duplex next to it.

She would still be cold, hungry and tired, he acknowledged. And now, before she had a chance to rectify any of those conditions, he needed to talk her into spending another few hours dealing with fallout from the latest moves of the madman who'd murdered her son.

"You ready?" he called, starting across the grass toward them.

Sarah turned, stopping to watch his approach. "Was that your partner?"

"Yeah."

"They ID the boy?"

Mac realized only now that he'd forgotten to ask. He placated his conscience by telling himself he was concentrating more on Tate than on his past victims. Mac's concern right now was preventing future ones.

"He didn't say. He wants me to come down there."

"To the park?"

"To headquarters."

"Tonight?"

"He says Morel wants to talk to me."

"Is that good or bad? For you, I mean."

"Good, I think. The media found out about the boy in the park. They know Tate did it, and now they know Tate's still here."

"The police have admitted that?"

"Not yet, but… I don't think they're going to have much choice."

"What does that have to do with you?"

"I was the lead detective on the murders. Before Tate was released."

"Before you destroyed the tape."

That hadn't been a question. And she wouldn't believe him if he tried to deny it.

"That was only part of the equation. Morel and I seldom see eye-to-eye. He didn't believe what I said about the damage to the camera. And I wasn't very respectful of his doubt."

"So now he wants you back because…?"

"Because he's been forced to admit we still have Tate

on our hands. Tomorrow he's going to be forced to admit it publicly."

"Any idea how long you'll be gone?"

"I told Sonny I was bringing you with me."

Her brow furrowed. "Me? Why?"

"I need you to tell them what Dwight said, for one thing. And for another, I don't particularly want to leave you alone."

She studied his face. "Not that I'm all that eager to be alone, but… You're thinking something changed tonight, aren't you?"

"Maybe it didn't. Maybe I just figured some things out I hadn't figured out before."

"Like what?"

"In the last week Tate has radically altered everything he normally does. When I ask myself why that's happened, I keep coming back to you. It's like he's obsessed."

"With me? With getting back at me for what I tried to do?"

"If so, he's got a peculiar way of going about it."

"Meaning what?"

"If he wanted to punish you for that, what's the worst thing he could have done tonight?"

She didn't say anything, but the answer was in her eyes.

"He didn't do that, Sarah. So if he *doesn't* want to punish you, then what the hell *is* he doing?"

"For one thing, he's still killing little boys."

"Just not one little boy in particular. And frankly, I want to know why."

* * *

"That's exactly what Dwight said," Sarah affirmed. "That the man who gave him the note told him to ask me how I liked what he did for me."

"And you took that to mean what?" Mac's superior asked.

"Him not killing Dwight."

"How would he have known that would be important to you?"

"Obviously he's seen us together. Leaving that other child in the park where I took Toby to play with Dwight indicates that he was watching me."

"Watching you *after* you tried to shoot him."

She glanced at Mac, seeking guidance about what she should say. She'd felt guilty that protecting her from that charge had gotten him suspended. If she now admitted that she had tried to kill Tate, would that make it harder on him?

His eyes were steady, giving nothing away. Still…

"I confronted him on the courthouse steps and shouted my son's name," she corrected. "After that, he left a message on my answering machine. I reported that to Detective Cochran, but no one believed it was Tate. I also thought he'd been waiting in my apartment the day my ex-husband was killed. No one believed that was Tate either."

"Because both of those actions would be very much out of the protocol Tate's crimes have followed. Maybe I could understand them if he were out for revenge for some threat you offered. As it is now…" Morel shrugged.

His dismissive attitude about what she'd told him infuriated her. If she didn't confess to a crime she could still be charged for, one for which Mac could be severely disciplined for covering up, then the police planned to do nothing to protect Dwight.

"I'm wasting my time here."

She had spoken directly to Mac. If he wanted to deal with these people in order to try and get his job back, that was his prerogative. The only thing she wanted, protection for Dwight, was clearly not on the table. And it wouldn't be unless she was willing to confess to attempted murder.

She still had Dan's pistol. If these bastards didn't intend to look after Dwight, she would do it herself. She began to push up from the wooden armchair she'd been directed to.

"Hold on," Mac said to her before he turned to his captain. "Are you more interested in playing one-upmanship with me and Mrs. Patterson or in catching Tate?"

The silence stretched long enough that despite the clarity of the choice Mac had presented, Sarah wasn't sure the captain was going to come down on the side of doing his job.

After a moment Morel said, "We discovered only tonight that Tate is still our problem. That's why I asked you to come down here, Mac. You say he's engaged in some very aberrant behavior since his arrest. What's *your* explanation for that?"

"I think he's playing to Sarah."

A strange turn of phrase, Sarah thought, for what had gone on. Maybe in cop-speak, it had a meaning she wasn't aware of.

"Trying to impress her?" Morel asked. "Like an adolescent with a crush?"

"I don't think that characterization is very far off the mark," Mac agreed.

"Exactly why would he do that? He's not sexually attracted to women. We have ample evidence of that."

Mac shrugged. "I think what he meant by 'what he'd done for her' was not killing Dwight Ingersoll. He killed the other boy instead and dumped him in a place Dwight and Sarah had frequented. Right across the street from the building where she lives. His victims are normally well hidden in out-of-the-way locations. Sonny said it when we were in the park. He said that body was like a gift. He meant a gift to the forensics guys, but I think it was also Tate's gift to Sarah. 'Look. I didn't kill the boy you care about. I killed another one in his place.'"

"A substitute sacrifice," Morel said. "That's almost biblical in its implications."

"I don't know what that means," Sarah said, drawing the captain's eyes back to her, "but I have to think the way he lured Dwight outside, making us all think something had happened to him… I have to think I was *supposed* to believe Tate had taken him. And I did."

"Then he shows up unharmed, with a message for Sarah," Mac added. "'Did you like what I did for you?' If that's not obsession of some kind, I don't know what is."

"I think he was out there tonight," Sarah said. "Watching the body. Maybe waiting for me to find it."

"You…felt him there?" Morel's question was dubious.

"I saw someone. Something," she amended, trying

to be fair. "It was dark enough that I couldn't be certain, but…if Mac's right about him being obsessed…"

Neither of them said anything for a few long heartbeats. Then Morel straightened in his chair, tenting his fingers so that they touched his chin.

"An interesting theory," he said. "I suppose we could debate the pros and cons of it. Or we could figure out how to use whatever connection Tate feels to Mrs. Patterson to our advantage."

"What exactly does that mean? Use the connection?"

Sarah could feel the distrust in Mac's questions. He had told her that he and the captain seldom saw eye-to-eye. Now she knew why. Mac was straightforward, perhaps to a fault, but you always knew where you stood with him. Morel, on the other hand, apparently liked to pontificate, to obscure his motives with double-talk.

"Tate continues to make contact, either directly or through a third party, with Mrs. Patterson. I'm suggesting that the next time he attempts to do that, we're waiting for him."

There was a moment of silence as both she and Mac absorbed what the captain had just said. Mac was the one who broke it, although she'd reached the same conclusion he had.

"You want to use Sarah to try and catch Tate."

"Since he seems to keep coming back to her…" Morel lifted his hands, palms tilted upward and to the side. A gesture of acquiescence.

"In other words, you want to set a trap for Tate," Sarah said, "and I'm to be the bait."

"I didn't think you'd agree to our using the Ingersoll child. He's the only other person in this city Tate has shown any interest in."

"You've lost your mind," Mac said.

"It's your theory, Mac. That he's obsessed with Mrs. Patterson. Given the situation, we'd be fools not to take advantage of that."

"Never mind that you'd put her at risk in order to do so."

"Right now every boy in New Orleans between the ages of five and fifteen is at risk. And we have no idea which of them he might choose next. Mrs. Patterson, on the other hand—"

"Trap him how?" Sarah interrupted.

Some emotion appeared in the captain's cold, mud-colored eyes and was then quickly veiled by the downward sweep of his lashes. Satisfaction? Or elation? she wondered. Not that it really mattered.

"I understand you aren't currently staying in your own apartment."

"That's right."

"We'd want you to go back there."

"You've lost your collective minds," Mac said.

"Go back there and then what?" Sarah asked.

"The next move would be up to Tate. If Mac's right, he'll make it. When he does, we'll be waiting."

"In my apartment?" she clarified.

"I think that might be too obvious. He's going to have to believe that you've gone back to your normal routine. Back home. Back to work. Back to the way you were living before your… What did you call it? Your 'confrontation' on the courthouse steps."

"If I do this—"

"You've lost your mind, too," Mac said to her. "You couldn't even walk into the place. Now you're proposing to move back in there and wait for Tate to do to you what he did to your ex-husband."

"If I agree to do this," Sarah went on, ignoring him to speak directly to Morel, "I have conditions."

"Which are?"

"You get Dwight Ingersoll and his family out of that building. Get them into an apartment in a safer neighborhood. One that's bigger and cleaner and near a better school."

She tried to think if there was anything else she could reasonably add, but she figured she shouldn't push her luck. Morel didn't strike her as someone who enjoyed having demands made of him.

"We don't have the authority—"

"You want to lure a serial killer who has been responsible for the deaths of at least a dozen young boys to a building where another young boy lives—a child Tate has already involved in a dangerous situation—and you're telling me you can't arrange to get him *out* of that apartment? I'm willing to act as bait in whatever trap you want to set. I'm not willing to do that until that family has been moved out of harm's way."

"I assure you, Mrs. Patterson—"

"Doing this is to your advantage, too, Captain Morel. If anything went wrong with your plan and something happened to that little boy, I think you would have a very hard time explaining things to the press.

"Or maybe that isn't a concern in the department?"

she continued, knowing that she'd hit on something Morel would have to react to. "How well it's protecting the most vulnerable in our society? Believe me, Dwight Ingersoll would fit that description. But maybe you guys think that if he got hurt in this operation, you could explain to everybody why you didn't think to get him out of there before you lured a serial killer into the building?" She looked from Morel to Mac's partner as she asked the last question. "And I want to make it very clear that I will see to it that if the Ingersolls *aren't* moved, you *will* all have to explain why to every reporter in this country."

Twenty-Two

Neither of them had said a word on the way back to Mac's apartment. Every argument, pro and con, had been made downtown.

Of course, the ultimate decision had been hers. She couldn't do much about the fact Mac didn't like the choice she'd made.

He unlocked the door, holding it open for her to go through. Toby looked up from his place on the couch, and then lowered his head as he prepared to go back to sleep.

Sarah walked on into the living room, but Mac stopped at the front closet to hang up his jacket, continuing to avoid her eyes as he had since they'd left Morel's office.

"Say whatever you want to say before you explode."

He put the jacket and hanger on the rod and then closed the closet door. Finally he turned, looking at her.

"I don't have anything else to say. You've heard how I feel. Probably ad nauseum."

"It's the right thing to do, Mac."

"Okay." He crossed the room and headed to the kitchen.

As she took off her own coat and laid it on the end of the couch, she listened to the water being turned on and then off. After a couple of seconds that noise was followed by the sound of a glass being set down in the porcelain sink. He was getting a drink, something he always did on the way to bed.

As he reentered the room, Mac was in the process of unbuttoning his shirt. "Mind if I grab a quick shower?"

"It *is* your shower."

"And it's your bedroom." Although the phrase "for the time being" hadn't been a part of that sentence, it hung in the air between them.

"What they want me to do gets Dwight out of harm's way," she said, unwilling to believe she couldn't make him see reason. "And it gives law enforcement the chance to remove a sadistic killer of children from the streets. How could I not agree?"

"Easy. You could say to them all the things I said tonight. They can use a ringer. They've done it before in this kind of situation."

Mac had kept arguing for that. All they needed, he'd said, was the *illusion* that Sarah was back at work and back in her apartment. They could easily use a policewoman to give Tate that impression. Someone of her general size and build who would wear her clothes.

"He's not that stupid, Mac. He wouldn't fall for it."

"He's obsessed with you. He'd bite."

"Yes, he will. *If* it's me. And when he does, someone will be there to take him down. And to protect me in the process."

"Things go wrong in operations like this all the time. No matter what they tell you, nothing comes with a guarantee."

"If there's anyone who understands that principle, Mac, it's me."

"Then don't let them put you in that position. They can do something else. Go in some other direction and get the same result."

"I want him, Mac. I want that bastard finally brought to justice. I wanted that enough to try to do it myself when the system failed. Why *wouldn't* I be willing to help them accomplish this?"

"Because you've sacrificed enough on the altar of Samuel Tate."

"I didn't *make* those offerings, Mac. He took them from me. And I couldn't do a thing about it. This time..." She stopped, fighting the emotion generated by the thought of finally getting payback. "Even if I didn't want this for myself, what kind of person would deny their help in getting that maniac off the streets? If I can protect Dwight or other boys like him and Danny, it would be criminal *not* to agree."

"Except it's not your job, Sarah. It's *their* job. They're just trying to make it easier by taking what is essentially a very dangerous shortcut."

"I'm not opposed to them making it easier, as long as they catch him. I don't understand why you are."

"Because I don't want anything to happen to you."

The words caught at her heart, but she couldn't let them influence her. She couldn't let *him* influence her.

"Then see to it that nothing does," she said. "Be there. Be there when he comes."

"That would make me party to what they're doing," he said stubbornly.

That had been Mac's last word in his boss's office. That he wanted no part of what they proposed. Although she hadn't expressed her dismay at the time, that was the one argument that had caused her to have second thoughts.

"They're going to do it with you or without you."

"Are *you*?" he asked.

"I don't want to. But…I don't think I have any option."

"And *that's* where we won't ever agree."

He moved past her to the bedroom, closing the door behind him. He had intended that gesture to make her feel shut out. Closed off from the support he'd provided since she'd been here. Understanding his intent didn't keep it from working.

She blew out a breath, too tired and too frustrated by his obstinacy to argue anymore. All she wanted was her own shower and some place to sleep. If she ended up sharing the couch with Toby, so be it.

She was right, and Mac was wrong. And she wasn't going to give in to his blackmail. If that meant she had to do this without him, then so be that, too. In the meantime…

She glanced at her watch and discovered it was only a little after ten. With everything that had gone on tonight, it felt much later.

Although it was early for bed, it was very much past dinner time. Maybe it was crass or unfeeling or something else emotionally unhealthy to think about food right now, but since she couldn't go to bed until Mac finished in the bathroom, so be it.

"Smells good."

It had. The smell of whatever Sarah was warming in the microwave had drifted back to the bedroom. He had intended to pull on the pair of sweatpants he'd slept in last night and roll Toby for the couch. Instead he found himself putting on a clean pair of jeans to join her in the kitchen.

She was sitting at the table, the takeout containers she'd stuck in the refrigerator earlier lined up in front of her. Across from her place was an empty plate and another set of silverware.

"I thought you might be hungry, too," she said.

"I didn't realize how much, until I smelled this."

He sat down, laying the paper towel she'd put beside his plate over his lap. When he looked up, she was watching him.

"I'm sorry." He hadn't intended to apologize. He still thought he was right, and she and Morel and the rest of them were wrong. That didn't mean they couldn't be civil to one another. After all, she was his guest.

And a hell of a lot more.

"I know you're just saying what you believe," she responded. "I can't fault you for that, but… I'm truly too tired to think about it any more tonight."

"Fair enough," he agreed, reaching over to grab one of the cartons.

As he spooned the contents, which looked like Mongolian beef, onto his plate, the aroma made his mouth water. He couldn't remember the last time he'd eaten. And he couldn't remember many times in his life when he'd been hungrier.

They ate in silence. Since she'd gotten a head start while he'd showered she seemed content after she was done to watch him finish off everything left on the table between them.

"Better?" she asked as he pushed his chair back a little.

"I may live."

It was the wrong choice of words. Despite the ease that seemed to have returned while they'd eaten, the phrase brought back all the issues they'd discussed endlessly for the last few hours. The ones that had created the barrier that now existed between them.

"Look—" he began.

"Don't. Let it go, Mac. At least let it go for tonight."

He shrugged agreement. What choice did he have?

"If I don't clear this stuff away, we'll be smelling Chinese for days." She rose, picking up as many of the empty cartons as she could carry over to the garbage can.

When she turned back to the table after depositing them, she said, "Why don't you let me take the couch tonight? It hardly seems fair that you don't get to sleep in your own bed anymore."

"Toby and I have an understanding. He sleeps on the floor, and he knows I'm not interested in any display of affection until after daylight." He pushed up from the table. "Go take your shower. I'll finish up in here. We'll both feel better after a good night's sleep."

She looked as if she didn't believe him, but she did allow him to take the remainder of the cartons out of her hands. Then she hovered beside his chair, watching as he disposed of the rest of the trash.

"Go," he ordered, when he'd finished. "You'll sleep better."

She nodded and then obeyed, finally leaving him alone. He thought about calling Sonny to see what he'd say without Morel listening to every word, but Sarah was right. He needed to let this go for tonight. Maybe if he slept on it, he could come up with some alternative solution that the powers-that-be would buy. One that didn't involve using Sarah as bait.

It seemed ironic that he'd been the one who'd pointed out to them that she was the only connection to Tate they had. At the time, he hadn't thought stating that obvious fact would work out like this.

He took a last look around the kitchen. It was better than he would normally leave it. He could load the few utensils they'd used into the dishwasher in the morning.

He turned off the light and went into the living room. By now, Toby was used to the routine. As soon as Mac appeared, he jumped down from the couch, ambling over to stretch out between it and the front door.

Mac checked the locks and then took the quilt he'd been using from the top shelf of the front closet, where Sarah stored it every morning after she'd folded it up. Normally that would have been a bit too much domestic tranquility for him, but having her pick up after him hadn't been too bad. Actually—

He shut down that line of thought. Whether he liked

having Sarah around or not was beside the point. She'd come here because neither of them felt it was safe for her to remain in her apartment. And now, if Morel had his way, she would be going back there.

He realized he was still standing beside the front door, the forgotten quilt in his hands. He carried it with him, laying his nighttime covering down on the couch as he walked past it and over to the bedroom door.

He hesitated a moment before he tapped on its hollow core with the back of his knuckles. There was no answer, which probably meant Sarah was still in the shower.

He released the breath he hadn't been aware he was holding and began to turn away. Midway through the motion, he changed his mind and his direction.

This time he didn't knock. Nor did he hesitate. He opened the door, stepped inside the darkened bedroom, and then closed it behind him.

The light in the bathroom was on, and he could hear water running. The mental images that sound produced were so clear he could almost see the beads of moisture on that alabaster skin.

She would have put her hair up, but tendrils, dampened by the steam, would cling to the slim column of her neck. When she raised her arm to reach for the soap in the corner rack, her breasts would lift into the spray.

He closed his eyes against the force of those pictures, only to have them replaced by others. Just as powerful. Just as provocative.

The last time he'd opened the door of the shower,

he'd found Sarah broken by grief and remorse. In need of his comfort.

Tonight, despite everything she'd been through, she was once more the woman he'd first seen pointing a gun at her son's murderer. A woman willing to lay her life on the line for what she believed was right. Willing to do what had to be done, even if it wasn't her responsibility.

In that earlier moment of weakness, Sarah had made him an offer. Although he'd accepted, he had understood from the first that what she'd given him that night had no strings attached. It made no promises.

Tonight, in admiration for her strength, he'd come to make a similar offering. No strings. No promises. Only the here and now. For however long the two of them found what they shared mutually satisfying.

He crossed the bedroom, the sound of the shower growing clearer with each step. As he walked, his fingers moved against the buttons of his jeans. When he reached the partially closed door of the bath, he stopped long enough to strip them off, leaving them behind him on the carpet.

He widened the crack between the door and its frame, and then, barefoot, he stepped onto the cool, smooth tiles of the bathroom floor. He could see her behind the translucent front wall of the enclosure, lifting her face to the spray. Her body was in profile, firm breasts jutting upward. Just as he'd pictured them in his head.

He must have made some sound. Startled, she turned toward him. "Mac?"

"Yeah. It's okay."

"What's wrong?" She pushed the sliding door open, unmindful of the spray.

When she saw him, her eyes made a quick tour down his nude body before, widened, they came back to lock on his. The knowledge of why he was here was in hers.

For a moment, there was nothing else there. Not even shock. Then her shoulders lifted as she drew breath. She didn't speak, waiting instead.

"Nothing's wrong," he said finally.

"Then…"

"It wasn't enough. The other night. That wasn't all this is supposed to be."

"This?"

"You and me."

He didn't say "us." She would have told him there was no "us."

She would have been right. They'd both been alone too long. Too self-sufficient. Too opinionated. Too damned stubborn.

That didn't mean that there couldn't be more than that one-night stand. The phrase echoed, the epitome of his adolescent dreams.

"What more do you want, Mac?"

Her eyes again made that downward journey. When they came up this time, there was a trace of amusement in their gray-green depths.

He didn't mind seeing it there. It was, he supposed, pretty damn funny that the only way they could manage this seemed to revolve around the shower enclosure.

"I don't know. All I know is what I want tonight. And so do you."

"Is this supposed to be another form of persuasion?"

"Would that work?"

"Depends on how persuasive you are, I guess."

"Fair enough."

He moved toward the shower, and her eyes widened again. He'd surprised her, and he liked that. It boded well for what he intended.

He stepped into the enclosure, pulling the door closed. Despite the fact that the stall was open at the top, there was an immediate sense of containment. As if they'd somehow managed to shut out the rest of the world.

Tate. Morel. The press. Everything else had been left outside.

Only the two of them were in here. Alone. Together.

And then he realized he'd been right about everything else he'd envisioned. Moisture glistened on her skin, adding to its pearllike luster.

With one finger he pushed a strand of hair off from her cheek. Then the thumb of that same hand began a slow, involuntary glide along the smoothness of her jaw and down the side of her neck. Her head fell back, her mouth opening on a sigh as her eyelids drifted closed.

His thumb continued to trail downward, tracing along the valley between her breasts. As it did, his fingers brushed over her nipple, feeling its instant response. Emboldened, they then cupped under the small, perfect globe, lifting it to his mouth.

Her flesh was warm and damp. Soft. The taste so sweet it literally took his breath.

His tongue circled the tautened bud, but he was too hungry for the slow, deliberate courtship he'd employed before. And she wasn't the woman she'd been that night. Fragile. Scarred. Scared.

The image of her stubbornly defying him tonight because she believed it was the right thing to do formed in his mind. His erection, already firmly engorged, tightened.

Maybe that's what had attracted him from the first. The same quality he would have admired in a fellow police officer. Or a combat vet. In anyone willing to stand up and be counted.

His lips fastened around the peak of her breast, suckling hard. With his hand against her spine, he guided her away from the wall with the spigots toward the smooth expanse of the longer side. Then, his mouth still engaged with worshiping her breast, he used his lower body to urge her back against the tile.

As soon as that contact between them had been made, he knew it was a mistake. He was too near the edge, and he wanted her far too much to take this kind of risk.

He eased away, trying to fill his mind with something else. With anything else. Anything but the fact of her body a fraction of an inch from his. Anything but the thought of burying himself inside her and staying there until neither of them could think about what had happened today.

Or any other day, he amended. He wanted to bury

himself inside Sarah until all either of them could do was feel.

Her hands had found his buttocks. Her nails dug into skin and muscle as she pulled him back against her.

He raised his head to issue a warning. Before he could form the words, her body surged upward, her mouth fastening over his as if she, too, had been waiting for this.

He could feel her nipples, hardened from his caress and slick from the combination of soap and moisture, slide across his chest. Another sensation to be added to the building chorus demanding relief.

He broke the kiss, lowering his face to find the curve between her neck and shoulder. Her head tilted, moving back and forth against his ear as his mouth nuzzled the soft, sensitive skin along her collarbone.

She moved suddenly, her arms locking around his neck. And then, using them to lever herself upward, she lifted her legs to fasten around his hips.

He raised his head then to look down into her eyes. They were closed, but her lips—only a fraction of an inch from his—were parted, seeming to invite his kiss.

As he leaned down to accept that invitation, her hand moved against him, grasping and then guiding him into the wet heat of her body. For an instant they both froze, from shock and pleasure.

Then she moved again, lowering herself onto his shaft, one slow millimeter at a time. His breath released in a long, low gasp, bringing her eyes open. At whatever she saw in his, the curve of her mouth increased, as did the pressure she exerted to pull him deeper inside.

She moved again, somehow able, within the restraints of their positions, to control the slow up and down motion of her body over his. She watched him as she did, seeming to anticipate the exact second when his quickly unraveling control reached the breaking point.

And then—suddenly—there was no further movement. No increase of the exquisite pressure her muscles had exerted. Nothing but some badly needed space and time to allow him to rebuild whatever control he could before the next onslaught of sensation.

He had come here prepared to take her. To show her that, despite her determination to do what she thought was right rather than what he believed was smart, he was in charge. At least of this.

He had discovered that he wasn't. Not by any stretch of the imagination.

When she began again that slow, seductive torture, he knew he should admit defeat. Which was also victory.

Unwilling or unable to endure any more, he gathered her to him, using his hands under her shoulder blades to lift her away from the wall. With them, he then pressed her downward. At the same time, he used the big muscles of his thighs and buttocks to drive his hips upward.

The gasp this time was hers. He caught it with his mouth, covering hers as again and again he pushed into her.

He broke the kiss only as the roaring cataclysm inside his body began. The force of it rolled over him in waves.

He could do nothing but cling to her as they rocked him. Leaving him mindless. Blind and deaf.

As his orgasm began to wane, allowing a partial return to sanity and consciousness, he became aware that Sarah had joined him. He opened his eyes to find that her head had fallen back against the wall behind her.

He held her through a series of shivering releases until, sated, she sagged in his arms. Then they rested together, their bodies joined as their ragged breathing slowed and finally steadied.

After an eternity, she leaned back against the tiles once more, blowing out a breath. "We might need to try that again sometime."

"To see if we can get it right?" When he smiled at her, her lips tilted in response.

"Can you do something about the water?" she asked.

"What water?"

She turned her head, looking at the now-lukewarm spray from the shower head that continued to pelt them. Mac knew from bitter experience it would soon become ice-cold. He reached over and turned the handle, cutting off the flow.

The sudden silence seemed deafening. A little intimidating.

"Have I convinced you yet?" he asked.

"No, but I have to say that's the best frigging argument I've heard yet."

Despite the seriousness of the subject, he laughed out loud. And Sarah laughed with him.

With the sound of her laughter, he realized that he didn't want to lose whatever this was. He didn't want to lose her.

Didn't want to lose her….

The words took on a life of their own. And in spite of her recent vote of confidence, he knew he hadn't changed her mind.

He couldn't. She wouldn't be Sarah if he could. Which meant…

Which meant it was up to him to come up with a solution that would put an end to Tate without placing her in greater danger than she was in already.

Twenty-Three

When the phone rang, Mac reached for the alarm on the bedside clock from sheer force of habit. The second ring brought him far enough out of the well of sleep to recognize the sound for what it was. By the third, he not only knew where he was, but who was asleep beside him.

As the memories from last night flooded his brain, he began to sit up, trying to untangle his legs from the long, smooth length of Sarah's. His hand, fumbling over the top of the bedside table, finally connected with his cell.

He opened the case and brought it to his ear. "'Lo?"

"Mac? Daryl Johnson here. I've got some new information on your guy I think you'll want to see."

It took him a few sleep-fogged seconds to place the name and then to identify the reference. "Something new on Tate?"

"Except that isn't his name."

There hadn't been a match in the databases for Tate's prints, but with the information they'd acquired at the time of his arrest, it had always been likely someone would eventually tie him to his past. Apparently the FBI had finally made that connection.

"Priors?"

"One very important one. Explains a lot."

"Want to give me the short version?"

As he talked, Mac was aware of Sarah sitting up in bed beside him. She pulled the top sheet up to cover her breasts.

In other circumstances, given what had happened between them last night, he might have found that amusing. Even slightly seductive. With the Bureau's profiler on the other end of the line, talking to him about the killer of her son, it was anything but.

"His real name is Nathan Burrows," Johnson went on, unaware of what Mac was dealing with. "Age thirty-three. Native of Wayne's Crossroad, Georgia. He was suspected of killing his mother and maternal uncle at age thirteen. No complete prints of any kind left at the scene, including the kid's, but they did get a couple of very incomplete partials. At the time of the murders, the boy disappeared, leaving the authorities to wonder if he'd been abducted by the killer. Now we know that he hadn't been because eventually he would reappear in a variety of personas and locations, the latest being Samuel Tate. The resemblance between the mug shots you guys took of Tate and Nathan as a boy are eerie."

"There's no doubt in your mind they're one and the same."

"Not for us. The methodology of the original homicide confirms what the picture and partials suggest."

"Did you say he killed his *mother*?"

Maybe if Tate's primary targets had been women, Mac might have expected something like that. Since it never had been…

"From what the locals pieced together—and this is by no means complete—the uncle had been abusing him for years. Whether that was with the mother's complicity or not, Burrows apparently blamed her for not putting an end to it."

"Jesus," Mac said softly.

"Yeah. Not that there's anything new about that. It's almost stereotypical, actually. Except for killing the mother, too, of course."

"So…he's just repeating with his victims what the uncle did to him." That hadn't been a question. That was always the pattern.

"He's assuming the control he didn't have as a child. And when he's done with them, he kills them just like he killed his molester."

Despite profiles and patterns, Mac knew that much of what the behavioral science guys put out was guesswork. Educated guesswork, of course, but they filled in a lot of blanks that no one who had not lived through the situation could possibly know.

"Anyway, I thought you might want to see what we have," Johnson went on. "I tried your office first, but they said you weren't in."

"Yeah. We worked late last night. I need to fill you in on that. You gonna be there the rest of the day?" As he asked that question, Mac glanced down at his watch.

It was after ten. No wonder Johnson was surprised to find he wasn't at headquarters.

"Most of it. Something else happen?"

"He did another kid, but...there are some twists to this one. Stuff I'd like to run by you. Let me get some final details from the techs, and I'll call you back."

"I'll be waiting. As bad as that is, it does give you some time to assimilate the new stuff before..." Johnson let the sentence trail, but they both knew what he was getting at. Before the next murder. With someone like Tate, the next one was inevitable. "Maybe there'll be something in here that will help."

"I'll get back with you as soon as I can," Mac promised. "Thanks for sending the stuff."

"Talk to you later then."

Johnson disconnected, but Mac held the phone to his ear a few seconds, trying to absorb everything he'd been told. Finally he closed the case and laid the cell back on the bedside table. When he turned, Sarah was looking at him, her brows raised.

"That was the FBI profiler who's been working with us on the Tate stuff," he explained.

"And?"

"They've matched the photographs we took of Tate to someone named Nathan Burrows, who disappeared at age thirteen from a little town in Georgia. *After* killing his mother and her brother."

"His *mother*."

Sarah's repetition didn't have quite the same note of shock his own had had. Of course, she'd had a few minutes to fit that word into possible scenarios. And given what they already knew about Tate…

"He killed his own mother," she repeated softly when Mac didn't respond.

"Apparently she knew her brother was abusing him and didn't step in to stop it. Or that's what the boy believed. He apparently hated her because she didn't do what she should have to protect him."

As he said those words aloud, it was as if the brain-fog that had dogged him during his conversation with the profiler lifted. More than that, he realized. It was as if everything he hadn't understood about what had happened yesterday suddenly fell into place. As if he'd been given the key to a convoluted puzzle that was no longer at all complicated.

Nathan Burrows's mother hadn't stood up for him. Weak and defenseless, he'd endured unspeakable horrors until he had reached an age and a level of fury that had allowed him to stand up for himself.

He had murdered his attacker, as well as the woman whose job it had been to not only nurture but also protect him. The woman who had failed to do that. A failure that had set him on the path to becoming Samuel Tate and all those other incarnations in which he had abused and then murdered defenseless children.

And through all those years, nobody had done anything to stop him. The justice system certainly hadn't. Not even when they had finally managed to apprehend him.

Then one cold, clear morning he'd walked down the steps of a courthouse, again a free man. A woman—a mother—had pointed a gun at him intending to bring him to account for what he had done to her son.

As the thoughts tumbled through Mac's brain, the sequence of understanding ran faster and faster. Each fit with the other until the picture they formed was unmistakable. And unmistakably correct.

Samuel Tate wasn't out to get revenge for what Sarah had tried to do. In his sick, twisted mind, she'd done exactly what a mother *should* do when someone hurt her child. Sarah had said no to him. She had screamed to her son's murderer, *No more. If no one else will stop you, then I will.*

"Mac?"

He raised his eyes, focusing on her face. The question he'd heard in her voice was reflected in her expression.

"What is it?" she asked. "What's wrong?"

"It isn't going to work."

"What?"

"What Morel wants you to do. It isn't going to work."

She shook her head, her lips forming a question she didn't speak aloud.

"He doesn't hate you, Sarah. And he doesn't want revenge. That isn't what he's doing."

"*Tate?* But… I don't understand."

"You *did* what his mother *didn't* do. You did what, in his mind, you were *supposed* to do. You stuck up for Danny."

Putting the realization into words made him more convinced he was right.

Sarah started to shake her head. Even as she did, something else was happening in her eyes. Some inkling of the chain of logic he'd just followed to reach this conclusion.

In response to what he saw there, Mac nodded. Encouraging her.

"He *admires* you, Sarah, for what you tried to do." He laughed, thinking how wrong they'd all been. "That sick, twisted bastard *likes* you. He isn't trying to hurt you. If anything—"

He stopped, not because he'd had sense enough to understand how this would impact her, but because of what he now saw happening in her eyes.

"Oh, my God," she said softly. "Dan. Oh, my God, Dan."

Tate had told Dwight to ask her how she liked his gift. They'd all thought he meant the gift of allowing Dwight to live when he'd had the boy in his clutches.

Tate's meaning had been more perverse than that. And far more diabolical.

For years, Sarah had blamed her husband for their son's death. And she hadn't been particularly shy about expressing her feelings. Samuel Tate had taken the culpability she'd assigned to her ex-husband one step farther.

Because he admired her, Tate had murdered the man she had always held responsible for her son's death.

"I'm telling you, Captain, this isn't about getting back at Sarah Patterson. Read the material Johnson sent. It's clear Tate *admires* what she tried to do. That he—"

"That's your opinion, Mac," Morel said, holding his

hand up, palm out. "And one the department doesn't happen to share."

Mac took a breath, trying to calm his frustration. He wouldn't accomplish anything by alienating Morel. He'd already done that, and it hadn't worked to his advantage.

"Sarah did what his own mother *wouldn't* do," he said, tempering his tone. "She stood up for her kid. That's what Tate's message to her meant. He killed Dan Patterson *for her*. Because she had blamed her ex for Danny's death. *That* was his gift."

He had asked Sonny to keep Sarah occupied while he tried to reason with their supervisor. This was going to be a hard enough sale without having to be constantly aware of the effect his words might have on her.

Although Sarah had accepted intellectually the reality of Tate's motives, he knew it was still hard for her to accept that her ex-husband's murder had occurred because she'd accused him of negligence that had led to his son's death.

"Last night you were equally convinced that the gift he'd referred to was letting Dwight Ingersoll live," Morel argued.

"Last night I didn't have access to the information the FBI provided us with today."

"Even if we accept that Tate admires the stand Mrs. Patterson took, I'm not sure how that negates our plans."

"He isn't coming after her. He doesn't want revenge."

"If you're so convinced of that, I take it you no longer object to her returning to her apartment?"

Was he sure enough of his conclusions to risk Sarah's life on their validity? His hesitation to answer the captain's question seemed to cement Morel's conviction.

"It's an admirable theory, Mac, but I find it difficult to believe Tate has set Mrs. Patterson on some kind of pedestal. He's as cold-blooded a murderer as it's ever been my misfortune to deal with. You think Tate killed the ex-husband because he admired her determination to blow his brains out. I think he was waiting for her, and Patterson showed up. He was in the wrong place at the wrong time.

"In any case, as far as the department is concerned," Morel went on, "nothing has changed. Your opinion is simply that, Detective Donovan. *Your* opinion." The captain emphasized the pronoun, indicating that he wasn't about to abandon the agreement he'd reached with Sarah last night.

"Then I want to be there."

"I don't think that's possible."

"You agreed to move the Ingersolls out of the bottom-floor apartment. Let me move in."

Morel laughed. "Tate isn't stupid, Mac. What makes you think he's going to buy a new tenant who looks remarkably like a cop?"

"That's the only way Sarah will agree."

"Really?" The question dripped sarcasm. "That isn't the impression I got last night."

"Things have changed."

Morel's mouth pursed, his eyes examining Mac's face. "I think I'd like to hear that from her," he said finally.

"Then ask her."

His supervisor's lips relaxed into a smile. "Oh, believe me, Mac, I intend to."

"What'd you tell him?" Sarah lowered her voice so that only Mac could hear the question. He had volunteered to walk her upstairs to Morel's office, giving them a few moments of privacy.

She hadn't been able to tell anything from his face when he'd come downstairs. Maybe that had been because Detective Cochran had been watching their every move. Or maybe it was because his expression had been so closed and hard.

"I told him you wanted me on site when you move back to your apartment."

"And he objects to that?" After all, it had been Mac who'd been adamant last night that he wanted no part of this.

"He thinks I look too much like a cop."

She laughed because Morel was right. "Don't you think Tate knows about…us?"

There had been a slight hesitation before she'd finished the sentence, but after last night there didn't seem to be any doubt that now there was at least some semblance of "us."

How long that would last hadn't yet been addressed. And she wasn't sure, knowing Mac's reticence, that it ever would be.

That was all right with her. What they had—a mutually satisfying sexual relationship—was all she wanted. She couldn't afford any kind of emotional involvement. Not at this point in her life. Not with her track record.

"I don't know what Tate knows," Mac said. "All I know is that you asked me to be there. That's what I told Morel you wanted. If it's no longer true, then tell him. He'll be more than happy to accommodate you."

"Don't," she said, putting her hand on his arm.

He pulled it away, but not before he turned to look down at her. "It's up to you, Sarah. You can do it their way or you can do it mine."

"I thought we were on the same side here. All with the same objective. Getting Tate off the streets."

"The difference is I'm on *your* side. They aren't. They're under a lot of pressure to get this done and to get it done quickly. You're their ace in the hole. They know that, but despite knowing it, they'll sacrifice you to protect themselves. Any day of the week and twice on Sunday."

"Mac—"

"Like I said. It's up to you. Make your case or walk away. But don't let them use you like they've used everyone else involved in this."

Seeing the bleakness in his eyes, she nodded.

Twenty-Four

Mac knew as soon as he and Sonny reentered Morel's office that he wasn't going to like the deal, whatever it turned out to be. His boss was looking too pleased with himself.

"Mrs. Patterson and I have come to an agreement about the arrangements. I have a call in to Special Agent Johnson, who, I'm hoping, will be able to help us in dealing with the psychology of manipulating Tate. If you're right, Mac, and be aware that I'm not conceding that point, then we may have to take some additional action to pique his interest."

"What kind of action?" Although his concern had been about being allowed to stay with Sarah once they'd put her back into her apartment, the last part of Morel's statement put that worry on the back burner. Behind all the possible idiocy the N.O.P.D. and the Bureau might come up with.

"As I said, we're consulting the FBI, both on your

read of Tate's motives and on what steps we might need to take if they agree with it."

"Steps to *make* Sarah his target?"

"Mrs. Patterson has agreed to help us attract Tate's attention. When we're sure about the best way to do that, everyone working on this will be informed.

"In the meantime..." Morel paused, seeming to expect Mac to ask additional questions. When he didn't, the captain continued. "Mrs. Patterson will return to work, under close police supervision, of course. Someone will watch her on her commute and while she's in the restaurant. We'll have officers posing as customers and kitchen staff, so that both areas will be covered. Since Tate's modus operandi doesn't normally involve home invasion," Morel went on, conveniently ignoring the facts surrounding Dan Patterson's death, "we believe any attempt he makes will be on neutral territory."

"And just for argument sake, what about while she's at the apartment?" Whatever pattern Tate had followed in the past, he wasn't adhering to it as far as Sarah was concerned.

"Since the Ingersolls will be relocated..." Morel tilted his head toward Sarah as if acknowledging that concession to her demands. "The landlord will take that opportunity to refurbish their apartment. Those doing the improvements will be our people, of course, who will monitor her apartment with surveillance equipment that will be installed under the guise of the renovations."

"And the cameras in Sarah's place?"

"Mrs. Patterson believes that, with proper training,

she'll be able to install those herself. If not, she can have a maintenance emergency. Something that will require the presence of a workman inside her apartment."

Mac couldn't find fault with that. And Morel was right. The equipment that would be needed on her end was the same type pubescent boys set up in the girls' locker rooms of countless high schools. He had no doubt Sarah would be able to handle its installation.

"The workmen will be there during the day. What about at night? You don't think Tate will buy that the landlord is paying overtime for these improvements?"

Morel shrugged. "A multitude of workmen will come and go throughout the day. I doubt anyone will be keeping count as to whether the number going in equals the number coming out."

"That's exactly the kind of thing Tate *would* do," Mac warned. "Ask Johnson, if you don't believe me."

"I'll put your question on the list. Although, considering your conviction that he's paid his debt, so to speak, to Mrs. Patterson, I would think you'd be less concerned about Tate's obsession to detail. Anything else?"

"I want to stay in that apartment during the operation. I'll take the night shift."

Morel's eyes lifted from the note he'd been making. "Mrs. Patterson has already expressed her preference."

For a fraction of a second Mac thought the captain was turning him down. Only when he replayed the words in his head did he realize they could just as easily mean Sarah had asked for him. Just as he'd urged her to.

"Does that mean yes?"

Morel's gaze shifted to Sarah before it came back to him. "I understood that was to be the arrangement."

"Thanks. I appreciate that."

Sonny was right. It never hurt to suck up, especially when the person you were sucking up to had just been forced to give you what you wanted.

"I assume that when I hear back from Agent Johnson I can reach you at Detective Donovan's," Morel said, his gaze again on Sarah.

"That's right." Her agreement had been made without any trace of embarrassment.

"Until then," Morel said, getting to his feet.

He reached across the desk to offer his hand. Sarah rose, too, and extended hers.

Morel held it a fraction too long before he said, "Please don't assume Detective Donovan is right about Tate. It would be a shame to let down your guard because of something that's only theory."

"I won't. Nor do I expect you to let down yours as far as the Ingersoll boy is concerned. Like you, I'm not totally convinced Mac's right. If he isn't, then Dwight is just as vulnerable as he ever was. You *do* have someone watching him?" There was a note of anxiety in her voice that hadn't been in her response to Morel's warning about her own safety.

"Twenty-four hours a day. We've also asked his mother to keep him home from school for the next few days so we can better keep an eye on him. I've already contacted the housing authority to find them accommodations that meet your specifications. You do understand that could take some time."

"As long as Dwight's being watched, I believe your timetable is more pressing than mine."

"I beg your pardon?" Morel looked genuinely perplexed by Sarah's comment.

Maybe because he'd become accustomed to the way her mind worked, Mac knew where she was going with that one. He also knew he was going to enjoy her explanation to his chief.

Probably a little too much, he acknowledged, biting the inside of his lip as he lowered his eyes.

"I read the morning papers while I was waiting downstairs. You let Tate go, and a few days later you have another victim on your hands. The press isn't very happy with the N.O.P.D. right now, Captain Morel. Frankly, neither is the populace. The sooner you get the Ingersolls into a safe environment, the sooner we can get down to what we're all interested in. Taking Tate off the streets again. And this time—hopefully—making it stick."

Sarah was too quiet on the way home. After she'd stood up to Morel, Mac had thought she was beginning to put the reason for Patterson's murder into perspective, but maybe he'd been wrong about that.

Along with a lot of other things.

"You okay?" He took his eyes off traffic long enough to glance over at her.

She'd been looking out the passenger side window, but at his question she turned. "I'm fine."

"Whatever Tate did, Sarah, you're in no way responsible for it."

"Just like Dan wasn't responsible for letting him walk off with Danny?"

Yeah, he'd been wrong about her putting things into perspective.

"Let it go, Sarah."

"Sure thing. It's only my son. And my husband."

"Ex-husband."

What the hell did it matter what she called the guy? She had divorced Patterson. Besides, the man was dead. Still her reference to him as her "husband" rankled.

"Ex-husband," she repeated obediently. "Poor Dan."

Mac said nothing. After all, Patterson *was* a poor, dead son of a bitch. That applied whether Tate had targeted him on Sarah's behalf or whether he'd just shown up in the wrong place at the wrong time.

"Does that bother you?" she asked.

"What?"

"That I called him my husband."

He thought about lying, but what was the point? Besides, he wasn't all that good at it. Certainly not with someone as astute as Sarah.

"Yeah. Yeah, it did."

"Because we slept together?"

He turned to look at her again. "He was your husband."

"I didn't mean him, Mac. I meant us. Does it bother you that I was married?"

"*I* was married. Does that bother you?"

"I don't know. Maybe. Some."

"Yeah?" Interesting. And encouraging. Which probably made him a poor SOB, too.

"Did you love her?"

"My wife? I thought I did. You love him?" He glanced over in time to see her nod.

Something weird happened in his gut. Because he was jealous of a dead man?

"I'm sorry," he offered, turning his gaze back to the road.

"Thank you. And I think you're right, by the way. For what it's worth."

He tried to fit that into the context of the current conversation, but there was only one place in which it made sense. "Right about Tate?"

"I can't feel sorry for him. But for a little boy…" She shook her head.

"Lots of children suffer much worse, and they don't turn out like Tate."

"Lots of children are murdered, and their mothers don't try to kill the bastard who did it. So what's your point?"

"I don't know. I'm not sure I had one."

After a moment she asked, "Do you think it will work?"

He hesitated, but he'd been considering that same question since they'd left Morel's. "I think that depends on whether the Bureau can find the right buttons to push."

"And if they do…" The words faded.

"If they do, Sarah, there's a chance Tate *will* come after you. After all, that's the whole point of this exercise."

It was well and good to accept in principle that something was going to happen. It was harder to accept the actuality that a man who'd killed more than a dozen people was going to make you his next target. In his opinion, she needed to do that.

"Better me than Dwight," she said. "Or someone like him."

"If we do nothing, there's every possibility Tate will move on. He may anyway."

He'd paid his "debt" to Sarah. Since Mac was now convinced the serial killer wasn't out for revenge for what she'd done at the courthouse, he could see no reason for the man to hang around New Orleans.

There were plenty of unsuspecting towns out there. Places where he could start over. Places where it would take a few missing kids before they figured out what was going on.

"I thought that's what we were trying to prevent," Sarah said. "Him leaving the area."

"That's what the Bureau is trying to do. All *I'm* trying to do is keep you from getting hurt."

She said nothing in response, turning her head to look out the window again. Maybe it was the personal direction his comment had taken. But if she didn't want him to feel personal about her, she shouldn't have spent the night in his bed.

"You said that stopping Tate was the department's job," she said after a moment.

"It is." The tight coil of fear in his gut loosened a little.

"You're part of the department, Mac. Even Morel admitted you have to be in on this."

"So?"

"So if all you're trying to do is keep me from getting hurt, you aren't doing your job. And maybe the rest of them aren't either."

"Sarah—"

"I don't have a choice, Mac. Especially if you're right. I used to say I had two kids to look after. Dan and Danny. That there wasn't a whole lot of difference in their maturity levels. Except Danny was more reliable."

"I don't—"

"I *knew* that about Dan. I said it to other people. Said it more than once. And yet I still let Danny go out with him. I pretended that he'd act like a parent. That he'd take all the normal precautions a responsible adult would take where a little boy was concerned. And I knew better. I knew better, and I still let it happen. I always said I was the responsible one. Dan wasn't. And if I really was—" Her voice broke.

For the first time he realized she was crying. "Don't do this to yourself."

"So what does that make me, Mac? If I was the responsible parent, and we both knew it, then what the hell does that make me?"

He had sense enough to know there was nothing he could say to assuage her guilt. Despite publicly blaming her ex for what had happened to her son that night, he understood that what she was feeling right now wasn't anything new.

This was something Sarah had lived with since Danny died. This was what had driven her to the courthouse that day. This was what would make her agree to whatever Morel asked.

There wasn't a damn thing Mac could do about her decision. All he could do was be there when all of it went down.

And maybe, if he was very lucky, he'd be allowed to pick up the pieces when it was over.

Twenty-Five

The worst thing about needing space from one another was that in their situation, there was no reasonable way to get it. With Morel's warning echoing in her head, Sarah couldn't suddenly announce she was going to take a walk around the block to clear her head. Sure, she believed Mac's theory made sense. But at this point it was, as everyone kept reminding her, simply a theory.

Finally she had retreated into the kitchen, spending a few minutes looking through its limited resources before she decided on how she was going to kill a couple of hours and get away from Mac at the same time. She couldn't remember cooking much of anything since before Danny died, but maybe it was like riding a bike, because the cake she was in the process of making burnt sugar icing for actually looked edible.

"Smells good."

She looked up to find Mac leaning against one side

of the doorway watching her. She had a feeling he might have been there a while, but the tricky icing had served its purpose. She'd been concentrating on it to the exclusion of everything else.

"Thanks."

She used the back of her wrist to push a strand of hair away from her eyes. As she did, she encountered a slight dampness at her temple. Despite the cold outside, between the residual heat from the oven and standing over the stove to stir the frosting, it had gotten uncomfortably warm in here.

"My mom used to bake cakes for our birthdays," Mac said. "I'd almost forgotten how good they smell."

"Your wife didn't cook?" She kept her eyes focused on the pan as she asked, suddenly conscious of the temptation Mac represented.

"Some. When we first married. You know how that goes. You both work. Gone all day. Nobody's got time or energy when it comes to fixing dinner."

"Yeah."

The silence built while she pretended to concentrate on her icing. She fought the urge to look at him again.

"Bribe?"

That brought her head up in a hurry. Maybe she'd been wrong before, she realized. Maybe Mac hadn't been there long. He seemed to have settled into position now, ankles and arms both crossed, his left shoulder propped against the frame.

"What?"

"I asked if the cake's supposed to be a bribe?"

"For *you?*"

He laughed. "Actually, I was wondering if you were going to take it to Morel tomorrow."

"To bribe him for what? He agreed to everything I asked."

"Then...a reward, maybe."

"It isn't for Morel." She returned her attention to the contents of the pan, which were, in fact, reaching the critical stage.

"Good to know."

She looked up in time to watch him turn and walk back to the living room. After a moment the television came on. As she continued to stir, she realized he was listening to a rerun of one of the popular forensics shows. Busman's holiday.

As she cooled the icing and then worked on assembling the cake, that program morphed into another. Some kind of cop show again, more action oriented than the first.

He was still watching that one when she carried the hunk she'd cut from the finished cake into the living room. Given the passage of time between her last effort at baking and this, she had been both pleased and surprised at how well it had turned out. Not only did the slice look decent on the plate, she'd tried a sliver in the kitchen just to make sure she wasn't going to be embarrassed when he tasted it.

"I told you it wasn't for Morel." She held the plate and fork out over the arm of the sofa.

Mac made no attempt to take it. "So *is* this a bribe?"

"No, but maybe it *is* a reward."

"For what?"

"For everything, I guess. Letting me stay. For getting on board with what Morel wants to do with Tate. For doing your job."

He nodded, finally reaching for the plate.

"Maybe most of all for saying that all you care about is protecting me," she added softly.

The motion he'd begun halted while he held her eyes. "I thought you didn't *like* me saying that."

"I liked it. I just said it wasn't your job."

"Whose job is it, Sarah?"

She laughed, the sound a breath, devoid of humor. "I honestly can't remember anybody in my whole life who considered that to be their job. My mom was a little too much like Mrs. Ingersoll. Maybe that's why I recognized the type so quickly. My dad disappeared before I had time to form any clear memory of him. Growing up, *I* protected me. I wasn't always successful at that, but...I managed to get by. I survived. By the time I'd realized Dan wasn't ever going to protect anybody, that it wasn't in his nature to think along those lines, it was too late to back out of the arrangement." She cleared the note of self-pity she could hear from her voice to go on. "So...like I said, you're a first for me. I thought that was deserving of some kind of celebration." She lifted the plate slightly as if to remind him it was there.

"Thanks," he said as he took it from her.

He cut a bite off the cake and then speared it with the fork. He lifted it toward her in a small salute before he put it into his mouth.

She could tell from his face that he, too, was surprised at how good it was. Stupid, maybe, but she enjoyed the feeling that small success gave her.

"It's great," Mac said, speaking around the mouthful. "Aren't you eating any?"

"I had mine in the kitchen. I wanted to make sure that I remembered how this was done."

At some point while she put on the icing, she'd realized that the last time she'd baked a cake was for Danny's eleventh birthday. She'd bought a pan in the shape of a football and had decorated it with fleur-de-lis. She wasn't sure the four boys he'd invited over got the reference to the Saints, but they'd all liked the cake. Chocolate with chocolate icing. The last thing she'd ever baked for him.

"I think I'm going to take a shower."

Mac looked back up at that, his eyes questioning.

"I need some space," she added.

As good as last night had been, this wasn't the time for physical intimacy. Unless maybe he just wanted to hold her. And knowing men as she did…

"I understand."

"There's more in the kitchen. I couldn't find a cake saver. I'll put foil or something around it later, but if you want another piece, all you have to do is go cut it."

"Thanks. You sure you're okay?"

She nodded, not trusting herself with the lie. After all, she *would* be okay. She was used to dealing with these feelings. For the first time in three years, she wouldn't be alone while she did.

"I'm fine. Maybe we can watch some TV together. Later, I mean."

"Anything you want," he said.

For some silly reason tears threatened. "Thanks, Mac. I just need some time and space for now." She'd already begun to head toward the bedroom when she turned to add, because it was true and because he deserved to hear it, "And to know you're here."

It was a long two days before Morel called back. When he did, he asked to speak to Sarah instead of talking to him. Mac didn't like that, but he handed the phone over without comment.

"Morel. For you. You want some privacy?"

"From you? Of course not." She put the cell to her ear and took a deep breath before she said, "Sarah Patterson."

Mac waited through the silences and her occasional agreements to whatever his boss was saying, trying to figure out from her expression what that might be. He had thought if he continued to look at her, she might meet his eyes, giving him an indication of what was going on. Sarah kept her gaze downcast instead, seeming totally focused on whatever she was being told.

"And that will all be completed by tomorrow?"

Another wait. During it he could hear Morel talking, but the words were unintelligible.

"I understand. I'll tell Detective Donovan. And thank you." There was a shorter pause before she added, "We'll see you in the morning, then."

She took the phone down to press the End button before she handed it back. "Dwight and his family are being moved out of the building this afternoon. Morel was able to get them into a three-bedroom apartment in one of the new public housing units built after the hurricane. There's a decent elementary school about three blocks away. Social Services is going to help them with some additional benefits that should, with the department's help, make it all work money-wise."

"Sounds good."

Almost too good, but he didn't tell Sarah that. He'd follow up on Morel's arrangements with one of the social workers he knew, someone who had worked closely with cases involving the department.

"And he wants to see us at ten o'clock tomorrow morning in his office," she continued.

"For what?" Mac could tell by her hesitation that he wasn't going to like this and that she knew it.

"Special Agent Johnson thinks you may be right. Even if you're not…"

He waited, but she didn't complete the thought. "If I'm not?"

"They want to try to flush Tate out. Make him act."

"Because they're getting absolutely hammered in the media."

"And because the FBI believes he'll soon move on. When he does, then everybody has to start over."

"So what's the plan?"

"I'm going to do an interview with one of the local stations. The FBI is working on the script."

"An interview about Tate?"

She nodded. "About the murders. About what really happened at the courthouse that day. Finding the body in the park. The station has promised to give it lots of play. Build it up. According to Morel, the fact that I've been mentioned in the press lately should also get the interview some attention from other media outlets."

"They want you to say publicly that you tried to shoot Tate?"

"I don't know. Like I said, Johnson's still working on the script."

"We need some kind of written immunity if they ask you to do that."

She nodded, her eyes holding his as if he were supposed to have all the answers. And he didn't.

While he didn't believe Morel was a big enough snake to put those words into the interview script, ask her to say them, and then charge her for what she'd done, that wasn't to say someone else wouldn't demand she be charged. It was hard to know how the media's collective minds worked.

Like Sonny had said that morning, if Sarah had succeeded in killing Tate, everybody would be better off right now. Everyone except Sarah.

All I'm trying to do is keep you from getting hurt. He still was.

"Better than demanding immunity," he amended, "we need to make sure that part isn't included."

"But that seems to be the primary reason he'd come after me."

"Or the thing he admires most about you. I'm betting it's the latter. And to keep you from any kind of self-incrimination, you sure as hell don't need to say anything about what you did on tape."

She nodded, as if that made sense. But for the first

time since they'd begun this, he sensed her uncertainty. Which would be a far more normal attitude about trying to make a serial killer target you than the determination she'd displayed before.

"Morel says they'll want me to belittle him. To make fun of him for picking on little boys. Challenge him that it's time to pick on someone his size."

"You, in other words."

"I can do this, Mac. I know I can. I *need* to do it."

He nodded, not because he wanted her to put herself at risk, but because he'd recognized that reality. If there was ever to be any chance that Sarah Patterson could become whole again, it hinged on her taking Samuel Tate down. The psychologists would probably have a field day with that logic, but now that Mac understood her sense of guilt about Danny's death, he knew he was right.

On some level, maybe not a conscious one, she knew it, too. That's why she'd been waiting outside the courthouse that morning when they'd released her son's murderer.

Mac had stopped her because he'd thought it was the right thing to do. Because he'd been trying to protect her. This time…

This time he was going to do everything in his power to do that again. And at the same time he was also going to do everything in his power to make sure that she succeeded.

Twenty-Six

"We can stop by and pick up anything you think they'll need at Wal-Mart. We could even do that *after* we see what Mrs. Ingersoll says." Despite his disclaimer, Mac took the exit that would carry them into the heart of the seedy neighborhood where Sarah lived.

Although she wasn't looking forward to entering her apartment again, if she was going to go through with Morel's plan, she knew she'd better get used to the idea. She also knew that having all the supplies Toby would need for the next few days would go a long way in convincing Dwight's mother.

"This won't take but a minute," she said.

"She isn't going to let him keep the dog, Sarah."

"You may be right. That's why we're going out there while Dwight's still at school. If she says no, we'll let Dwight have the visit with Toby I promised the other night, and then take him to the vet."

Boarding the big dog wasn't something she wanted

to do, but Mac had been adamant about the impossibility of either of them caring for Toby, especially about taking him out for the twice-a-day necessity walks, while the operation to catch Tate was ongoing. It would be too dangerous for Sarah to attempt those without surveillance, which would add to the possibility of Tate figuring out he was being set up.

That was something she knew Mac believed was going to happen anyway. Something he might even be counting on.

"I know you're worried about leaving him at the vet's, but he'll be fine, I promise."

Despite how ridiculous she knew the comparison was, all Sarah could think about was Toby looking out at them from that cage at the Humane Society. And how much he loved his daily romp in the park.

"I know. But it won't hurt to ask Mrs. Ingersoll. All she can do is say no. You can wait for me out here," she offered, as Mac pulled up to the curb outside her apartment building.

He'd agreed with her assessment that coming back here prior to the beginning of the sting would present no problem. And he'd promised her that no one would be able to follow them from here to the Ingersolls' new address.

Of course, if Mac's theory was correct, Tate was no longer interested in Dwight. Not unless she managed to make him furious at her.

"I told you the other night, you don't have to prove anything to me," Mac said. "Toby and I are coming with you."

"You sure they haven't changed the locks?"

"That's supposed to finally happen this afternoon."

She could hear the disgust in Mac's voice that it hadn't been done when he'd asked the department to see to it after Dan's murder. Maybe, since everyone seemed to have known she wasn't living here, they'd felt there was no hurry.

Now, of course, there was. Tate wasn't stupid enough to believe she would move back into her apartment with the key she'd lent Dan still missing. That would be a dead giveaway to what they were about.

Mac handled getting Toby on his leash and out of the car. The dog took the opportunity to relieve himself on the patch of dead grass out front and then happily followed them inside. He stopped at the door to what had been the Ingersolls' ground-level apartment, looking at it as if he expected it to open.

"Not today, buddy." Mac pulled him away to head toward the stairs. Toby started putting on the brakes as soon as he realized their destination. "Somebody else who isn't eager to revisit…"

"The scene of the crime," Sarah finished when he hesitated. "Can't say I blame him." She put her hand on the dog's head. "One more time, Tobe. Then we'll find some place better than this, I promise."

She took a breath, catching Mac's eyes as she released it. She shook her head at his look of concern and preceded them up the stairs.

When she reached the top, she stepped aside to allow him to insert the key she'd given him the other night. The dog cowered behind Mac's legs as he unlocked the door.

"Poor baby." She reached down to grip Toby's collar

to drag him forward. "He really is terrified of this place."

Together they got the big dog inside. Mac closed the door, holding him while she walked into the kitchen.

She took a garbage bag out of the cabinet under the sink and began putting cans of dog food into it. When she'd finished with those, she added an unopened sack of dry food and then picked up Toby's bowls from the floor.

As she came back into the living room, she realized Mac and Toby were no longer by the front door. "Mac?"

She looked through the peephole to see if he'd taken the dog into the hall. It was possible Toby had gotten too upset being inside, but surely Mac would have said something to her first.

"Ready?"

She turned to find him coming down the hall from the bedroom, Toby close on his heels. "What were you doing?"

"Just taking a look around."

Something about Mac's face belied his explanation. He'd told her the other night that he was going to check to make sure the department had had the place cleaned up.

She'd assumed, since he hadn't said anything when he'd come back downstairs, that they had. But maybe, like replacing the locks, they hadn't yet gotten around to that either.

"Everything okay back there?"

Without thinking about what she was doing, she started toward him. Mac stopped her by reaching out to take her arm.

Shocked, she looked up into his eyes. "What's going on?"

"He's been here."

He's been here. The only possible explanation for that phrase—

"Tate?" She tried to wrench her arm away, but Mac tightened his hold.

"You don't want to go back there."

"What the hell has he done?"

Was this something to do with Danny? Like the message he'd left on her machine. Whatever it was—

"Let go, Mac." Deliberately, she kept her voice soft.

"No."

"Whatever's back there, I was meant to see. It isn't going to change anything, but… I need to know what he did."

He held her eyes for a long time, but they both knew she was right about this. If Tate had left her another message, she needed to know what it was. Maybe there was something about this one that would be as important as the one he'd given Dwight. Something that only she would understand.

Finally, Mac released her. As soon as he did, she wondered if she'd lost her mind to want to go back there. Whatever Tate had done, she should let the cops handle it. As Mac kept reminding her, that was their job. Their responsibility.

A word that seemed to be cropping up a lot lately. One that had always been the watchword of her life. And now…

She took a step forward and then another, forcing

herself to walk down the hallway. The first time she'd done it since they'd discovered Dan's body.

Another body? Was that what Mac had found?

She quickly dismissed the possibility from her mind. If this were anything like that—another child or a victim of any kind—Mac would never have let her come back here. Not alone.

This was something else. Something Tate had intended just for her. And that was the reason, of course, he'd placed whatever this was in this particular setting. The most intimate room in the apartment.

When she reached the doorway, she hesitated, aware that Mac had not left his position at the end of the hall. He had told her the night Dwight disappeared that she didn't have to prove anything to him. She still didn't. She could turn and leave now. Let someone else deal with this.

Instead, she reached out and turned on the light, fully illuminating the bedroom that had been dimmed by the closed blinds. Her gaze swept the room, no longer disordered in any way, before it returned to the one thing that was out of place.

Dwight's half-inflated pink ball sat between the two pillows on the bed. Just in case she'd had any doubt Tate had been the one who'd talked to Dwight? Had he realized during that brief conversation that the child might not be the most reliable witness?

His previous message had been intended to inform her that Dan's death had been a gift. This one apparently conveyed the same intent, just in case she hadn't gotten the memo.

And this time he was letting her know that his gift

had been exactly what she'd suspected it to be at first. He'd had Dwight in his hands and let him go. If he had so desired, it might just as easily be Dwight's body on her bed as Toby's ball.

Whatever reaction this was supposed to evoke, it seemed to have backfired. All she felt was a rage almost as great as when she'd learned Tate had killed her son.

He had murdered another innocent child just to point out to her how magnanimous he was being in letting the boy she had befriended live. If the bastard expected her to feel gratitude for that—

She took a breath, deeper than the one she'd taken prior to forcing herself down the hall. Then she marched over to the bed and snatched up the lopsided sphere, carrying it with her.

When she reached the place where Mac stood in the hallway, she picked up the garbage bag she'd filled with Toby's food and tossed the ball inside. Mac would probably have wanted the technicians to look at it. But what could any of that forensic mumbo-jumbo matter now?

They knew who their enemy was. And they both knew what they had to do to defeat him.

"This would only be for a few days." Sarah held the sack of things she'd gathered up during their trip to her apartment. "I have everything Dwight would need to look after Toby right here."

"Look, I know you mean well. And it's not that we don't appreciate what you all did for us." Dwight's mother made a vague gesture toward the living room behind the small foyer where the three of them stood. "But he's already too attached to the animal. He's doing good here. Adjusting real well." She turned to Mac, as if asking for his help in convincing Sarah.

"Dwight will be under constant surveillance until this thing is over." Whether Mac thought this was a good idea or not, if it would make the next week or so easier for Sarah, he was willing to add his powers of persuasion to hers. "The officers will go with him whenever he needs to take the dog out. I know he'd enjoy having Toby as a companion. Despite adjusting well, Dwight is in a new place without his friends."

He was aware that Sarah glanced at him when he said the last. Like him, she probably doubted that Dwight had had any friends to miss.

"I can't take the dog. It's too much responsibility for him. You both know—" Beverly Ingersoll stopped, seeming reluctant to characterize her son further. "And with my mother to look after, getting her adjusted to the new place, I have all I can handle."

Mac glanced over at the old woman, who was again watching the blaring television. She seemed oblivious to the rest of her surroundings, new or not.

"Having the responsibility would do Dwight a world of good," Mac urged. "He has to grow up sometime, Mrs. Ingersoll. And he loves Toby. He'd want to take care of him."

"It won't cost you anything," Sarah said. "If you use up the food I've brought, all you have to do is speak to the officers, and they'll resupply you."

She looked at Mac again, as if seeking his agreement. Considering that Morel had already expended so much of the department's resources on this family, he couldn't imagine those arrangements couldn't be made.

"And I'm sure the department would be willing to *pay* you whatever it would cost to have the dog boarded," Mac said. "We just feel Dwight would take better care of him than a kennel."

"They'd *pay* me to let the dog stay here?"

Mac could almost see the wheels turning behind those slightly widened eyes. Avarice might succeed where gratitude seemed to be failing.

"I'll see to it," he promised.

"Dwight would probably like to have him," the boy's mother conceded.

"If the officers see that Toby is being well taken care of, they'll give you the boarding fee. If Dwight proves incapable of looking after him, as you fear, then they'll take the dog to the kennel." That arrangement should ensure the woman wouldn't "accidentally" let Toby get lost, Mac thought.

He wasn't sure why he was so cynical about Beverly Ingersoll. She wasn't wearing the ratty bathrobe today. She was dressed and her personal grooming seemed to have vastly improved, maybe in response to their improved living conditions. Even the old woman, at least what he could see of her, seemed better cared for.

"Okay, you can leave him," the boy's mother agreed. "Dwight'll look after him. I'll see that he does. It's not good for an animal to be neglected."

"Could we wait for him?" Sarah asked, her voice hopeful.

"He's staying late today for Scouts. The troop meets there at the school. One of the officers thought it would be good if he joined. You just leave the dog and his food here, and I'll make sure Dwight understands what he needs to do."

Mac glanced at Sarah, afraid she'd protest. She nodded instead, holding the bag out.

As Mrs. Ingersoll took it, she added, "My daddy had hunting dogs when I was growing up. We lived out in the country. Better than the city. Better times, too. People weren't so wicked back then. I know what to do for dogs. I'll show Dwight."

"Thank you."

Sarah's gratitude had seemed genuine. As she turned toward the door, Mac reached out to open it for her.

"What I said the other night..." Given the subject, Mrs. Ingersoll's hesitancy was understandable. "I'm sorry. I didn't mean anything about your boy. I was just scared. Terrified that Dwight—" Surprisingly, the hoarse smoker's-voice broke. "I'm sorry."

For a moment neither of them moved. Then Sarah reached out to put her hand over that of the other woman. "I know. Keep him safe."

Beverly Ingersoll's chin quivered. "I know you all don't think much of me. I don't think too much of myself," she said with a watery laugh. "But...Dwight's all I've got. Whether you believe it or not, I love him. And I do try. It's just so hard sometimes."

Sarah nodded, squeezing the hand she held. Then she released it and opened the door, stepping outside before Mac could get there.

"I'll explain everything to the officers," Mac said as he handed over Toby's leash. "Don't worry. They'll take care of both of them."

As he closed the door, he knew the vision of Beverly Ingersoll, Toby's leash in one hand, his supplies in the other, with her senile mother rocking in the background, would ensure that he didn't forget to make those arrangements.

Twenty-Seven

"Most serial killers were victims themselves at some time in their lives. According to the FBI, Tate was, too. They think that's why he continues to act out the pattern of abuse he was subjected to. He was brutalized as a child by someone older and stronger. That's what Tate does to his victims. He's totally incapable of sustaining any kind of adult relationship, so that's really all he can do." Sarah seemed to look directly into the camera as she said the last. "He's nothing but an impotent coward who targets defenseless little boys like my son."

"You're convinced Tate's still in this area?"

Tall and dark, the female reporter made a good foil for Sarah's size and coloring, almost emphasizing her physical fragility. A fragility that would surely resonate with the station's viewers. Mac wondered cynically if Johnson had advised the department about that, too.

"Both the FBI and the New Orleans police believe

he is. There's no doubt that the boy found in this park was murdered by the same man who killed my son."

The two of them were standing near the oak where that body had been found. The reporter had already gone into Sarah's role in its discovery.

"How did the police determine that? I understand this isn't anything like the usual locations where Tate leaves his victims."

"No, it isn't. However, the methodology used in this killing was exactly the same as in the others."

Although this part of the interview sounded rehearsed, Mac thought Sarah had made all the points she'd been instructed to make. And in spite of the fact that he was admittedly prejudiced, he thought she'd come across as both sympathetic and strong. The only time her emotional vulnerability had been evident had been when the reporter questioned her specifically about the circumstances surrounding Danny's death.

"So they expect him to strike again?"

Mac wondered if that question had been in the script. The probability that Tate would kill again wasn't one the department would want to dwell on.

Sarah nodded. "Some other child. Another little boy. Tate doesn't have the guts to do anything else."

On the advice of Daryl Johnson, they had avoided any mention of the murder of Sarah's ex-husband. After the discovery of the last victim virtually across the street from Sarah's apartment, there was little doubt in anyone's mind that Tate had been the perpetrator. For the purposes of this interview, however, tying Tate to an adult's death did them no good.

"Although there was a lot of media coverage when you confronted Tate at the courthouse the morning after his hearing, you've kept a relatively low profile since your son's death. So why speak up now, Mrs. Patterson?"

"Since the FBI discovered Tate's real identity, there's been an attempt by some in the media to portray *him* as a victim. As just another abused child. They've said those things as if that excuses what he's done. I just want to remind everyone that nobody murdered Samuel Tate when he was a child. Maybe, as they say, he *was* sexually molested. If so, I'm sorry for that, as I would be sorry for any child in that situation. But you have to remember that Tate got to live out his life. My son didn't. He was only eleven years old when Tate kidnapped, tortured, and then killed him. Any sympathy anyone has should be directed toward Danny and Tate's other victims and certainly not toward a cruel, spineless monster like their murderer."

The camera cut away from Sarah's impassioned face and back to the reporter as she finished up the segment. "Sarah Patterson has shared her personal nightmare with our viewers because she doesn't want the focus to be on anyone other than the true victims of these crimes—the more than a dozen little boys Samuel Tate has murdered in various locations around the country, including here in the greater New Orleans area. The N.O.P.D., who are working in conjunction with other agencies, both locally and nationally, are devoting a huge percentage of their manpower and resources to the ongoing search for this dangerous serial killer. If you have any information that might be helpful, please call the number that appears on the bottom of your screen. In the meantime, we'll continue to cover this developing story for you. Back to you, Andrea."

After the cameraman signaled the jump back to the studio had been successful, the reporter leaned forward to give Sarah a hug. Whatever words the two exchanged were too low for Mac to hear, but he knew Sarah had felt a rapport with the woman during their first interview.

Maybe that's why they'd been able to arrange this second one so quickly. That and the media's still-intense interest in rehashing the ineptness of the police in Tate's bungled arrest.

As Sarah approached the spot where he was standing, Mac smiled at her. "Good job."

"I embellished on the FBI's text a little. Your profiler friend might not approve."

"You got the spirit of it right. I don't think anybody is going to object to you calling Tate a monster."

"Except—hopefully—Tate. How soon do you think we can expect some reaction?"

The first interview had been three days ago. Sarah had gone back to work and back to the apartment two days before that. Morel had kept to the plan, rotating a small group of undercover officers in and out of the old building in the guise of doing renovations on the now-empty downstairs apartment.

Mac had moved in there the same day Sarah had once again begun living upstairs. The cameras were in place in her apartment, and he'd spent the last five nights watching Sarah sleep, all the while thinking about the times they'd done that together in his bed.

So far, there had been no reaction from Tate. In all honesty, Mac wouldn't be surprised if there never was one. He couldn't believe Tate wouldn't recognize Sarah's taunting for exactly what it was.

"Johnson may have given Morel some kind of guess on a timetable," he said aloud. "If so, nobody's mentioned it to me."

Sarah took a breath, turning to look at the television crew who were in the process of packing up their equipment. "I wish this was over."

"We've done what we can. Nobody can force Tate to react. There's no guarantee he's even seeing these interviews. He could be a thousand miles away from here by now."

Sarah turned back, her eyes meeting his. Their color seemed intensified by the paleness of her face, as did that faint dusting of freckles across the bridge of her nose.

"He's still here, Mac. I can feel him."

That was a little too new age for him. He would have thought it would be for someone as pragmatic as Sarah, but he didn't argue with her. He was aware, as he had been since all this had gone into play, of the effort she was making to maintain control.

"Then I hope he heard every word you said."

"No matter what, promise me you'll get him, Mac. Promise me."

"I'm going to do my best. I can promise you that, Sarah. All he has to do is give me the chance."

Tate didn't, however. Not in the remainder of that week. Nor through the next.

During the third week of the operation, Mac realized he'd become a prisoner of the role he'd chosen. He spent his days tossing and turning on a cot in the back bedroom of the downstairs apartment while the fake workmen hammered and painted and traipsed in and out of its front door.

While someone else looked out for Sarah.

He awakened a dozen times a day, drawn out of what passed now for sleep by nightmare images of Tate doing to Sarah what he had done to the children he'd murdered. After those dreams, he would lie awake, listening for the other cops to leave and for the front door to open so he could track her footsteps as she went upstairs.

When she reached the apartment on the third floor, she always called his cell. Since the department listened in on everything coming in or going out on her land line, the message, too, was always the same. *I'm home.* Short, to the point, and impersonal.

As hard as it was to know that during the day she was out in the world where Tate could get to her, it was almost harder to endure the nights, knowing she was only a couple of flights of stairs away. He could watch her prepare her solitary dinner from the department-stocked items in the freezer of her refrigerator. He could watch her undress for bed. He could even watch her sleep.

Watch her…

He walked over to the kitchen counter and poured one of the dozen cups of coffee he would consume tonight. The heavy caffeine intake might explain why his sleep was so broken during the daylight hours, but he couldn't risk changing the cycle he'd now established. He didn't sleep well during the day, so he needed the jolt the coffee gave in order to stay awake at night. After all, Sarah's life depended on him doing that.

He carried the mug back to the fold-up table where they'd set up the monitors. He was in the act of putting the coffee down on the morning paper someone had left in the apartment today, when, out of habit, he glanced at the screen.

Sarah was not in bed. The covers had been thrown back, and the pillow still carried the imprint of her head, clearly revealed by the camera.

Bathroom, he thought. She's gone to the bathroom.

Despite that logical explanation, a knot of cold fear formed in Mac's stomach. He didn't take his eyes off the monitor, willing her to appear in the doorway to the bath.

What seemed like an eternity of seconds ticked off in his head before he realized he hadn't thought to look at his watch as soon as he'd discovered she wasn't in bed. He had no idea how long he'd been waiting. However long it was, it was more than time enough for Sarah to go to the bathroom and return.

Maybe she was sick. Or maybe—

Unwilling to play that guessing game, Mac bolted for the front door, unholstering his weapon as he ran. Morel had assigned an unmarked patrol car to this block. Should he call for backup or simply follow his instinct and get upstairs as fast as he could?

He went with his training, jerking his cell out of the

case on his belt. He flipped it open, and then, with the same hand in which he held the phone, worked the locks to throw open the door.

Sarah stood on the threshold. She physically recoiled when the door opened, her shock as great as his at finding her outside.

His eyes searched her face before they quickly lifted to scan the foyer behind her. Nothing—no one—was out there. Nor was anyone on the stairs leading up to her apartment.

Whatever was going on, whatever had brought her here, the first thing he needed to do was get her inside. He reached out and, still encumbered by the cell he held, pulled her into the apartment by putting his arm around her shoulders.

He propelled her on past him and into the living room. He closed and locked the door before he turned to question, "What's wrong?"

"Nothing. I—"

"Sarah?"

"Nothing. I woke up and thought about you being down here and me being up there. I just thought…" She crossed her arms over her body, hunching her shoulders. "I'm sorry, Mac. I didn't mean to frighten you. It's stupid, I know, but I just wanted…" She shook her head again. "I don't know what I wanted."

"You're okay? You sure?"

She nodded. He snapped his phone closed, causing her to jump at the sound.

"I thought he was here." Fear made his voice too harsh.

"Tate?"

"I got up to get some coffee and when I went back to the monitors, you weren't in bed. I was on my way up there. I was about to call for backup." He held up his cell to her, as if to make his point.

"I'm sorry. I didn't think. I just woke up and… I didn't want to be alone."

"This isn't part of the deal."

"What?"

"With Morel. Nobody's supposed to know there's anyone *in* this apartment."

"Nobody does. There's no one out there, Mac. I looked before I came downstairs."

"The department's put a lot of time and effort and money into this plan, Sarah. You agreed to it. You can't risk everything now because you can't sleep."

"Who's going to know, Mac? Who's ever going to know that I came down here?"

"Sarah—"

"Isn't there *just* as much danger of someone seeing me go back upstairs? What's an hour spent together going to hurt anything? I'll be careful, I promise. I *was* careful."

"That isn't the point."

"I *know* the point, Mac. I get it. But…I'm not sure I can do this anymore."

The confession she'd just made was, no doubt, a sign of her desperation. Still, Mac knew her well enough to know that she'd never forgive herself if she blew this.

It was up to him to help her through whatever emotional upheaval she was experiencing right now. That's what he'd signed on to do, even if he hadn't been on board with the original concept.

"Every stakeout's like this," he said. "Every one of them. The waiting. The boredom. The sense that you're wasting your time."

"I can't even do my job. I can't remember what people order. I can't think anymore."

"You don't have to. All you have to do is wait. Tate's the one we want to be thinking."

"Morel thinks I should do another interview."

Mac wasn't sure how the captain had communicated that suggestion. Maybe by phone. Or through one of the cops who guarded her during the day. However the message had been sent, he wasn't thrilled about being left out of the loop.

"How do you feel about that?"

"I just want this to be over. Do you think he's gone?"

He was beginning to wonder. In some ways that would be good news. In others, at least as far as his relationship with Sarah was concerned, it wouldn't be. She, even more than the police, needed closure with Tate. The only way for her to get that was if he were dead or behind bars.

"I don't know," he admitted.

"So how much longer will they make us wait for him to do something?"

Sarah's use of the word *us* had probably been unconscious. Or maybe she wasn't thinking of the two of them in any way other than their working together. Which was all they were supposed to be doing right now.

"You'll have to ask Morel. Right now—" He hesitated, because her eyes had come up. "Right now, you need to go back upstairs. And you need to stay there. As far as the world is concerned, this is an empty apartment. If anybody sees you coming to this door, *anybody* in this building, then this operation is over. And with it, so is any chance to trap Tate. You don't want that, Sarah. Neither do I. We need to at least give this our best effort."

"Five minutes. That's all I'm asking. I just need somebody to talk to."

"Sarah—"

"What difference can it make whether I go upstairs now or five minutes from now? If anybody saw me come down, the damage is done. But they didn't, Mac. I swear. I looked. It's three o'clock in the morning. Even in this dump nobody's up at that hour."

He couldn't argue with her logic. Either she'd been seen or she hadn't, and there was nothing now he could do about it either way.

"What do you want to talk about?"

"I don't care. Just…talk. Talk to me."

It would have been much smarter if he'd done what she told him to do. Smarter. More professional. Whatever.

Instead, he slipped his weapon back into the shoulder holster and walked over to where she stood. Her head lifted, chin tilting upward as he approached.

By the time he got there, her lips had parted. They were at the perfect angle for him to lower his head and put his own over them.

Her arms fastened around his neck, just as they had the last time he'd held her. Her kiss revealed the same pent-up hunger he'd fought through those long, lonely nights as he'd stared at the monitor while she slept.

He had already acknowledged that letting her stay wouldn't be the smartest thing he'd ever done. But by God, now that she was here, there was no way in hell that he wasn't going to assuage the desire that virtually vibrated through her body.

As well as assuage his own…

Twenty-Eight

The sounds were so familiar that, although Mac heard them, they didn't cause him to react. Every morning he'd been here, he had heard the noise Morel's men made as they unloaded their tools from their utility trucks in preparation for coming into the apartment they were supposedly in the process of renovating.

With the second clank of metal against metal, however, his eyes opened. They went immediately to the heavily curtained front window, the same one through which Dwight had waved at him that first day.

A thread of silver outlined the edges of its covering. *Morning.*

On the heels of that realization came another. Sarah's body was still spooned next to his on the pile of drop cloths he'd arranged on the hardwood floor for the makeshift bed they'd made love on.

"Get up," he urged, scrambling to his feet.

Despite the darkness in the apartment, he located his jeans. Hopping first on one leg and then the other, he struggled into them. Fumbling around on the floor, he finally found his shirt. He'd pulled it off last night without unbuttoning it. Getting it back on without taking time to do that now was considerably more difficult.

"What's wrong?" Sarah sat up, looking around with the befuddlement of someone too suddenly awakened from a sound sleep.

"The day shift is outside."

Mac wasn't sure if she grasped all the implications of their mistake. He wasn't certain he did either.

He did know that if Morel got wind that Sarah had spent the night down here, he was going to be royally pissed. Maybe angry enough to renege on the deal he'd made with Sarah to let Mac have this particular duty.

The white nightgown he'd helped her take off last night was easy to find despite the lack of light. He scooped it off the floor and tossed it toward her. Sarah made no move to pick it up, simply looking up at him as if she still wasn't sure what was going on.

"Get dressed," he ordered.

"What are you going to do?"

"Stall them. I'll keep them outside while you get up the stairs."

She nodded, finally reaching out to pull the gown towards her. He didn't stop to watch her put it on. He walked over to the window instead, carefully easing back the covering enough to see the street outside.

One of the now-familiar white trucks was parked at

the curb. An officer, disguised as a workman, was unloading items out of its bed into a carpenter's carry-all.

Mac let the drape fall over the window again before he turned back to Sarah, who had finally gotten to her feet. She was still holding her nightgown to the front of her body. Eyes wide, she was watching his every move.

"Give me a couple of minutes to engage him in conversation. Then crack the door and make sure the foyer's clear. If it is, get back upstairs."

"Should I pick this up?" She indicated the pallet of painters' cloths where they'd made love.

"Leave it. It doesn't matter."

The important thing was for him to get outside before the officer entered the building. Once that happened, there would be no way Sarah could escape upstairs without being seen.

As he crossed the room, Mac picked up his weapon from where it lay on the floor next to his side of the "bed." He shrugged into the holster as he approached the door.

Through the peephole, he checked out the foyer. From this less-than-perfect vantage point, it appeared to be empty. Faintly, from outside, he heard something that sounded like the lift gate on the truck being slammed shut, pushing him into action.

He slipped the .38 out and opened the apartment door. Leading with his weapon, he took a single step forward, visually scanning the areas he hadn't been able to see through the fish-eye view offered by the peephole.

When he'd verified that the foyer was empty, he glanced over his shoulder to nod to Sarah, who was still hovering on the pile of drop cloths. He gestured her forward with his left hand before he stepped through the door and then closed it behind him.

He reholstered his weapon as he walked toward the front entrance, trying to think of some plausible reason that might have sent him out to meet the arriving workmen. Something that would also keep them outside for the next few vital seconds.

When he opened the outer door of the building, the cold was like a physical force, especially after the near-fetid warmth of the foyer. Despite having closed the truck's lift gate, the cop he'd seen through the window was hunkered down beside the carry-all, fiddling with his tools. As he did, he whistled, the sound low and tuneless.

Maybe he was waiting for the rest of the crew to show up. If so, Mac might not have to come up with a story that would keep him outside. He eased a breath in relief as he walked down the sidewalk toward where the man stooped.

"Morning," he called, his breath feathering in front of him in a small, white cloud.

The policeman didn't respond. Once away from the wire-caged lights on either side of the building's entry, Mac realized it was earlier than he'd thought.

No wonder the cop was waiting for the rest of the crew to show. It was barely daylight. With that thought a sliver of unease touched Mac's spine.

Through the window of the downstairs apartment he

had watched the officers assigned to play workmen go through this drill a dozen times. They parked in this exact spot. Unloaded tools from the back of the truck, just as this guy was doing. Wore that same white coverall...

Despite that litany of sameness, the radar Mac had acquired through his years in this job told him something wasn't right. He'd reached the curb before that conviction grew strong enough to cause him to reach toward the butt of the .38 that protruded from his shoulder holster. It was a motion he would never complete.

As if he had eyes in the back of his head, the workman bending beside the workbox sprang to his feet at the same instant Mac's forward progress began to slow. There was no hesitation on his part.

Unlike Mac, he had known what was about to happen. He'd been prepared for it.

As the man sprang up, he brought with him whatever he'd been concealing at his feet. He swung the object in a lethal arc, one which had begun with his first movement.

The end of what he held connected with the bent elbow of Mac's right arm. The hand that had been reaching for his weapon went numb, but his mind seemed to be processing information at warp speed.

The dark, thin face of the man who wielded what he'd now identified as a shovel was instantly recognizable. Mac barreled into him, trying to grab at the implement before Tate could hit him with it again. In response the killer raised the wrench he'd concealed in his other hand and brought it down in a vicious blow against the side of Mac's head.

Mac struggled to hold on to consciousness as the air thinned and then blackened around him. His good hand fastened on the lapel of Tate's coverall, fingers digging into its fabric in a futile attempt to hold himself upright.

The wrench was raised once more. Although Mac was distantly aware of its descent, mercifully he was not aware as it once more connected with his temple.

When Mac closed the door, leaving Sarah alone, his action seemed to destroy the paralysis created by being jerked out of the first sound sleep she'd managed in almost three weeks. She realized that she was still pressing her nightgown against her breasts. She held it out before her, trying to orient the garment so she could slip it over her head.

It was wrong-side out, no doubt the result of Mac's help in removing it last night. Fingers trembling in haste, she reversed it and then put it on.

As she stepped off the pile of drop sheets, she saw Mac's T-shirt and briefs lying beside them on the floor. She stooped, gathered them up, and then pushed them under the edge of the stack.

It wasn't until she'd reached the door to the apartment that she realized her mistake. This place would be full of policemen in a few minutes. It was entirely possible someone other than Mac would separate and then move the painters' cloths. If they did, wouldn't they wonder what Mac's underwear was doing underneath them?

She looked back at the pile Mac had told her to leave alone. Even without the evidence of the clothing, it would be obvious what they'd been used for.

She knew there was bad blood between Mac and his supervisor. All Morel would need to hear was that Mac had been sleeping on the job and the deal she and his boss had made would be moot.

She crossed the room again, conscious as she did of the precious seconds ticking away. Mac had said to give him a couple of minutes. She wasn't sure if he'd meant her to take that time frame literally, but surely he would keep the cop outside long enough for her to do something about the cloths.

She pulled the top one off the stack, dragging it as quickly as she could toward the kitchen. Since Mac had brought them into the living room, she wasn't sure of where they'd been previously. Maybe whoever had been assigned to work here yesterday wouldn't remember either.

Aware of the passage of time, she rearranged the drop sheets quickly, spreading them throughout the two rooms. As she worked, she listened for the distinctive creak the front door of the building made. She left what had been the bottom sheet in place in the middle of the living room, retrieving the underwear from beneath it. Then, bunching the clothing up in her hand, she headed back toward the apartment door.

Maybe she'd been slow on the uptake when Mac had left, but she understood his urgency now. She'd forced Morel's hand to get Mac reinstated. The captain wouldn't hesitate to suspend him again if he had any idea what they'd done last night.

As Mac had, she looked out through the peephole. There was no one in the foyer. She turned the dead bolt and then the knob, opening the door wide enough to allow her to see the main entrance.

As she peered through the crack, the door to the building began to open. Panicked, Sarah eased hers closed again.

Mac? It had to be, she reasoned. He wouldn't let anyone else inside. Not without giving her warning. If any of the workmen had entered the building with him, he would be talking to them, loudly enough to be sure she'd hear.

Although she listened, her ear pressed against the wood, no further sound came from the foyer. There had been none after that familiar snick of the mechanism of the entryway door engaging.

Another tenant leaving? It was possible, she supposed, except that after living here all these months, she knew their habits. No one in the building got up this early. Or came home this late.

Which left the question as to who had come through the front door. She stood on tiptoe, putting her eye against the peephole again.

The foyer still appeared deserted. If Mac *were* out there, he would either have come into the apartment by now or he would have said something to her. Called her name. Done something to let her know it was him.

She took a step away from the door. At the continuing silence, fear of something other than Morel's displeasure began to coil in her gut.

Why couldn't she see whoever had come in? Was he hiding from her? *And if so, why?*

There wasn't a single possible answer to that

question she liked. She took another step back, trying to decide whether to reach out and throw the dead bolt.

Its sound would give away to anyone outside that the apartment was occupied. If whoever had come in the front door was not one of the officers, however, it would provide an extra barrier of protection.

Suddenly she realized that she didn't know whether or not the dead bolt could be unlocked with the key that worked the main lock. The chain around Dwight's neck had held only one. The fact that the boy came and went while both his mother and grandmother were inside the apartment argued that the dead bolt could be manipulated with the same key.

The locks hadn't been changed when the police took over the apartment. She would have noticed. The faux-brass shine of the new ones they'd installed on her apartment upstairs were a dead giveaway.

Dead...

She ignored the mental echo as her mind sorted through the possibilities. Morel's decoy workmen, at least some of them, would have been given keys. Mac would too, since he'd been staying here.

That had probably been in the pocket of the jeans he'd slipped on before he'd gone outside. If Mac wasn't with whoever was out there...

As if the last piece of some difficult puzzle had suddenly fallen into place, she knew who was outside the door. And if she was right, he would have Mac's key.

From the time she'd spent here on the night Dwight had gone missing, she knew there was no back entrance to this apartment. There were only the front door and the windows, which, if they were like those in her apartment, had been painted over so many times they'd be impossible to open.

She hesitated, unable to decide if it would be better to go out into the foyer to confront Tate there or stay where she was. Even if she somehow managed to get past him and escape out the front door, he'd come after her. If she screamed for help, would anyone in this neighborhood get up and come outside in response to her cries? Would they even bother to call the police?

At least here there was a door between them. Some kind of barrier.

One to which he has the key.

Somewhere to hide.

Empty rooms with no furniture in them to offer the possibility of concealment.

Something to use as a weapon against him.

Something? When every item that would normally be in a home had been packed and moved with the Ingersolls? There would be no wooden block of butcher knives in the kitchen. No shears. No ice pick.

But the officers assigned as workmen had left things here, she realized. Like the drop cloths she and Mac had used last night.

The sound of a key being inserted in the lock made the decision for her. If she were going to find something that could be used as a weapon, it would be here rather than in the foyer.

Twenty-Nine

Acting instinctively, Sarah avoided the exposed kitchen, running for the back of the apartment instead. The room Dwight had shared with his grandmother was the first she came to in the short, dark hall.

She ran past it, heading for the smaller room, the one Mrs. Ingersoll had used. Maybe there would be a privacy lock on its door. Something—anything—that might give her a few more seconds. Then she stopped, so suddenly her bare feet skidded over the wooden floor.

As she'd passed Dwight's bedroom, her brain had subliminally recorded the existence of another stack of drop cloths, similar to the ones Mac had piled together in the living room. And beyond them, some unidentifiable shape had been silhouetted against the light seeping into the room from the single window.

She reversed directions, sliding into the larger of the two bedrooms just as the front door opened, the creak seeming to echo throughout the empty apartment. She closed the bedroom door, which she discovered had no privacy lock, probably because of the mental condition of Dwight's grandmother.

In the dimness, she frantically pushed aside the drop cloths to get to whatever else the cops had left here. Since all the work on this apartment was bogus, everything the department brought in and out during the last three weeks would have been for show. Despite the fact that they were part of the deception, however, the tools themselves had been real.

A wooden carry-all she discovered partially hidden under the plastic yielded a hammer. She laid it out as she continued to search for something that wouldn't require her to match Tate's longer reach in order to use it against him.

Physically, she was no match for the bastard. Mentally…

Still sorting through the tools, she remembered those long, sleepless nights before she'd gone to the courthouse. Nights when she'd imagined killing him. Had dreamed about it. A hundred times in her mind she'd visualized his head exploding as the bullets she'd fired from Dan's gun impacted.

Tate was nothing more than an animal. A vicious, brutal coward who had murdered more than a dozen children. But he'd never been driven to kill any of them as strongly as she'd felt compelled to try to put an end to his existence.

She moved away from the carry-all, having exhausted its possibilities. In the darkness, her fingers brailled a band saw. Although she was familiar with its operation from the years she'd worked with Dan to build up his father's business, she couldn't imagine how she might use this to kill Tate.

Air sobbing in and out of her lungs, she crawled over to the next object, carrying the hammer with her. Despite the noise she herself was making moving over the plastic sheets, she imagined she could hear Tate moving around the apartment, a soft scuffling sound that came from beyond the bedroom door.

She tried to control her breathing as she ran her fingers over the remaining objects. As she touched the last of them, her heart began to race.

She knew instantly what she'd found. More importantly, she knew how to use it.

Discarding the hammer, she examined the nail gun by touch, familiarizing herself with the model. Which, to her relief, was very much like the one she'd used during those long summers when she'd worked shoulder to shoulder with Dan.

And then, on top of that realization came another. Tate was outside the bedroom door.

She didn't know why she was so sure. She couldn't see him. She hadn't heard anything outside clearly enough to be this certain. All the same, she knew he was there.

Maybe the evil that emanated from him was that strong. Because she also knew the second his hand closed around the knob.

The door opened, the squeak of its hinges subtle in the darkness. She laid her finger over the trigger. And for the first time she realized that, since it had never really been intended for use within these walls, her weapon might not be loaded.

It was too late to look for anything else. Like that morning on the courthouse steps, all that was left for her was to act. *Shoot. Don't talk.*

A shape, far less distinct than those that had attracted her attention here, was coming toward her. His progress across the room seemed incredibly quick. The distance between them had been cut in half by the time she got her weapon into position.

Although she couldn't be certain what would happen when she pulled the trigger, she aimed at the widest part of her attacker's body. She placed one finger against the guard, an awkward positioning, but one which would have the same effect on the firing mechanism as if she were pressing the gun against a board.

Lesson learned from her last, failed attempt, she didn't open her mouth, allowing her finger to squeeze the trigger instead. For some reason she would never understand and could not possibly have explained, whoever had left the nail gun here had taken time to insert a coil of nails.

She could feel the small percussion as they were fired. The rushing figure now seemed to loom above her, but she continued to apply a steady pressure against the trigger.

She had no idea how rapidly or how powerfully this model was capable of spitting out missiles, considering her misuse of its design. All she knew was that Tate's forward progress suddenly faltered.

He changed directions, staggering against the wall. Encouraged, she continued to fire, refusing to think about what the nails could do to flesh and bone.

Nor could she think about Danny. Not even about Mac.

She had to finish this first. Only when it was over—

She jerked her mind away from that thought. She couldn't afford to think about anything beyond what she was doing—directing the hail of missiles that followed the man who now careened from one side of the room to the other as she targeted him.

Suddenly the gun went quiet. For a second or two she continued to press the trigger, but nothing happened.

The coil of nails had been used up. And unless she wanted to search through the items she'd scattered around in her haste to find this one…

As she waited, the silence in the room was almost complete. She could hear her own breathing.

And then, when she held her breath, she could hear Tate's. Ragged. Almost gasping.

She kept her empty weapon pointed at her son's murderer as he leaned against the wall. In the few minutes it had taken her to find and then empty the nail gun, the bedroom had grown lighter. She could see her son's murderer more clearly now.

After a long time he put his right hand flat against the wall. As if that effort were far more exhausting than he'd expected, Tate seemed to rest a moment, gathering strength, before he straightened his elbow, pushing himself upright.

Black splotches covered the front of the white

coverall. His body had even left a smear of darkness on the pale wall. Still, he managed one swaying step and then another.

Despite his injuries, he was coming for her. Sarah lifted her eyes from his blood-soaked clothing to focus on his face.

Contorted by pain and effort, his features bore little resemblance to those of the man she'd accosted on the courthouse steps. Only one thing seemed the same. His unwavering determination to claim another victim.

Not me, you bastard. You've taken enough from me. More than enough. And now, when I've finally found something to make life worth living again...

She blocked that unwanted admission. She didn't know if Mac were dead or alive. All she knew was that she was. And that she wouldn't allow Tate to steal her life from her, too. Not if she had to finish him off with her bare hands.

She laid the nail gun down and scrambled to her feet. The growing light from the window behind her revealed the hammer she'd found first lying in front of her.

Her eyes never left the man who continued his staggering progress toward her, one hand over the spreading red stain on his torso, the other clutching the knife he might have used to butcher her son. As she watched his approach, she raised the hammer, prepared to fight him to the death.

Suddenly Tate stopped, gripping the blood-soaked fabric that covered his chest. His mouth opened, so that for a heartbeat she thought he was going to say something to her.

Shoot. Don't talk.

Instead, he leaned forward, a froth of bloody fluid pouring from his mouth. She backed away, her gaze automatically lowering to watch as it splattered over the white drop cloths at her feet.

When she lifted her eyes again, Tate was in the process of falling forward. He made no attempt to break his fall, hitting the floor face-first. The knife he'd held landed near her feet.

Hammer raised, she waited, expecting him to move again. To get up. To do something.

Unable to believe it was finally over, she edged around him, avoiding both the blood and the weapon he might have used on Danny.

And on Mac? Had he used that same knife to kill Mac?

The question mattered far more to her than whether or not Tate was dead. If he wasn't, he soon would be. Either here and now or by the State's command. And either way…

That wasn't nearly as important as getting to Mac.

She had tried so hard not to care. To keep him as well as the feelings he evoked at a distance. She had never wanted to love him because she knew what happened to everything she'd ever loved in her life.

Please, God, don't take Mac, too, she prayed as she ran through the echoing rooms of the empty apartment.

Please, dear God, don't take it all away from me again.

Thirty

There was no good reason for Tate to have left Mac alive. As she ran, Sarah couldn't think of a single scenario that would make that action plausible. And no reason to hope Tate had done anything other than what he'd done in every other situation in his entire life: destroy whatever lay in his path.

Yet she still ran. She threw open the front entrance to the building, letting the door bang back against the brick facade.

The tiny apron of winter-dead grass that served as the complex's landscaping lay empty before her. As did the sidewalk and the street. If Mac were out here somewhere—

"Mac?" And then louder. "Mac? Answer me."

Her breath caught on a sob, but her eyes were dry. Her tears had been used up during the past three years so that now, in this final betrayal, there were none left.

She had known that if she loved him, this would

happen. Yet once again she'd fallen victim to the hope that it would be different. That this time—

She stopped at the end of the walkway, the emptiness of the street a reflection of her own. "Mac?"

The wind carried the sound of his name away as soon as she uttered it. She turned her head, looking at the vacant lot next door. Would Tate have dragged him there? Would he have taken time?

The word reverberated. How much time had elapsed since Mac walked outside?

Her eyes went back to the utility truck. A carpenter's carry-all sat on the sidewalk beside the left rear wheel. Between that and the tire, as if it might have been dropped in the killer's rush to get inside, lay a spill of white.

Drop cloth, she realized as she drew closer to the vehicle. One exactly like those inside.

Most of it lay in the gutter, trailing under the truck, but part of it had caught under the toolbox. Only when it fluttered in the next cold draught did she grasp the significance of that. The wooden carry-all had been placed on top of the plastic to hold it in place.

She dragged the toolbox off and onto the grass. Then she knelt beside the drop sheet.

Even this close, it was difficult to tell that the cloth hid something because its plastic, stiffened by the freezing temperature, was bunched against the tire. From the vantage point of a passing car, it would have been impossible.

Hands trembling, she reached out and lifted the edge of the sheet. Beneath it, Mac lay on his side, his back to her, his body curved into a near-fetal position.

"Mac." She whispered his name because it was obvious he wouldn't answer.

She pushed the drop cloth further back, stretching forward so she could see his face. In the pale winter sunlight it looked gray and lifeless.

The hair at his temple was matted with blood. It had run down into his ear and then onto his neck, pooling finally on the pavement.

She touched his head, her first instinct to succor him. Then, steeling herself, she put her fingers under his jawline, feeling for a pulse.

After a moment she closed her eyes, her body sagging in relief. Beneath the sticky warmth of the blood on his neck, she could feel a heartbeat. In her admitted inexperience, it seemed strong and steady.

Mac was alive. And it was up to her to keep him that way.

She began to search his clothing for his cell, gingerly at first and then with a greater urgency. She found it in his shirt pocket.

Hands shaking, this time in haste, she slipped the phone out and opened the case. She punched in 9-1-1 with her thumb, her other hand resting on Mac's hair.

"Just a few more minutes, baby," she whispered as she listened to the rings. "Just hold on and somebody will be here. Just a few more minutes, I promise you."

"I realize this is probably not the best time..." Captain Morel lifted his brows questioningly.

Why not? Sarah acknowledged. The sooner she gave them what they wanted to know, the sooner she could get back to the only thing that was important. Besides, answering Morel's questions might help occupy the endless hours while Mac underwent the surgery necessary to repair the damage Tate had inflicted.

She gestured toward the plastic-covered couch opposite her chair. Mac's boss glanced at Sonny Cochran, who'd been hovering beside his elbow, before they both awkwardly sat down on it. For a long time neither of them spoke.

Into that uncomfortable silence Sarah finally asked the question she'd wondered about since she'd had time to think of anything other than making sure Mac survived. Now that was out of her hands. And beyond her control.

"Is he dead?"

Morel's mouth opened and then closed. Then he glanced at Sonny, who shrugged.

"You didn't know?"

"If I knew, I wouldn't have asked."

"Believe me, Mrs. Patterson, Tate is dead."

She nodded. One less thing to think about. Maybe, given the situation, that wasn't necessarily a good thing.

"Can you tell us what happened?"

She considered lying to him. Not because she cared what Morel thought about her, but because she wasn't sure how the truth would affect Mac.

Still, coming up with a plausible explanation for why she had been in the downstairs apartment was something she hadn't had time to think about. Besides, what possible difference could any of that make now?

"I couldn't sleep, so I'd gone downstairs some time

before dawn. I don't know...maybe three o'clock. Maybe a little later. Mac didn't want me to stay, but I begged him to let me. I just didn't want to be upstairs alone."

As she said the words, she wondered if she'd had some premonition of what Tate was planning. Just as she had known he was outside the apartment door—had sensed his evil—had she known he was going to choose that night, after all the other nights they'd waited on him, to come?

"Something woke Mac at daylight. He thought it was the workmen. He didn't want them to come in and find me in the apartment, so he went outside to meet them. He told me to give him a couple of minutes and then to go upstairs, but...when I opened the door of the apartment, someone was coming in the entrance to the complex."

She stopped, realizing how near a thing that had been. And Tate had already made sure Mac wouldn't be able to help her.

"I thought it was Mac, but when he didn't say anything, I looked out the peephole. The foyer was empty. I thought it might have been some of the other officers." She stopped, shaking her head at the memory. "I waited a little while for them to come into the apartment, wondering why Mac hadn't stopped them outside. And then...then I knew who was out there."

"You knew it was Tate?"

"If it had been Mac, he would have said something. And he would never have let the others come in with me there without giving me some warning, so... I knew it had to be Tate. And I knew he'd have Mac's key. I thought about trying to get out of the building past him, but..." She shook her head again, thinking about that choice, too. "I decided to try to find something in the apartment to use against him."

Those minutes of terror while she had looked replayed in her memory. And when she'd found her weapon...

"At first the only thing I could find was a hammer, but then I uncovered a nail gun somebody had left. If it was loaded, I knew it would be more effective. That it would take away his physical advantage."

"I'd say highly effective." For the first time, Morel smiled at her.

"When did you learn how to use a nail gun?" Sonny asked.

"My husband owned a construction business. Ex-husband," she amended, remembering that Mac didn't like it when she referred to Dan as her husband. "Danny and I helped out when we could."

"So you were alone in the apartment? With Tate, I mean."

"When I killed him?"

Morel nodded.

"We were alone. Is there... Is there some problem with what I did?"

Mac had told her that if he hadn't stopped her that first day, the police would have charged her with attempted murder. But surely after he'd assaulted Mac and broken in—

"There's no problem, Mrs. Patterson, I assure you. We're just trying to piece together everything that happened. The press is going to be very interested in learning how Samuel Tate was killed. I'm afraid that the media attention is going to be even more intense than what you were exposed to before."

"Are you going to tell them about…? Look, I don't care for myself. I don't owe anybody an explanation for how I live my life, but Mac… Mac tried to get me to go back upstairs." If she had, she realized, she might be dead right now. They might both be. "I don't want him to be reprimanded or publicly embarrassed because of something that wasn't his fault."

"I don't think anybody's looking to place blame or cause either of you embarrassment. The department as well as the FBI is relieved to have Tate off the streets. The fact that you are the one who made that happen, considering your connection to him…" Morel shrugged. "You can see why this is going to appeal to the media. I'm afraid there's very little we can do to shield you from their interest in this story."

She shook her head. "I don't expect you to shield me, Captain Morel. I do expect you to take care of your own. Take care of Mac. Other than that…" She hesitated, realizing again how little else mattered. "Other than that, I don't give a damn what you or the department does. Just see to it that Mac doesn't suffer, or by God, I'll make sure the press asks all those questions you don't want to answer."

"Mrs. Patterson—"

"Like how Tate got around all your supposed safeguards. Or how he found out exactly how your 'workmen' dressed and what kind of trucks they drove and when they arrived."

"If that's intended to be a threat—"

"You bet your ass it is. You take care of Mac, and I'll take care of your department's reputation. What's left of it. Otherwise..."

She let the rest trail, knowing she'd pushed this as far as she should. Mac had warned her that Morel was capable of digging in his heels, even when it wasn't to his advantage.

"Detective Donovan is a valued member of the N.O.P.D." Morel's tone was as smooth as the one he had used to address the media during the height of the previous frenzy about Tate being released. "One who was instrumental in bringing a serial killer to justice. Believe me, Mrs. Patterson, I'll be the first to acknowledge that publicly."

"And privately?"

"As I'm sure you know, Mac and I haven't always seen eye-to-eye. I doubt that will change. But neither will anything else. Whatever I am, I'm not a vindictive man."

Or a fool, Sarah thought, looking into his eyes. Morel would do whatever he needed to do to protect the department. And in this case, that meant keeping her happy, which meant that at the very least Mac's position was safe.

She had little time to enjoy that momentary satisfaction. The door of the private waiting room where they'd been directed to avoid the hordes of reporters haunting the hospital's corridors opened.

Despite his scrubs, the man who entered looked far too young to be a doctor. And considering the time frame the nurse had given her for the surgery—

"Mrs. Patterson?"

Sarah nodded, not trusting her voice. Had he come to tell her that Mac hadn't made it? That in the course of what she had already been told would be a long and delicate procedure—

"How is he?"

At Morel's question, the doctor's gaze shifted to him. "Are you a relative?"

"I'm Detective Donovan's superior."

The man nodded. "Then I can tell you that the surgery went well. Much better than anyone expected, actually. He's already been taken to recovery. Someone will come for you," he said, his eyes shifting back to Sarah, "just as soon as he's taken to the NICU."

"NICU?" Morel repeated.

"Neurological Intensive Care. As with any head injury, your officer will be carefully monitored for the next few days."

"But…?" Sarah stopped, almost afraid to put her question into words.

"No buts. He's doing good. Real good. You hang in there now, you hear?"

She nodded again, swallowing against the unwanted rush of emotion. "Thank you."

"You bet. They'll come and get you as soon as they get him settled."

Sarah hadn't realized that she'd fallen asleep. And she wasn't sure what had awakened her. But when she opened her eyes, Mac's were open, too, and he was looking at her.

She stood, taking the single step that separated her from his bed. The staff of the intensive care unit had tried to throw her out after visiting hours, but she'd refused to leave.

She knew all about rules and regulations. She also knew far too much about loss. And that there wasn't a cop in the greater New Orleans area who would have forcibly removed her from this room.

She was almost afraid to touch Mac, surrounded as he was by wires and monitors. His eyes, looking remarkably focused, considering everything, tracked her approach.

"Hey," she whispered, bending down to brush her lips over his.

She took his hand, avoiding the clip around his finger. Its warmth was comforting. As was the slight squeeze he managed in response.

His mouth moved. She leaned down again, trying to pick up what he was saying.

"You okay?"

She straightened, relieved that the question made sense, even in this context. He hadn't asked why he was here. Maybe that was a sign he remembered something of this morning's events, although the nurses had cautioned her that he would probably suffer some memory loss due to the injury.

"I'm fine."

He appeared to nod before his eyes closed again. His tongue rimmed his lips, undoubtedly dry after the anesthesia. While she was trying to decide whether to leave him to ask for some ice chips, his eyes opened again.

"Tate?"

This time sound accompanied the movement of his mouth. Her eyes filled with tears she blinked to clear.

"He's dead, Mac. It's over."

She had characterized Tate's reign of terror over her life as a long nightmare. It had been. But now…

Now there was something better in her future. The fact that Mac was cognizant enough to ask that question proved it.

"Good." Only one word, and as soft as the last had been.

With it, her tears threatened again. This time because she knew it would be.

Epilogue

"My friend Ricky likes him, too. We take him to the playground in the afternoon after school and throw the ball for him. Ricky brings a tennis ball from home. It's easier for Toby to handle."

Sarah glanced at Mac, wondering if he, too, saw what she considered to be marked differences in Dwight. Were those the result of the department's financial support or the family's access to more social services?

Whatever the reasons, the child's hair was now neatly trimmed, and he had a new jacket. One that actually fit.

Of course, it was probably too much to expect Mac to pick up on those subtle signs of change. He'd only been out of the hospital for a little over two weeks now.

According to the doctors, the prognosis was for a complete recovery. And that was happening faster than anyone had had any right to expect.

"You taking good care of him?" Mac asked, stooping to scratch behind the dog's ears.

"I walk him in the morning, real quick because of school. Then we play outside most afternoons. Us and Ricky. Then my mother and me take him out before I go to bed. Usually that's just to the lawn outside the apartment, but he doesn't seem to mind."

"And your mom?" Sarah asked. "Does she like Toby better now?"

"She still fusses some about the dog hair and stuff, but she doesn't really mind. He keeps Nana company. She likes him, too. She can't remember his name, but she knows he belongs to us."

At that Mac's eyes lifted to hers. Sarah knew what he was suggesting, but she quickly looked away, smiling at Dwight instead.

"I'm proud of you for taking such good care of him, Dwight. I knew I could depend on you."

"Yes, ma'am." The boy beamed, seemingly unmindful their original agreement that he keep Toby was to have been of short duration.

"How's school?" Mac asked. "Making good grades?"

"I like it better than my old school. The kids are nice to me. And so is my teacher."

They already knew Dwight had found a friend. Someone named Ricky, who brought Toby tennis balls to play with.

Sarah wasn't sure she could credit all that to Toby's influence, but it was clear the boy was happier here than he'd been before.

Mac got to his feet. She watched the process, amazed at how far he'd come in such a short time. He raised his brows as he looked at her, tilting his head slightly.

When Sarah had called today to tell Mrs. Ingersoll they wanted to come over, Dwight's mother mentioned how attached they'd all become to Toby. Especially Dwight. She'd even gone so far as to express her concern about how he'd deal with Sarah taking the dog back.

If that's what you intend to do, she'd finished, her intonation as questioning as Mac's expression.

Was it what she intended? Right now, Sarah wasn't sure what she wanted to do about Toby. It was clear that he, too, was happy here. And even clearer that Dwight was flourishing in this new environment and ecstatic to be able to claim ownership of the dog, even temporarily.

"Sarah?"

Mac's question exacerbated the ongoing internal debate. She knew exactly what he wanted her to do.

Not because Mac didn't have his own affection for the big mutt, but because he believed it was the right thing to do. To give Dwight, who had had so little, permanent ownership of the animal that seemed to symbolize the positive changes these last few weeks had brought to his life.

Except she was finding that it wasn't easy to give Toby away. He'd been Danny's dog. Chosen by him. Named by him. And loved—dear God—so loved by him.

Toby was the only connection she had to him now. The only physical link to another little boy who had once been her whole world.

She looked at Mac, her eyes again filling with tears that had been too near the surface lately. At Morel's insistence, both she and Mac had seen a psychologist to help them deal with what had happened that day. Despite the counselor's assurances that her emotional reactions to everyday events were perfectly normal right now, she still felt like an idiot. Or a coward.

While the media extolled her courage on a daily basis, she, at least, knew the truth. All she wanted to do these days was to have Mac hold her while she cried and cried and cried.

There had been so many things during the past three years she had thought would be impossible for her to do, yet she'd gritted her teeth and found the resolve to do them. But this… This was too hard. Too unfair.

"Dwight, I'm glad you've enjoyed keeping Toby," she began. "I really appreciate it."

The boy's eyes had suddenly lost the joy that had shone from them. But Dwight, too, knew too well life's unfairness.

He nodded, manfully controlling his own emotions as he bent, once more putting both arms around Toby's neck. He buried his face in the thick ruff of the dog's coat, hugging him as if he couldn't bear to let go.

He did finally, standing up and holding the leash out to her. "Thank you for letting me keep him. He's a very good dog."

"He belonged to my son." She said the words as if they explained anything. As if that made what she was doing right. "Toby's all I have of his now."

"I know. He's yours. My mother and I talked about

it. That this was just temporary." He said the word carefully, as if he'd recently learned it. "Just until you got everything settled at your apartment."

She glanced at Mac, hoping for remission for the guilt she felt. That wasn't in his eyes, although love and acceptance were.

And there was something else she recognized. Not because it was familiar, but because she felt the same emotion for him. Whatever she decided today, Mac would never, by word or deed, indicate that he thought she'd done the wrong thing.

She had every right to try to hold onto the little she had left of what her life had once been. How could anyone blame her for that?

She reached out, taking the lead from Dwight's hand. "We'll bring him to see you, Dwight. As often as we can."

That was something else that was new in her world, she realized. Speaking in the first person plural.

The boy nodded, his eyes again dropping to the dog. Toby looked from one to the other of them, as if trying to figure out what was going on. His tail no longer wagged as it had almost nonstop since their arrival.

"You ready to go home, Tobe?"

His ears perked at the familiar diminutive, but then his eyes went back to Dwight.

"Go on." Dwight spoke directly to the dog. "I'll see you again real soon. Me and Ricky will throw your ball for you. You don't have to be sad, Toby. It'll be okay. It'll all be okay."

The brown eyes fastened on Dwight's thin, pale face,

trying to understand what he was saying. Just as they had always fastened on Danny's.

Sarah again thought how different the two boys were. Her son had been tanned and robust. Vibrant and full of life. So confident that he was loved and always would be.

He had been. He always would be. And she didn't need Toby to help her remember Danny.

It was time to let the bad memories go. To remember only the good ones. Danny's love for Toby was certainly one of those. And the right thing to do—

She looked at Mac again, the same love shining from his eyes that shone from the dog's as he looked questioningly at this child, who needed him more than hers ever had. When she smiled, a little tremulous, Mac answered it, understanding exactly what she was thinking.

She turned back to Dwight, knowing this last sacrifice was not only necessary, but empowering. Freeing.

"Your mom said that she really wouldn't mind if you wanted to keep him. Would you like that?"

"Keep Toby?" Hope and disbelief mingled in his tone. "Forever?"

'Til death do us part…

She wasn't sure why that bit of the marriage vows echoed in her head. Maybe because that's all anyone could ever count on. A minute. Or an hour. The transient, wonderful joy of each day's living.

'Til death do us part. And beyond.

She nodded, the love she felt for all of them, the living and the dead, crowding her throat too thickly for words.

It seemed they weren't necessary. Whatever answer

Dwight had sought, he found in her face. He knelt again, wrapping his arms around Toby's neck.

Over the tableau the two of them made, she met Mac's eyes. When he nodded, she knew that whatever mistakes she'd made in her life, this hadn't been one of them.

"Let's go home," he said.

Wherever that was, with Mac there, finally it would be.